Not Safe For Work

ALSO BY ISABEL KAPLAN

Hancock Park

Not Safe For Work

Isabel Kaplan

MICHAEL JOSEPH

PENGUIN MICHAEL JOSEPH

UK | USA | Canada | Ireland | Australia
India | New Zealand | South Africa

Penguin Michael Joseph is part of the Penguin Random House group of companies
whose addresses can be found at global.penguinrandomhouse.com

First published in the United States of America by Henry Holt,
an imprint of Macmillan Publishing Group, LLC 2022
First published in Great Britain by Penguin Michael Joseph 2022
001

Printed and bound in Great Britain by Clays Ltd, Elcograf S.p.A.

The authorized representative in the EEA is Penguin Random House Ireland,
Morrison Chambers, 32 Nassau Street, Dublin D02 YH68

A CIP catalogue record for this book is available from the British Library

HARDBACK ISBN: 978–0–241–53724–4
TRADE PAPERBACK ISBN: 978–0–241–53725–1

www.greenpenguin.co.uk

Penguin Random House is committed to a
sustainable future for our business, our readers
and our planet. This book is made from Forest
Stewardship Council® certified paper.

ONE

THE THING ABOUT LOS ANGELES IS THAT IT'S awful and I hate it, but when I'm there, nowhere else exists, and I can't imagine leaving. It's a difficult place to be old or sick or fat or poor or without a strong social media presence. It's not an easy place to be young, either.

After college graduation, I postpone my return from Boston by one week, then two, cat sitting for a professor. It's the second week that drives my mother over the edge. She calls, she emails, she accuses me of loving the professor's cat more than her. She says don't I know how hard she has been working, how lonely and depressed she has been, how she has been counting down the days until my return.

I get sick upon arrival, aching limbs at baggage claim blooming into a fever by the following day. Garden-variety virus, but it hits my mother's sweet spot. "You're run-down, poor baby. I'll take care of you," she says.

My father sends a "welcome home" text. *Hope to see you for dinner soon*, he writes. He doesn't ask where I'll be living or if I'd like to stay with him. I suspect he doesn't want the infringement on his space, his freedom.

It's strange being back in my mother's house. She has just finished renovating, and it barely looks familiar, though somehow items from long ago—CD players, pants from GapKids—

have resurfaced in the new version of my old bedroom. The sight of them is unsettling.

My parents divorced when I was ten, during the summer before fifth grade. They were civil, but it was terrible. My mother suggested we go on a diet together. "It'll be fun," she told me. "You'll look great for the start of the school year." She said she knew I had been overeating because I could tell she was unhappy in her marriage. This was news to me. She taught me all about calories and the places they hide. I dipped carrots in Dijon mustard while my friends at day camp traded Skittles and M&M's, candy coatings melting in a rainbow smear on their palms.

My weeks were split between my parents. My father kept the house in the Hollywood Hills, and my mother moved to an apartment in Santa Monica, across the street from the beach. There was an infinity pool on the roof and towels were provided. She called it Heartbreak Hotel.

A few nights a week, I would ride my scooter to the Third Street Promenade with my mother and younger brother. While my brother browsed the toy store, I punished myself in the basement fitting rooms of GapKids, trying on jeans two sizes too small and watching my stomach pucker as I did up the button. I practiced sitting casually on the bench in the fitting room, as if I were on a playground bench at recess. I made believe I was talking about normal things with my classmates and kept an eye on my stomach in the mirror.

My mother moved several times over the next five years, a real tour du West LA, before landing back in Santa Monica, two miles east of Heartbreak Hotel. When I think back on those years, I remember a choking sensation. My father's silence, my mother's longing, my brother's rage. My bottomless hunger. My psychiatrist kept increasing dosages, switching medications. Trial and error, she said. I would stare at the tapestry behind her head and say, week after week, "I want to stop falling asleep in class."

The day my mother moved into this house was also the day I got drunk for the first time. Early evening, a bottle of Grey Goose on the kitchen counter, carton of orange juice next to it. I helped myself. "If you drink that screwdriver, you can't drive," my mother said. I said I didn't care, and I drank that one and then another and another until the floor tilted. I was fifteen. I couldn't drive at night on a learner's permit anyway.

My parents were both from New England, high-achieving youngest children of long-suffering Jewish immigrant mothers. A perfect match on paper. My mother moved to Los Angeles for my father, a literary historian who moved for his research, wooed by a trove of archives acquired by USC. My mother often said that my father was the only person who would willingly relinquish tenure at Harvard. It took me a long time to understand the double-edged slice of that comment.

My mother never liked Los Angeles, but she also never left. She stayed for my brother and me, so that our lives would be stable and we could have a close, or closer, relationship with our father. She made do with what she believed to be a pale imitation of the career she imagined having in Boston, where her star was on the rise and her expertise—as a lawyer and legal activist doing groundbreaking work on victims' rights and rape laws—was more highly valued.

Until I went to college, I didn't know where my mother ended and I began, a lack of differentiation more common in toddlers than teenagers. It was a problem my mother didn't recognize as such, which was of course part of the problem. Her life's purpose was to sacrifice and provide for me, and mine was to make her feel sufficiently loved in return. What could possibly go wrong?

Growing up, I assumed I would become a lawyer, like her, or go into politics, become an advocate for issues affecting women. A public feminist, broadly conceived. But a Capitol Hill internship the summer after freshman year—when Democrat dreams of single-payer health care were shattered—disillusioned me about politics and I realized I didn't actually want to be a lawyer.

I spent much of college trying to develop my own interests and a fundamental sense of self. The only thing that didn't feel like a hand-me-down was my love of words, my belief in the power of storytelling. Before benzos and SSRIs, I had books and TV. I was never a movie person. I preferred ongoing narratives, parallel realities to dip into alongside my own. Different stories for different moods, like vitamins to address certain deficiencies. I became an English major. I read a lot of novels.

I liked Cambridge, the unfashionable bookish atmosphere, the red bricks and history. I considered academia. As a trial run, I took a graduate seminar on intertextuality, which involved endless discussions about "the literary word as an intersection of textual surfaces" and "'textasy' as the 'release' of the subject in a sexual or textual 'coming.'"

I spoke exclusively in fragments, stringing together phrases I barely understood. The professor was invariably pleased with my insights. She complimented my analytical clarity. So much performative nonsense, and to what end? All to spend a decade picking at the carcasses of my favorite books and competing for underpaid jobs in places I don't want to live? I might as well work in television.

I grew up in the shadow of Hollywood, both figuratively and literally, the sign itself visible from the rooftop playground of my elementary school. I hid behind the role of Smart Girl, smug with intellectual superiority. I was meant for Harvard, not Hollywood.

But Harvard was its own Hollywood, I learned, just with different jargon and celebrities.

So, really, why not television?

It's the golden age. Everyone's talking about the quality of the writing, the power to catalyze social change, even. Prestige dramas are the new social novel, my thesis adviser assures me. *The Wire* is *Middlemarch*. Why write academic books about increasingly esoteric subjects for an audience of approximately twelve when I could be a part of this creative renaissance? It's what I want—what I've always wanted. I ran in the other direction out of insecurity, not disinterest.

And so, though I am daunted by the prospect, I move back to LA.

That I get sick upon return is, in its way, a blessing. It helps me skip past the claustrophobia and panic that typically smother me upon arrival, a cling wrap that I have to claw my way through. Or maybe, I think, as I roll over in bed and wave my arms in search of a cool patch of sheet, mood softened by an Ambien-NyQuil haze, maybe I've grown.

As soon as my fever breaks and my head clears, I start job hunting. For what job, I'm not sure. I meet with everyone I know and everyone they know, shuttling from sleepy production company offices in the valley to crowded backlot bungalows to try-hard offices in Hollywood where I struggle to sit in a dignified position on the neon foam amoebas that someone deemed a step up from regular old chairs. I feel guilty about using connections, but there's no apparent alternative. This is a town full of people with connections.

Most of the people I meet are producers. Few have produced anything of late.

Somebody advises me, early on, that when the assistant offers water, I should always accept. My car fills up with plastic bottles, rolling on the floor of the back seat. I have coffees, many coffees. I nod and smile until my cheeks hurt.

A writer whose daughter went to my elementary school and with whom my parents are friendly asks if I've thought about working in development. "That's where the power is," she says. "Hollywood needs more smart executives. If you want to make change in a big, noticeable way, really impact how women are portrayed on television and what stories get told, you need power."

She tells me about a meeting she had that ended with her saying yes, she would be delighted to work on a network drama called *Marsipan* (logline: "Decades after humankind has conquered the red planet, a diverse group of colonists form Mars's first 'Reduced-Gravity Bake-Off'").

I learn that development is the department in charge of coming up with new shows—television's editorial department, so to speak. It's a job with a real career path, a ladder of executive positions to climb. It sounds like something I could be good at, something I might enjoy.

Production companies have development departments, as do studios and networks. If she were me, the writer says, she'd want to be at a network. At a production company or a studio, you're closer to the material, but you're still a seller, you have no control over what ends up on air. But at a network, you're in the buyer's seat; you hold the keys to the castle.

Development. The idea takes root, the appeal obvious. I have an answer now, to the question of what I want to do.

———

MY BIGGEST BREAK comes in July in the form of a meeting, arranged by my mother, with her old friend Robert Baum, the longtime chairman of XBC. XBC is the youngest of the big broadcast networks, known for edgier programming than the older stalwarts. In advance of the meeting, I watch as many XBC shows as I can. I worry too much about what to wear. I read interviews with Robert, who is in his early seventies and comes across as charismatic and good humored. It's often noted that he is the kind of boss who inspires great loyalty from his employees. He has been at the network for over twenty years and shepherded many of the biggest early-aughts hits to prime-time success, ambitious, character-driven shows that seemed risky at the time, better suited to cable. Now, after long runs, nearly all those shows are off-air, and, like the other broadcast networks, XBC is struggling to compete with digital and streaming services and cord-cutting millennials who don't watch live TV. Robert's a member of the old guard, but he's not considered out of touch. He knows he's part of a changing landscape, and he's ready to change with it. Most important, my mother says, is the loyalty aspect: it shows he's a good boss, that his top executives have been at the network so long.

Robert's office is perched on the top floor of the executive building on XBC's affiliated studio lot. I have been on a studio lot before, though only a few times, and I feel self-conscious and scrambled by the protocol. The building's lobby is all white and polished marble and well-dressed people moving with purpose. Next to me in the elevator: a woman so thin, she looks flattened. Flawless blow-dry, icy-blue blazer, and a familiar face. Veronica Ross, I realize. President of XBC, a regular feature in various "Women Who Are Changing Hollywood" roundups. I've read about her. Have fantasized, tentatively, about becoming her. She does not make eye contact with me or appear to register my presence in any way. I look down at my feet, the toes pinched and aching in my mother's heels, which are too tight even though we theoretically wear the same size. ("So they're a little tight; are you planning to run a marathon?" my mother said after condemning all the shoes in my closet.)

Veronica strides ahead of me down the hall, into the waiting room outside Robert's office, where two assistants sit at side-by-side desks.

"Morning, Veronica," one of the assistants says. Veronica barely stops to nod.

I take a seat on the couch across from the assistants and pretend to check my email, to have somewhere to direct my eyes. *Relax. Try to relax. You probably don't look as dumpy or desperate as you feel.*

Twenty minutes later, Veronica strides out, and shortly thereafter, one of the assistants tells me to go on in.

The office itself is huge. An imposing desk, two leather couches, and a handful of tastefully upholstered armchairs. A well-curated coffee table featuring carefully fanned copies of *Variety* and *The Hollywood Reporter*, a signed football in a case, and two glass bottles in the shape of handguns, filled with golden liquid.

"Tequila," Robert says. "The only kind of guns I'm allowed to have in here."

He is shorter than I was expecting, based on his online head-shots. What my mother would call a Jewish five-eight. Meaning five-six. His voice is what strikes me most. Deep, booming, and Boston accented. He sounds like my mother in a way few people in LA do. I remember my mother telling me that the first time she heard Robert speak, she went up to him and said, "Are you by chance from Salem?"

"How did you know?" he had asked.

"You sound just like my father, and he was from Salem," my mother said.

Now, as I sit across from Robert and give him a little spiel about myself, he interrupts me. "You sound just like your mother," he says. "It's wild."

"Thanks," I say.

"Do you get that a lot?" he asks.

"I do."

I don't think the two of us sound that much alike, but there must be things I don't notice. Inflections. Intonations. Also, I don't really know what my own voice sounds like.

"I love your mother," he says.

"Join the club!" I say, shifting my legs in a futile attempt to dislodge the underwear that has migrated uncomfortably from ass cheek to crack. "And I love XBC," I add. "I admire the way you built the brand and pushed the limits of what broadcast can do." I couldn't sound more like an anonymous cover letter if I tried.

"So you want to polish brass on the *Titanic*, do you?" he says.

"I hear it's the fastest ship afloat."

He laughs, and I feel a quick flash of relief. "If anyone avoids the iceberg, it'll be us," he says. "But only time will tell."

"I have time."

"Let me guess. You watch more cable than broadcast, right? That's your profile. More shows every year full of young people getting naked and doing drugs, and that's fine, some of them are very good, but all the fear-mongering articles fawning over premium cable and asking, 'Is broadcast dead?' Nobody mentions the numbers! Cable, you're in the hundred thousands. And that's a hit. Us? Millions. Not a competition! You want viewers? We've got viewers."

"Where's that story?" I ask.

"You're telling me! These cable honchos, they think it's edgy to show people shtupping on screen. You know what's edgy? Being provocative without cheap tricks. That's what we're about. I don't want fluffy schlock or another *CSI* set in god knows where because they're running out of good cities."

"I love *Justice Served*," I tell Robert. It's XBC's cop show, one of Robert's biggest successes. For a show about violent crime, it's strangely soothing to watch, in large part due to the formulaic structure of the episodes. You know the first suspect is a red herring and that there will be a big twist forty minutes in. Final scenes are always in the courtroom—justice is not necessarily served, because that would be too predictable, but things work out often enough to sustain hope. I'm not the only one who likes this show—it's hugely popular, into its sixteenth season now. The chemistry between the two detectives, Newman and Coffey, is what keeps it going. It's been will-they-or-won't-they for years, but they haven't so far, and there's something commendable in that. Blake Peterson's rugged, short-fused Detective Newman is the more popular of the two, but I've always liked Coffey best. The actress who plays her is muscular in both body and attitude. Alluring because of how much on-screen space she takes up, not how little. She's nearly the same size as Blake Peterson. I get his appeal, I guess. I wouldn't *not* fuck him. But I feel no desire to talk to him, no sense of an interesting person behind the part. Then again, I've always had the tendency to ascribe more dimension to women and to objectify men. Problematic, sure, but in this male-dominated hellscape of a world, what's so wrong with a little overcorrection?

This I don't say to Robert Baum, of course. I'm no fool. I tell him only how much I like the show and congratulate him on its recently celebrated milestone: fifteen years on air.

"The little show that could," he says. "Newman and Coffey are keeping XBC alive."

I tell Robert about my interest in development and, god help me, about how my undergraduate thesis on representations of gender-based oppression in the works of George Eliot furthered my belief in the social and political power of fictional narratives.

"Over my head," Robert says, with a laugh. "I was always a Hemingway fan myself."

I smile and nod, glance over at the tequila guns on the coffee table. Figures. "He's good too," I say. I've never liked Hemingway. All the tortured masculinity and bitch-goddess women, though yes, fine, the man could write a great sentence.

Robert goes on to explain that he isn't kept apprised of all the comings and goings on the assistant level, but he knows there is fairly frequent turnover, and I sound like I have the drive that it takes to succeed. His cheeks pinken as he leans over to pick up the phone on a side table. "Can you leave word from me for Diane in HR?" he says, presumably to one of the assistants beyond the door.

He returns the receiver to its cradle and presses a button on the wall. The door to the waiting room swings open, which I take as my cue to depart. I stand. "You're a good one, I can tell," he says, remaining seated. "And if we don't snap you up, someone else will."

The buoyancy lasts for a few days, until I go in for an HR meeting, which is in a different building with different parking and entrance instructions, so I arrive feeling just as frazzled as I did the first time. I meet with two women in HR, neither of whom are as encouraging as Robert. They both remind me that I am underqualified; they usually require agency experience. The first woman, Diane, an EVP with a large office, though not nearly as large as Robert's, asks how I feel about doing personal tasks.

"I'd prefer to do professional ones?" I answer.

She nods, thinking.

Afterward, a lower-level executive with a smaller office and only one guest chair asks if I have experience booking travel and making reservations.

"Yes?" I say.

HR sends my résumé to an executive at the affiliated studio who is hiring an assistant, and I have a good meeting with him, though the oligarchic power structure through which this studio and XBC are intertwined but somehow independent remains opaque to me. The executive gives me a script to write coverage on, and I spend a long, careful time on it. The job goes to someone else, a friend of his current assistant.

There are more meetings that go nowhere, other leads I follow up on. Hours spent smiling and nodding and hearing people say,

"You sound great; you're so impressive." Another assistant job that I get close on, two rounds of interviews, but it goes to someone with more experience.

My mother calls Robert Baum again in September, ostensibly to talk about whether he might have legal business for her (no, not right now, but she's at the top of his list), but mostly to follow up on my behalf. He promises to check in on the situation, which sets off a chain of events leading to a call from Diane in HR, who offers me a floating temp position in the development department. It's only temporary, she explains, barely a step above an internship, but if I impress the executives, I'll have a better shot of landing a permanent assistant job when one opens than I would if I were an external candidate.

I accept immediately.

The weekend before I start work, my mother and I get our nails done together for the first time in years, and I allow her to convince me to put acrylic tips on my ravaged stubs so that I will look like an adult woman. My mother has worn acrylics for decades. Deep red, usually, though sometimes pink. When she is anxious or stressed, she tears them off. Throughout my childhood, there were nails everywhere: in purses, pockets, around the house. Sometimes, if it was just one or two nails, she would save them in her wallet and bring them to the salon for reattachment. I often accompanied her. Before the divorce, it was I Love Nails on Beverly. After, across town, Tracy's Nails on Montana.

"Me again," she would say, voice ringing over the front door bell's chime.

"Full set?" they'd ask.

I began tearing off my nails around age ten, but these were my real nails, not fake tips. A brief satisfaction, though sometimes too much would come off, raw pink skin exposed. Sometimes blood and a throbbing that would linger. I stopped enjoying trips to the nail salon. But I accompanied my mother for a long time because I would go anywhere and everywhere with her.

I have not been to Tracy's Nails in years. "All grown up!" Tracy says to me. "You look so much like your mother."

"Prettier than I ever was," my mother says.

"The same!" Tracy says, passing her sister-in-law, who has been tasked with my hands, a basket of gel nail polish samples for me to consider. Plastic wheels of nails, more shades of red than anyone could possibly need.

"You know what my mother told me when she was born?" my mother tells Tracy. "She said, 'She looks just like you, but with much finer features.'"

"Well, that was Nana being a bitch," I say, relinquishing my hands to the sister-in-law.

"How old are you now?" Tracy asks me.

"Twenty-two."

"She just graduated from Harvard!" my mother adds, loud enough to prompt congratulations from the rest of the salon. The woman two stations to my right, who is wearing a sweatshirt that reads NAMASTAY IN BED and fur-lined Gucci slides, leans over to ask if I grew up here and what schools I went to. I answer, giving the names of my private elementary and secondary schools. She nods with obvious approval and I feel conflicting zaps of satisfaction and disgust. I glance down at her feet, the overflow of fur. It looks like she stepped on a couple of squirrels.

These days, my elementary school has a lower acceptance rate than Harvard. When I, at two years old, was wait-listed along-side the son of one of the most famous actors in Hollywood, my mother went as far as calling the White House for a letter of rec-ommendation. I felt out of step with my classmates, who brought in their parents' Academy Awards for show-and-tell.

"We're not like them; we're not from here," my mother would remind me. But I *was* from here.

Many of my classmates' parents weren't from LA either, this being a city people come to, not from. But my parents weren't here for *the industry*. Therein lay the difference.

I didn't enjoy elementary school. I wanted more rigorous aca-demics. When presented with suggested research topics like *dino-saurs*, *ballet*, and *Shirley Temple*, I opted for *underrepresented suffragettes* instead. I gave a presentation on Eleanor Roosevelt, including exten-sive discussion of her sexuality and rumored relationship with Lorena Hickok. I asked to do my sixth-grade book report on *Lolita*. My poor teachers.

"You must be so proud," Tracy says to my mother.

"Of course. We had a lovely time at graduation. She gave one of the commencement speeches!"

Nothing to do but smile. *Lovely* is not the word for it.

A month before graduation, after I told her I'd been selected as a commencement speaker, my mother said she didn't think she could come. That the whole experience would be too painful for her, prompting traumatic memories of her own college graduation, which Nana didn't attend because my mother couldn't secure a ticket for Nana's new husband.

"So you're telling me that your mother's failure to put you first and attend your graduation hurt you in a lasting way, and as a result you're going to do the exact same thing to me?" I cried into the phone.

"No, no, no!" she cried back.

Both of us beside ourselves with frustration.

"I've always been there for you. Nana was never there for me."

"I know."

"My college graduation was different," my mother reminded me. "I had just been raped." She sat on the platform in her borrowed robe, struggling to find a comfortable position, ass still sore from the shots they gave her at the hospital. No mother in the audience to show her support.

My mother was raped in a Boston parking garage five days before her college graduation. This is something I've known for as long as I can remember. I knew about rape before I knew about sex. Before I fully understood the mechanics of it, at least. I didn't know this was unusual, either. There was a song called "It Wasn't Me" that came out when I was in fifth grade. I thought it was about a lousy rape-allegation defense: *She saw the marks on my shoulder (wasn't me). Heard the words that I told her (wasn't me). Heard the screams gettin' louder (wasn't me).* I shared my interpretation with my classmates, who went home with questions for their parents.

I grew up hearing my mother talk openly about rape—in speeches, on TV, on the radio, with friends. As a child, I didn't have any objective understanding of her prominence, but I did know that she was famous enough to be recognized in public fairly regularly. It was because of a book she published just before I was born called *Simple Rape*, which led to a regular column in a big newspaper, a weekend radio show, TV appearances, and lots of panels and lectures and advisory boards. She practiced law, too, but selectively, focusing on sexual assault and gender discrimination. Passion projects.

"What's a complicated rape?" I remember asking when I was eleven.

"Simple rape is the most complicated kind," my mother said. She explained that a simple rape is when the victim knows her attacker, and he doesn't beat or threaten her with a weapon. It's the most common form of rape. Comparatively few people are raped by an armed stranger, as my mother was. An armed stranger who also stole her purse. Because of this, the police believed her. If the rapist were someone she knew, a boyfriend or acquaintance, a man with a good reputation, they would have been more critical, she explained. Same goes with a jury.

How inspired I was by my mother's ability to turn her trauma into fuel. To transform an experience in which she was believed into a weapon to use on behalf of those who were not. Her own rapist was never caught. She went on to law school, then cofounded the first nonprofit legal center dedicated to victims' rights. Then, collecting all she'd learned from her experience as both victim and advocate, she wrote *Simple Rape*, an examination of the ways the law mistreats rape victims.

She came to my graduation in the end.

I made a reservation for dinner at a restaurant in Boston for my parents, brother, and me. New England seafood meets New American, somewhere well reviewed and recommended by a friend but, unbeknownst to me, located just a few blocks from the original location of my mother's victims' rights law center. A painful reminder of the world she left behind, the life she might have had. "How could you have chosen this restaurant?" she said. "How could you do this to me?"

How could I have known?

My brother, newly nineteen, radiated fury. He was on a confusing new diet of exclusively chicken and eggs. "Your brother can't have anything on this menu. Did you even think about him?" my mother said. "Of course not. You only think about yourself."

There were many tears, from everyone but my father, who refused to engage and made eye contact only with the branzino on his plate. We left before dessert. I was too drained to party hop with my friends. It was then that I decided to stay in Boston a little longer, to recuperate before returning to my mother once more.

"Doesn't that look better?" my mother says now, after the UV light machine dings and I remove my newly dried glossy-nailed hands. "Not too long, very natural."

She is right, they do look better like this. It's harder to type, though. The nails make contact with the keys before the pads of my fingers do, and it's a foreign and frustrating feeling. My mother assures me that I will get used to it. I'm not writing anything lengthy these days anyway, just cover letters and networking emails.

Now that I am back, now that she has, for the moment, what she wants—which is me, close to her—we are in a period of calm; we are even having fun. We go shoe shopping, get stoned, order sushi, and watch *Justice Served*. We are, together, indomitable. Pity the poor shmuck who tries to pull one over on us at the car dealership. The look on his face when we jab back. We know nothing about cars but everything about the sounds of sexist condescension.

My mother takes it a little far, with vague threats of a lawsuit, and I feel a familiar blend of pride and panic—pride in her strength and panic at her potential for overkill, like the time she wrote a nationally syndicated column about IBM's poor customer service when her laptop died.

Maybe the problem was that I've never had an independent life in LA. The catch, the question to which I don't have an answer and so am trying not to ask: Is it a life of my own if I need her help to create it?

TWO

IT IS HARDER TO GET ONTO A STUDIO LOT THAN INTO the halls of Congress. I know it's ridiculous, but it's still exciting. My name in the system, the gate lifting open. Development is in the same building as Robert's office, directly across from New York Street, which is a block full of building facades, complete with a fake diner and fake subway stop, dark green railing and bright red dot for the 1 train on the sign above it.

On my first day, I check in with the department coordinator, who is to be my supervisor. Her name is Allyn, and she seems surprised by my presence. "Oh!" she says when I show up at her desk. Her eyes perfectly lined but lips bare and chapped. She looks at me for so long, I begin to wonder if I forgot to say hello out loud. "Are you starting today?" she asks.

She rustles up an old laptop from a filing cabinet marked INTERNS and sends me off to an empty cubicle in the front bullpen, down the hall from her desk, with a printout of instructions for setting up my email. "These instructions probably won't work, but you should follow them so when you call the IT help desk later, you can say you tried everything."

I spend the next three hours trying and failing to set up my email. A welcome break when Allyn invites me to join her for lunch in the building cafeteria. Once we are seated, she tells me to turn around. In the booth behind us, Robert Baum drinks green Gatorade out of a wineglass. The cafeteria only has compostable plastic cups. "That's the chairman," Allyn says. "He brings his own glasses. Sometimes he likes to eat lunch down here, like he's one of the people."

It has been a few months since I met with Robert, and I don't know that he'll recognize me on sight. After all, think of how many people he meets on a daily basis. I am reluctant to reveal my connection, lest it change how Allyn treats me.

Over lackluster salads, Allyn gives me a brief rundown of the department, a flurry of names and titles. She speaks quickly and often begins in the middle of a thought, as if I know who or what she is talking about without her needing to explain. I appreciate the chattiness and the instant intimacy—Allyn is close to six feet tall and the kind of beautiful you might presume to be bitchy—but I also don't understand most of what she's saying, and I'm hard-pressed to figure out whether this is because I know so little about TV or because Allyn has omitted a critical part of a sentence or story. Allyn is twenty-seven, and she recently received a title bump from Assistant to Coordinator, which means she is responsible for "doing more grids and tracking, you know," though she still performs assistant duties as well. She keeps saying "you know" about things that I absolutely do not know.

She has been at the network for two years; before that, ICM, and before that, the University of Indiana, where all her siblings also went and in the vicinity of which her entire family lives. Her family was surprised by her decision to come out to LA, and she suspects they still think it's a temporary plan, that it's only a matter of time until she decides to move back home, marry some guy, ideally her high school boyfriend, who is the most boring person who ever lived, and start popping out babies.

"Please tell me you were prom queen," I say.

"Only homecoming," she says. "It was stupid."

"All-American girl! Student body vice president?" I venture.

Her eyes widen, true surprise. "How did you guess?"

Friendly, fun, and inoffensive. "Just a hunch," I say. I was student body vice president too, but of a different sort. At my all-girls high school, I was more respected than I was popular: people joined the extracurricular clubs I led but didn't invite me to the best parties. I didn't bother running for president; the field was too crowded, and I knew I would never win. In my campaign speech to the student body, I mentioned that I'd had a rough month, that my boyfriend had dumped me and started dating one of my best friends. The sharp intake of breath from five hundred female mouths. "But it's okay," I added. "I'm okay." I got a standing ovation then, right in the middle of the speech. It was my mother's idea to mention the breakup. I balked at first, concerned it was a cheap and desperate gambit. Also, the girl in question was in the audience. But my mother said it would work, and she was right.

"Where are you from?" Allyn asks.

"Here," I say.

"Here?" She looks around the room.

"Not this cafeteria. But a few miles east."

"Oh, wow," she says. "Almost nobody is actually from here, but the ones who are . . . You're lucky. It's an advantage. When I got here after college, I didn't know anything. I didn't even know all the things I didn't know, you know?"

Allyn tells me she's hoping that after a year as a coordinator, she'll be able to make the jump to manager, which is the most junior executive position. She also tells me that the department head's assistant is burned out and trying to find another job. Gregory, the department head, is super demanding and kind of a dick, she explains, but he's also one of the youngest department heads in town and on his way up. "It's a tough desk and a big jump up from being a temp, but if you can pull it off, you'll really impress people," she says.

"How do I do that?" I ask.

"Well, his assistant calls in sick all the time and honestly is so lazy these days, so you'll definitely get a chance to cover that desk. Just make sure you learn the basics first, on less scary desks, like calls and scheduling and expenses and stuff. That way, when you get to Gregory, all you have to do is not fuck up in a major way. Being an assistant isn't hard work, it's just a lot of it."

On our way out, we pass Robert, and he smiles in a general way at both of us. "A sight for sore eyes," he says. "How's it going?" This question, I think, is directed at me. Whether it means he knows who I am or vaguely recognizes me and feels that he should, I'm not sure.

"Great!" I say. "Day one!" Almost immediately embarrassed by the pathetic ring of my voice.

"Try the soup," he says, with a lift of his plastic spoon. A drop of orange liquid plops from spoon to table, landing dangerously close to his white button-downed stomach, which protrudes up against the table's edge. "Pumpkin bisque. It's delicious."

"Will do," I say as if I haven't already eaten and am not holding the remains of my lunch en route to the trash.

"He can be awkward," Allyn says when we are alone in the elevator, "but he means well, and he's very friendly."

That afternoon, I spend a full hour troubleshooting my email issues over the phone with the IT help desk. Given that I have literally no other work to do, the inefficiency of the technicians attempting to gain remote access to my laptop is more endearing than frustrating. By three p.m., my email is up and running. A message from HR is waiting in my inbox. I click it open and follow the link to a mandatory online training that turns out, inexplicably, to be an hour-long course about stairs: how to build them and how to use them. A question-and-answer section at the end of each unit. *Stairs have multiple components. Look at these stairs and identify the individual components. How can you ensure that you use stairs safely? What are the best practices for using stairs? Select all that apply.*

In the underground parking garage that evening, I walk up to the wrong silver Prius twice. It takes me too long to find the exit, stuck on P3 no matter which way I turn. I feel like I'm trapped in an Escher print. When I finally make it out and join the sea of cars inching westward on Pico, I call my mother. I tell her that nobody seemed to know what to do with me. That I felt strange and shy and had absolutely nothing to do.

"First days are always like that," she says. "You just have to be assertive. Did you see Robert?"

"I did, actually. At lunch." I tell her about the Gatorade in the wineglass and that he called us "a sight for sore eyes."

"And?"

"That's a weird thing to say, right? Isn't it a comment on our appearances?"

"He's seventy. It's an old-fashioned saying. I'm sure he didn't mean anything."

"I suppose."

"Did it make you uncomfortable?"

"No," I say. "But I was already uncomfortable. I was uncomfortable all day."

"Nadine says you don't know how to handle discomfort. It's
something you need to work on," my mother says. Nadine is my
mother's psychiatrist. She is also, separately, my brother's psychiatrist. And my father's. She was my psychiatrist too, throughout
high school, until I got to college and found a psychiatrist of my
own, Susana, who, unlike Nadine, had the unimpeded emotiveness
of a Botox-free face, and helped me realize that there's something
ethically murky about individually treating all members of a family.
The number of arguments that have started with "Well, Nadine
says . . ."

I flick my turn signal on and move into the right lane. "Home
soon," I say.

That night, I look over my notes from the day, a list of words and
phrases Allyn used in ways I didn't understand.

- *pods:* "Gregory's switching up the pod coverage."
- *overalls:* Shopping overalls? Big overalls? Covering overalls?
        Not clothes.
- *auspices:* "Always check the auspices."
- *freeballs:* "We're getting more freeballs."
- *competitive (noun):* "It's important to be good at competitive."

My job is to cover the desks of assistants when they are out.
This means jumping in at a moment's notice with no preparation.
I am anxious when the phone rings, because every call brings
questions I cannot answer and people calling for someone who is

not me. And there are so many buttons. I've been warned about dropping calls. I don't want to do this; I don't know how to pick them back up again.

My cubicle is wedged awkwardly in the middle of the front bull-pen, with a small gap between the edge of my desk and a long glass cabinet filled with Emmy Awards. There is just enough space that people think they can pass through the gap but not enough for them to actually do so. In order to get through, they have to flatten them-selves against the edge of my desk. Every time this happens, I turn and make awkward eye contact.

If all the assistants are in the office, which they usually are, I have nothing to do. When I ask Allyn if I can help her with any-thing, she says, "Why don't you catch up on our shows?" and hands me a pile of DVDs. I spend most of my days watching television on the sluggish intern laptop. The dramas are full of misanthropic men and mysterious, wounded women. The comedies, schlubby dads and uptight moms. Two pilots from last season concern the hijinks of characters who used to be fat. That's their sole personality trait. One is called *Former Fat Kid*. It got a series pickup but was canceled midseason; the ratings were terrible and only getting worse.

Zach, the department's most junior executive, instant messages me to ask if I want to grab coffee one afternoon. He sits at the cubi-cle across from mine, and I know him by sight, but we have never had a conversation. I say yes, of course. It's a sunny day, and we bring our coffee outside, to a table in the courtyard. There's another cafe-teria with more outdoor seating across the courtyard, but it is cur-rently being used as a film set. A Middle Eastern café scene, lots of actresses in hijabs. Zach is a blend of relaxed and on edge, alternat-ing between lounging back in his chair, legs spread, and leaning forward, elbows on the table, knees bouncing, hands around his coffee cup. He's wearing Ray-Bans, the classic Wayfarers, which he pushes up onto his forehead every few minutes only to bring them back down over his eyes shortly thereafter. He takes up a lot of space.

When he asks how I got the job, this newly made-up floating temp position, I don't know what to say other than the truth: through Robert, connected by my mother.

"Wow," Zach says. "Who's your mom?"

I say her name but with a question mark at the end.

"Is she in the industry?" Zach asks.

"No. She's a lawyer and legal commentator?"

"Oh," he says, and I can tell, with this, that he has written her off as irrelevant to his life. Which, fair enough. "So you're a Robert hire, huh?" he says. "This changes things."

"What do you mean?"

"I was going to ask if you'd be interested in being my de facto assistant," he says, explaining that he's too junior an executive to be officially allotted his own assistant. "But I feel bad," he adds, "taking up your time with menial tasks. You're clearly too smart for what I'm offering, destined for better things."

"No, please, I have to start somewhere, right?" I say. I badly want a place, a position, something with more solidity. A chance to prove myself.

Zach says he knows how important it is to have a mentor in this business. He wants to pay it forward. "What do you say?"

Yes. I say yes.

The next morning, I find Allyn perched on the edge of Zach's desk, laughing. "I miss having you as my cubicle neighbor," Allyn says. Her boss, a VP, recently moved to a bigger office toward the back of the floor, which necessitated a move for Allyn from the front to the back bullpen.

"You're telling me!" Zach says.

"Lunch, please?"

"Absolutely," Zach says to Allyn. Then, to me, "This girl's the best."

As I sit back down at my desk, my computer pings with a message from Zach: *I SO DON'T miss sitting next to Allyn. She's such a ditz. Constantly interrupting me with stupid stuff.*

Shortly thereafter, Allyn messages me: *Love Z & good starter desk but he's a whiny baby.*

"Relationships are everything in this industry," Zach tells me that afternoon. "It's important to find the people you can trust." He has come over to help add his extension to my phone. I roll my chair back to make space for him.

"You'll listen to all of my calls," he says. "You'll probably think I sound like an idiot sometimes."

"I'm sure I won't," I say.

He spends all day on the phone, mostly talking about nothing, with agents, producers, managers, and studio executives. A lot of gossip, a lot of "Love it, love it," and "Let's set it up, bro."

I keep my ears open for gossip about Robert, but there isn't much. The person I hear the most about is Veronica Ross. I consider my sexism radar finely tuned, and it goes off immediately when Zach and Allyn describe Veronica. *Scary, aggressive, cutthroat, bitch.* I know the double bind faced by women in leadership positions. I am prepared to assume the best of her. I like the idea of working at a network with a woman president.

Veronica has been at the network for fifteen years, which is a lifetime as far as these things go. She got her start in publicity before moving to development and programming—a move akin to going from cheerleading to varsity football—and there are rumors about how she managed to make that switch. That she's a favorite of Robert's is clear enough. But why? She does everything he says. But doesn't everyone? I hear occasional speculation about who she might have slept with, and every time I'm included in such a conversation, I can't help myself and my curiosity; I let it go on for a certain amount of time, to hear if any new names come up, before I offer a general defense. "Women are more likely to sleep their way to the middle than the top," I say. It's one of my mother's oft-repeated maxims. Another being: There's a special place in hell for women who don't support other women. The other assistants respond with mild amusement. I suspect that if I keep this up, it will be catego rized as my shtick and codified into my office personality.

I learn as much as I can as quickly as possible. I am encouraged to ask questions, but I understand that it's important to ask the right questions, to avoid revealing the depths of my ignorance. The person I feel most comfortable asking is Allyn; she always responds warmly and without judgment, though her explanations tend to engender more confusion than clarity.

In broadcast television, the year is divided into four seasons. Pitch season, development season, pilot season, and staffing season. Pitch season coincides with summer and early fall, development season is fall into winter, pilot season is the end of winter and early spring, and staffing season is mid- to late spring. There is also off-cycle development—more and more of it these days—but the creaky old infrastructure remains, rusty but without obvious replacement.

I've arrived at the tail end of pitch season and the beginning of development season. The project Zach is most excited about, at the moment, is called *Olympus*. The premise: What if the Greek gods had to go undercover and pretend to be humans, passing as a family running a Greek restaurant?

"Why do they need to go undercover and run a Greek restaurant?" I ask when he first tells me about it.

Zach shakes his head. "It's complicated. Listen, I heard the pitch and it's great. I can't wait for the outline to come in. I think you'll like it. We've been trying to crack the Greek mythology arena for a while. Think about it: Greek mythology is like the OG of preexisting IP. It's gold."

"Midas touch," I say.

He gives me a strange look.

My mother keeps encouraging me to get to know the executives. I struggle to explain the impossibility of this task, the meaninglessness of the phrase "get to know." What exactly am I supposed to say? How? When? I am used to working hard and standing out. But I am used to classrooms, homework, textbooks. "Read scripts and send your notes to all the executives," my mother suggests.

I tell her this would backfire in a mortifying way. I can't quite articulate how I know that, but I do. It has to do with hierarchy and respect and understanding the pecking order. Reading the room. A room that has yet to acknowledge my presence. Success will require carefully calibrated pressure, not blunt force.

The morning after Mitt Romney bungles a debate question about pay equity with a boast of "binders full of women," Zach calls in sick with a hangnail.

"A hangnail?" I repeat, looking down at my own hands under the harsh fluorescent office lighting.

I have stopped tearing my real nails off only because I have fake ones to focus on. If and when I tear those off, I can go have them replaced. The biggest thing keeping me from tearing is the knowledge that one missing nail will expose the shameful artifice of it all. It's not such a mark of progress, really. It's only that my hands look better, less ravaged, throughout the whole cycle. When I look down at them, I feel less ashamed and more like an adult. Specifically, my mother.

"It's very painful. I'm worried about infection."

"Oh no," I say. *A hangnail?*

"Don't worry, I already called the dermatologist, and she can take me in an hour." He asks me to clear his morning but not tell anybody why. "I trust you to be discreet," he says.

I open his calendar: two calls and two meetings before lunch. His afternoon is open. Could this not have waited until after lunch?

I instant message Allyn. *If you have to reschedule super last minute, how much explanation do you give?*

We're the network, she replies.

I add a few question marks. No response. I don't want to be annoying, but I also don't want to fuck up. Zach's first call is in half an hour. I pick up my phone and dial Allyn's extension, which by now I have memorized.

"We're the network," she repeats. A crackery crunching sound in my ear as she takes a bite of something.

"Meaning?"

"We're the buyers. We don't have to explain."

———

I DON'T KNOW WHAT TO DO or how to be. I've figured out the phones, though, which is a start. What buttons to push in which order. Zach sends me the link to a website where I can order stationery, business cards, even. He suggests I add *Office of Zach Daniels* to my email signature. It's a mutually beneficial setup, though I still feel like a fake assistant, imposter syndrome as bright as the yellow backing of the ID badge that highlights my temp status. These early weeks pass slowly, full of anticipation and uncertainty.

I try to get a handle on the things within my control. Like my health. I've been light-headed and exhausted and having frequent night sweats, which could be anxiety or antidepressant side effects, but it's been a long time since my last checkup. Susana has been on me to get my blood levels tested to rule out a medical issue. So I schedule an appointment for the afternoon of an off-site executive retreat, and after a day of doing not much in the office, I head to Howard's office in Beverly Hills. The building is flanked on one side by Judi's Deli, which has the best tuna salad in the city, and on the other side by a nail salon that always has paparazzi waiting outside, just in case.

Up to the waiting room, check in, say hello. Howard is both my primary care physician and a family friend. He hears my voice and comes out to give me a big hug. "Come, come, come," he says, herding me into Room 2. "It's been too long!"

Howard is a few years older than my parents. He wears his khaki pants belted high over his stomach and thick black orthopedic sneakers. "See any good movies lately?" he asks right after sticking a thermometer in my mouth.

I point to the thermometer. He taps his head, says "Duh," and pulls it out.

"Don't you want to finish taking my temperature first?" I ask, but he waves me off.

He decides he'll draw my blood himself so that the two of us can keep chatting. I have doubts about this; I remember struggles in the past. Sure enough, he has trouble finding a vein. After several ineffective pricks, he calls for a nurse. The whole time, I look away, at the beige wall, stucco ceiling, crinkled paper covering the green vinyl beneath me, anywhere but at my right arm, extended out, hand in a fist to plump my veins. I focus on speaking calmly because I am an adult and adults are not supposed to be troubled by needles.

As a child, I had a theory about the nurses who administered shots and drew blood. I thought it was a power trip for them, a chance to get back for all the shots they received. I suspected it was part of the appeal of becoming a nurse.

Howard asks if I'm feeling okay, and I say yes, generally, I guess, I just don't sleep well sometimes or I sleep too much, and I'm always tired but can't fall asleep without medication, and since getting back to LA, I often wake up in the middle of the night drenched in sweat. But that might all be psychological, right?

He asks if I want to step on the scale.

I say I will if he needs me to, but I'd rather not. He says fine, checks a few more things, shines a light in my ears, down my throat.

"I think that covers it," he says.

"So I look okay?" I ask.

"Well," he says, drawing it out, "I don't know if you'd be interested, but there's this new thing I've discovered. I've been using it myself, and I have to tell you, it's pretty incredible."

"What is it?"

"Technically it's for type two diabetes. It regulates blood sugar."

"Do I have diabetes?" I ask, alarmed.

"No, no, but off-label, it's proving really effective for weight loss."

A rush of static fills my head, high frequency buzzing between my ears.

"Do you—do you think I need to lose weight?"

"Only if you want to. I just noticed you seem to have gained a little through the hips and thighs." Something must change in my face because he adds, "I didn't mean to upset you! I just discovered it myself and want to spread the wealth."

"How does it work?" I ask weakly.

He says I wouldn't believe what an effective appetite suppressant it is and proceeds to walk me through his daily meal plan in great detail, from his breakfasts of half a grapefruit or a single scrambled egg with a dollop of ketchup to his evening chicken breasts, cooked with just a splash of olive oil, a dash of salt and pepper. I am contemplating whether there exists a more depressing meal than a single egg with ketchup when I hear him say, "It's just one injection a day."

"Hold on," I say. "Injection?"

"It's a teeny-tiny butterfly needle, much smaller than any of the needles here. You barely feel it."

I tell him I'll think about it and get out of there as fast as I can. I was planning to stop by Judi's for tuna salad, but now I don't.

While waiting at red lights on the way home, I do a Google search of the medicine and find some stuff about it being used as a treatment for obesity in nondiabetic individuals. Okay, so yes, I must have gained weight in the past year, but I am not obese. Howard didn't even weigh me! Since fifth grade, I have considered getting dressed to be an exercise in camouflage, though Susana has made a valiant effort to help me understand that I don't perceive my own body accurately. I may have been overweight once, during those difficult early years of adolescence, but I am not trapped as that girl.

Except now this. Here is someone who is not me, someone who is my doctor, telling me I might want to inject myself to lose weight. It is a desperate measure—does that make it a desperate time? Plus, muffled: the usual crap about how I am more than my body and think of the energy I've wasted on hating it and the beauty myth and the patriarchy and so on.

By the time I get to my mother's house, I am angry. In the blur of my indignation, I nearly trip over a huge box outside the front door—the new living room rug. Abraham, the pug, is insufficiently potty-trained. My mother has resigned herself to replacing the area rugs every so often. She says it's my fault, and she might be right, since I was the one who advocated for a dog when I was in high school, knowing I'd be leaving for college and wouldn't be there to see it through.

When she gets home from work, I follow her into the kitchen

to tell her about my afternoon. I want to hear her say that I don't need to lose weight and I certainly don't need to inject myself to do it. If she says it, maybe I'll believe it.

But she doesn't take my side. She says I am being unfair to Howard, who was just trying to be a friend.

"He's supposed to be my doctor, not my friend!"

She thinks I'm being childish and melodramatic when I say I want a new doctor. A new doctor won't be available the way Howard is, reachable by text, day or night, she reminds me. She herself has sent many a late-night text to Howard over the years.

"Do you think I need to lose weight?" I ask.

"Don't start. Please, let's not start this again."

"Is that a yes?"

"I think you should do whatever you want. And I think I shouldn't get stuck in the middle of it. You're beautiful. You've always known that."

It's a funny thing, the writing, and rewriting, of history.

Here is one version:

My birth is the greatest gift of my mother's life. I am spoiled by my parents, who give me everything I ask for and cannot bear to see me cry, my mother in particular. These are the happiest years of her life. She never imagined that someone might love her as much as I did.

She wanted to protect me. She tried so hard. The best schools, the best therapists. All the books and toys I ever wanted. My father would only buy me one book at a time, but not her, no, she would never say no to my love of reading. She was nice to my father after the divorce. She didn't want me to feel like I had to choose.

You are beautiful. You are brilliant. You are special. You can accom-
plish anything. You'll never get a boyfriend if you don't lose weight. You're
a spoiled, selfish bitch. You're thoughtful and kind. You're thoughtless and
cruel. You're too sensitive. You're entitled. You have never known pain.

"Lots of people have had worse mothers than you," she says
sometimes. "Like me."

————

MY FRIEND GEMMA and I decide to get an apartment together.
Gemma is my oldest friend, though she has not always been my
best. We were classmates from ages two to eighteen, a period
riddled with competition and dysfunction. I was arrogant and
she was cruel; I compulsively followed rules and she caused constant disruptions. We were regularly forced together for group
assignments.

College was good for us, individually and together: a pressure
valve, released. Over the course of academic breaks, we circled
back toward each other. She is newly into meditation and crystals and unpronounceable supplements, working at a chakra-based
mindfulness start-up.

I introduce the prospect of moving in with Gemma to my
mother during a Saturday nail salon trip, a deliberate location
choice. She surprises me with her support. Perhaps she knows that
some concessions must be made. That I require at least the illusion
of independence. She says she knows I am an adult and deserve the
opportunity to be my own person, and she is happy to help. She
always wished she had parents who could support her, and she's
glad to do that for me. She's a partner at a top-tier corporate firm
now, a job she took when my brother and I were in high school and

she was looking down the barrel of dual college tuitions. She hates the soulless cases that have swallowed her days, leaving her with limited time for the pro bono work and writing she cares more about, but this is where the money is. "It's all for you and your brother," she tells me. I feel both guilty and grateful.

We find an apartment in West Hollywood, in a little pocket where several small Russian mom-and-pop shops still stand, interspersed among trendy new bars and restaurants. The rent is so reasonable that my mother asks if I'm sure it's safe. "It's walking distance to Whole Foods," I say.

"Who would walk to the market?" my mother says. "How would you get the bundles home?"

The emptiness of the new apartment is soothing at first, then overwhelming. There is so much I need. My mother and I go to Bed Bath & Beyond, the temple of domestic consumerism, where there are so many options that I am tempted to turn around and leave empty-handed. My mother is enjoying this, propelling me forward through the gauntlet of the store. Rows of bedsheets, swatches of fabric to touch, but they all feel so similar. Do I want white with blue borders? Black? Gray? No borders at all? "It's not so hard; just choose what you like," my mother says.

"But I don't know what I like," I say, only understanding that this is the problem as the words tumble out of my mouth.

"Of course you do," she says.

She tells me to get a nice pillow, not one of those cheapo ones piled high in the bin. "You can get a couple of those, too," she says, "to fill out the bed and for when someone sleeps over, but for you, a nice one, a good one, the difference is real."

Again, the options. The question seems to be: What kind of

sleeper am I? Side, back, or stomach? It's not back, I know that much. But beyond that, who knows? The options for side and stomach are different. Also, is it unethical, the goose feathers, the down?

That night, I get in my new bed and savor, for a moment, the luxurious feeling of fresh bedding before leaning over to turn off the bedside light, which, like my mattress, is on the floor for now. I roll over and try to pay attention to what my body is doing, to what feels most comfortable.

What I find is this: I sleep on my stomach, in the "ready" position. The position you are supposed to take if you are asleep and wake to find an unwanted man on top of you. Legs spread a bit, one straight, the other frog-legged up. From this position, you can easily dig your feet into the mattress and use your lower-body strength to roll to one side and thrust the man off you.

At my high school, self-defense was the most popular PE elective. Male instructors in padded suits came in each week to role-play sexual assault scenarios. They would say awful things and try to scare us. The point was to practice in an adrenalized state so the actions would become muscle memory. I learned what to do with a man I didn't want on top of me before I learned what to do with a man I did.

I have no idea how long I've been sleeping like this.

———

"THE THING I TRY TO REMEMBER," Allyn tells me while we are standing in line for the food trucks that drive onto the lot every Friday, "is that nobody in our department is cool. Everybody used to be a weird kid who sat in front of the TV at night and thought, 'These are my only friends.'"

I have chanced a comment about the fact that none of the executives acknowledge my presence—not in an "oh, they've noticed me, but they don't know who I am and don't think it's worth learning" kind of way, but rather in a way that makes me feel like I am literally invisible.

We're in line for sushi burritos. I squint to make out the menu. I've been trying to eat more healthfully, though my problem is one of quantity, not quality—it's the end-of-day attempt to plug my leaking emotions with whatever food is on hand.

Allyn makes a face. She's beautiful even in her attempts at grotesquerie. She does not look like one of the weird kids she is describing. File it under appearances, deceiving.

"That's insightful," I say.

"Is it?" she says. "I don't know. It's just my version of imagining everyone in the audience in their underwear. If someone is being a dick or talking down to me, I try to think of them as socially awkward third graders who never learned better. If anything, they learned worse. Actors, it's a different story, and on the business side, I don't know, we don't really interact with them. I mean we do, all the time, but it's like we live in different countries. What we do in Creative, nobody just falls into this. It's way too hard. You do it because there's nothing else in the world you want more." She pauses, looks at me for a moment. I try not to grab for my shirt hem or readjust my hair or betray the splitting seams of my composure. "Sorry. I don't want to scare you or make it sound like you'll be asked to kill someone. It's a lot of shit work, yeah, but obviously enough of us think it's worth it, and you deal with the shit so one day you can do the better shit and make someone else do your shit, but hopefully without being such a dick about it."

She asks how long my temp assignment is for, and I say, honestly, that I don't know.

"Fair enough. Nobody seems to know anything about what's going on around here, only that if we don't come up with some hits, heads will roll. You're lucky not to be starting at an agency, and to be coming in at a time when everything's up in the air. Could create an opening for you."

"That's the hope," I say. We pause our conversation to order the burritos and then step back to wait for our numbers to be called.

"If I were you," Allyn says, "I'd do everything you can to avoid ending up at an agency. It nearly broke me. But be careful about what you say, and to who—not now; when you're basically an intern, it's fine that you don't have agency experience—but if you're going for a desk. They think of agency time as a rite of passage, something they had to suffer through, and so you should too."

"Like hazing."

"It really isn't terrible here. Other places are way worse. It's just, to do well, you have to be willing to make it your whole life."

"I am," I say quickly and easily. I want that single-minded devotion. I always have. It's the only way I know how to be. How to feel like someone worth being. I am not intimidated by Allyn's comments. What she has described is an environment in which I know I can thrive.

———

I CALL HOWARD'S OFFICE and ask the receptionist to send in a prescription for the weight loss injections, speaking in hushed tones as I walk through the grocery store. I buy vegetables and kombucha and ancient grains that I don't know how to cook. I stop by the drugstore on my way home. At the pharmacist's counter, I offer my name and date of birth. When they come up blank, I look furtively behind me to ensure nobody is within earshot before I whisper the name of the medication. I think about the groceries in the car and feel virtuous. So many colors, so many leafy greens. I consider signing up for yoga. There's a hot yoga studio just a few blocks away. But how hot?

Later that night, I sit cross-legged on my bed and open the box of needle tips. I think of the laser face peels that turn my mother's skin red. Eye lifts and face-lifts, the incisions involved. Waxing and threading and cupping. This is nothing. You are strong. You are steel.

I think of Veronica Ross with her blowout and blazer, the whiff of frost and confidence. I want that. Not to look like her, exactly. But to walk into a room like her, protected by an impenetrable wall of self-assurance.

I spend a lot of time hating my body, but the truth is that, on some level, I also know I'm pretty in a fairly conventional, heteronormative, patriarchal Western beauty standards kind of way. And yet, when I look in the mirror, I am full of self-loathing. It's a high-wire balancing act of mixed messaging—no easy feat, but I have so many years of practice.

I realize that people probably don't register my weight one way or another. But they don't know how long it takes me to get dressed in the morning. They haven't scrutinized the extra flesh on my hips, the way my belly button squints instead of stretching taut, or the dimples of fat at the tops of my thighs. They don't understand the lack of control I have always felt over my eating habits. The persistent sense of teetering too close to the edge. If I could just take a few steps back.

I am pursuing freedom. I am taking control. I uncap the medicine pen, click the needle into place, and stab my thigh.

———

THE *OLYMPUS* PILOT OUTLINE comes in. Zach is nearly giddy when I hand him the pages, still warm from the printer. His baby. "You should read it too," he tells me, and so I do.

It's a blend of soapy family drama and police procedural and fantasy. The gods posing as restauranteurs are drawn into a murder mystery after a young woman is found bludgeoned to death in a back booth one morning. Patriarch Zeus is the chief suspect. He can't account for his whereabouts the night before because the truth is he spent the night in the form of a swan, fucking his mistress, Leda.

"This is hilarious," I say to Zach, lobbing my words up above the frosted plastic partition that separates our cubicles. I hear the squeak of his chair wheels on the plastic carpet cover as he stands up. He comes around to my cubicle and perches on the edge of my desk. I swivel to face him. "Do you like it, though? It's good, right?" he asks.

He looks suddenly young and vulnerable. He cares what I say, what I think. I know not to make too much of this—it's more about a desire for validation generally than specifically from me, but it's hard not to lunge at the bait. I am full of need myself.

The problem is, it's not good.

The story makes little sense. If they're gods, why can't they figure out who the murderer is? What happened to their powers? Why did they get expelled from Mount Olympus? There are so many unanswered questions, only glancing references to a "mysterious incident" to be unraveled over the course of the season, the obliqueness of which seems like a red flag that the writers haven't settled on what said incident is.

Or maybe it's good. Who am I to judge?

What I say in the end: "Zeus can't reveal where he was because he doesn't want to be outed as a shapeshifting god, or as a rapist?"

Zach gives me a look. "What are you talking about?"

"Leda and the swan. That's a rape story. Zeus rapes Leda."

"No, it's not," he says.

"Zeus rapes a lot of women," I say. Everyone knows Zeus is a serial rapist. *Does everyone know Zeus is a serial rapist?*

"What? Who?"

"Who" is right. Someone as a bull, or a cow—what was her name? Something with just vowels. Does he rape Persephone? No, Persephone is his daughter. He raped her mother? Demeter? This would be a good moment to have my answers straight.

I google *Leda and the swan* and click on the Wikipedia link at the top. Zach leans in to read over my shoulder. He's not inappropriately close, but I feel hyperaware of his proximity.

Leda and the Swan is a story from Greek mythology in which Zeus, in the form of a swan, seduces or rapes Leda.

"Seduces or rapes," Zach repeats. "Huh."

"There are others. I can't remember them off the top of my head, but it's a thing."

"But it's just one interpretation, right? It says there, 'seduces or rapes.'"

"Sure, but it's a pretty common reading. I think."

He pulls away and sits back down on the edge of my desk, drumming his fingers on its surface, metabolizing this unwanted complication in front of me. "But he's not a rapist in our show, and I bet the average American doesn't know as much about this as you do."

I've been here just two months, and already I have heard so much about this mythical average American viewer, whom nobody knows and everybody wants to satisfy.

"Maybe not."

"Definitely not."

"Okay, sure. I guess where I'm going is, this outline is light on character development. And if the gods aren't defined within the world of the show, viewers will interpret them based on prior knowledge, and we clearly don't all come in with similar preconceptions. This reads differently if you think of Zeus as an amoral autocrat as opposed to a more benevolent father-figure type. Sorry. I don't know if this makes sense. Maybe it's not relevant."

"No, no, it's an interesting point," Zach says, my self-deprecation triggering a certain softness. "It's good that you're passionate. Listen, if you write that up—nothing long and complicated, just what you said—I'll flag it for Gregory when we go over notes."

"Of course!" I say, with a little too much enthusiasm.

———

IT'S NOT SO BAD, REALLY, the needles. They don't hurt, not like I expected. It becomes mechanical—peeling the paper covering off the needle tip, inserting it with a click into the medicine pen, removing the plastic cover, pricking my thigh and pressing down on the plunger, checking the numbers on the side to ensure I'm injecting the right amount.

I throw the needles away in my bedroom trash, but the medicine pen has to be refrigerated. I store it behind the butter, which sits on its designated shelf inside the refrigerator door, unsalted and untouched. I haven't figured out what I'll say the pen is if Gemma finds it and asks.

Many nights, we stay up late, talking about how much we've grown. Congratulating ourselves on the maturity of our friendship, on the adults we are becoming. We drink cheap wine and talk about the past.

"I was so angry," she says.

"Me too, but I didn't understand it or think I had any right to be," I say.

"I thought if I wasn't going to be loved, I should do something to become unlovable. It hurts less if there's a reason for it, you know? I felt more in control."

"I thought I would only be lovable if I was perfect. But I wasn't perfect. I couldn't be."

"Nobody can."

Gemma has been losing weight in a fairly dramatic way. She has always been big, someone about whom people would say, "She has such a pretty face." But now the weight is coming off. The reason for the weight loss is clear: she has mostly stopped eating. She eats a lot of seeds, measuring them out into tiny Tupperware containers. One night, she offers me a bowl of dry oats. "Is that dinner?" I ask. She nods.

I feel like I should say something, but also, who am I to say anything?

"I had this extraordinarily transformative moment," Gemma tells me one night as she opens the living room window to retrieve the crystals she left on the outer windowsill to "charge" in the sun, "when I realized that food is for fuel, not pleasure."

"But can't food also be for pleasure?" I say. "In moderation?" This seems like an argument someone would make.

———

I DECIDE TO FOCUS ON getting into better shape. Thanks to the injections, I have very little appetite for food, and some of my clothes are loose. But my body looks the same to me. While I was away at college, a whole new world of boutique fitness blossomed in LA. It seems like all the women in the office attend workout classes—everywhere I go, I overhear conversations about SoulCycle versus Flywheel versus Pilates versus barre. I envy the smug post-exercise satisfaction of the women I see waiting in line to order iced almond milk lattes or green juices at cafés throughout the city. It's something in their faces. And their bodies, too, of course: the lean muscles, sculpted arms, yoga pants, and loose tanks with sports bras showing underneath. They exude an expensive sort of wellness. There is a buoyancy to them that I crave.

I've heard about some of these classes. The intensity, the number of calories burned per hour. I can't even jog for ten minutes straight. Here in LA, workout classes are filled with people who are paid to be beautiful. It's an impossible point of comparison. I have no idea what many of the class titles even mean: Yoga Booty Ballet, Cellulite PlateFIT, Aerial Hoop, The Rocket.

I start slowly, with gentle-sounding yoga classes. Pilates one Sunday afternoon, which is harder than I remember it being the last time I did it, in eighth-grade PE. My abs burn and I'm not sure what they mean by "tilt your pelvis" or whether I'm doing it correctly. I can't make it through the hundred without collapsing on my back. Another weekend, yoga at a studio that boasts an "immersive" experience using something called Yogascape technology, which turns out to be akin to a glorified screensaver—alternating underwater, beach, and mountain scenes projected onto one of the walls of the darkened studio.

At The Bar Method, the instructor says to sit down and "three-quarter-lengths your legs," as if that's a verb I know what to do with. There are so many props—full mats, booster mats, mini mats, rubber balls, rubber bands.

I end up at hot yoga by mistake. The class description didn't mention the temperature, it just said hip-hop, which seemed daring enough on its own. I only learn about the heat when I get to the studio, where the wall behind the front desk reads 99 PROBLEMS BUT A BRIDGE AIN'T ONE in bold font. The placid woman doing check-in assures me I'll be fine, 105 degrees only *sounds* like a lot. The infrared heating system makes a world of difference, she says.

I do downward dogs as "Ms. New Booty" blasts through speakers in a candlelit, black-walled room. I sweat from places I have never sweated from before and have to close my eyes when I bend over to stop the sweat from clouding my vision. I get so hot that I'm cold. Goose bumps prick my arms; my arm hair stands on end. It's a wonderful feeling, and I relax into it, but in the back of my head I think, isn't that how heatstroke feels too?

After ImprovYoga, I resolve to read class descriptions more carefully. I assumed the "improv" referred to yoga flow sequences.

I discovered otherwise when, halfway through the class, the instructor transitioned from Savasana to theater games.

My pants are too big for me now. I go shopping for new workout clothes. Leggings and those flowy tanks with the low sides that I've seen so many people wearing.

———

WHEN PEOPLE ASK ME what working in Hollywood is like, I say it's like middle school, if most of the classes were recess and lunch.

There is no official dress code at XBC. I learn by observation. Sneakers are fine for men but rarely worn by women. (Veronica pays attention to shoes, Allyn tells me.) Jeans are worn by all. When in doubt, think fashionable. Corporate cool.

In high school, I wore a uniform five days a week, so my closet was limited mostly to weekend clothes. I couldn't and didn't compete with my richer, trendier classmates, carrying books in beat-up Louis Vuitton totes, shoving Burberry scarves into their lockers. There was nothing I needed that I didn't get, but I didn't have a drawer full of, say, $200 sweatshirts designed to look pre-worn, adorned with holes. My mother was an expert consignment shopper, with an eagle eye for discounts. She'd lend me accessories as needed. I kept up well enough.

Harvard was comparatively unfashionable, and I loved it. Sure, there were the rich preppy kids, the ones in Loro Piana or Nantucket Reds, neither of which were on my radar before college. But by and large, Harvard was a place of fleeces and practical shoes. I relaxed quickly and happily into a life of sweatshirts and snow boots. I stopped highlighting my hair. None of my new college friends did, and I didn't think they were less attractive for it. All this felt, stupidly, like a revelation.

It becomes quickly clear that my collection of college clothes and random, inexpensive business casual left over from summer internships won't get me far at XBC, where the women in the office play a never-ending compliments game. One woman compliments the other, usually on an item of clothing, but other things related to appearance work too. Woman Two says thank you and immediately pays the compliment back with one of her own.

"I love your shirt."

"Thanks! I love your dress. So cute."

It sounds ridiculous, but everyone does it. It's like saying good morning. Allyn is an expert. She's great at quickly homing in on a new item of clothing, a different shade of lip. Specificity suggests sincerity, I realize. And maybe it is sincere. Maybe I'm the asshole here. It's best to be the first one in with a compliment. Return compliments run the risk of sounding fake.

My mother offers to take me shopping. "Please, let me; it gives me pleasure," she says. It's hard to know how to handle this, her desire to buy things for me. I suspect I am doing it wrong. There will be strings attached, I know there will. And yet. I am making twenty dollars an hour, pretax, and I want to fit in.

Most assistants receive parental support of some sort, I am learning. How else could anyone accept a job at an agency with its starting ten-dollars-an-hour salary? Allyn bemoans the dearth of culture in her Midwestern upbringing, but there's plenty of money there. Her father works in pharmaceuticals.

I say yes to my mother, yes to new clothes, new shoes. To highlights and manicures, to items from her closet. I say yes, and in the office, I begin to receive compliments. I learn to play the game.

I could come up with theories, if pressed, about the forces to which I am succumbing. But it's easier not to, and there's nobody to urge my eyes to the light. I still talk to Susana on the phone, but she is three thousand miles away.

In Boston, being from LA was part of my identity, and this I could handle. I felt in control of the narrative, apart from the place. I surprised myself by sometimes even feeling abstract affection for the city and its idiosyncrasies. But now I'm back and it's like being trapped in the middle of a Jell-O mold, trying to swim to the surface for air without knowing for sure which way is up.

Things are better with my mother, though. I go over for dinner after eleven-hour workdays, we get our nails done together. She tells me about her terrible cases and advises me about asserting myself in the workplace. We get stoned and watch TV, often still *Justice Served*. An easy choice, and there are so many episodes. "My only happy moments are when I'm with you," she tells me, and I feel a familiar blend of tenderness and terror.

Then I go home, back to my apartment. And in the morning, I do not have to first stumble to her bedroom to gauge her mood, to determine if this is going to be a good or bad day. Anyone less brilliant than her, and less widely respected, could not get away with the schedule she keeps. Her headaches, which come during periods of stress or depression, have grown more debilitating over the years. She doesn't always go into the office, and she often sleeps during the day. She works in fits and bursts so productive that people think she must have been up all night, glued to the computer. A brief that would take someone else ten hours takes her two. She specializes, now, in crisis management, helping high-profile companies who find themselves in various forms of trouble. She knows not just the law, but also how to shape a narrative.

Maybe this is the answer, living near—but not with—her. Maybe it doesn't have to be so hard. She is thrilled to have me back. And it's nice to have somewhere I can go, someone I can call, if I need to. To feel like I'm not going it alone.

THREE

O NE SATURDAY IN NOVEMBER, THE WEEK AFTER
Obama's reelection, Gemma drags me to a biweekly dance
party in Echo Park called Bootie LA. She befriended one of the
door guys on a previous visit, and he waves us forward, allowing us
to skip the line. I can feel the eyes on us as we cut ahead.

"Didn't ask to be born under the patriarchy, but as long as we're
here," I say.

Inside: a wave of heat. There's a fog machine and dancers in dis-
cordant outfits leaping, twirling, gyrating. A woman in a tutu and a
dinosaur mask, a man in red-and-white-striped footie pajamas and
a Where's Waldo? hat, a guy in a pink leotard with a Hula-Hoop.
The uninhibited nature of their performance is entrancing. I wonder how drunk or high I might have to be to shed my inhibitions,
to try dancing like that. Whether I'd even be capable of letting my
body be liquid like theirs.

In ninth and tenth grade, my friends and I went to under-
eighteen nights at a rotating series of Hollywood clubs, hosted
by companies with names like Seduction and LA's Realest. The
parties attracted high schoolers from all across LA. We would
stand in a circle on the dance floor and make smallish suggestive
movements with our hips, waiting for the heat and pressure of a
body against our backs, hands on our hips. Instead of turning to
look at the boys, proper etiquette required relying on our friends'

facial expressions to indicate approval or disapproval. Extrication always proved tricky. Because although these boys were strangers we would likely never see again, and they never even asked if we wanted to dance in the first place, we didn't want to offend them. The most effective strategy was to claim a need to go to the bathroom. It didn't occur to me that I might simply turn around and say "I don't want to dance" until college. I didn't enjoy these parties, exactly. I went in order to be objectified, in abject search of validation from boys who didn't know me.

The dance floor at Bootie LA is too hot and crowded to remain comfortable for long, so we make our way out onto the smoking patio to get some air. Gemma decides to bum a smoke. The first person she asks—a clean-cut guy in a button-down—shakes his head, but the friend to his right obligingly pulls out a pack. As the guy with the cigarettes flicks his lighter, the first guy turns to me.

"Don't smoke either?" he says.

"Not cigarettes." I smile, and he laughs.

"Me either."

"Have you been to Bootie LA before?" I ask.

"Nope, Bootie virgin. My friends have been talking it up for a while. You?"

"Same."

"What do you think?"

"Kind of reminds me of a big college party."

"I hadn't thought about it like that, but you're absolutely right. Really brings me back," he says. He looks older than me, but it's hard to guess by how much. Probably just a few years. He's cute, though sweaty. Then again, so am I.

"Long time ago?" I tease.

"Eons," he says.

"Where did you go?"

"I went to school in Boston."

I laugh and shake my head. "Seriously?" I say.

"What?"

"Me too," I say. "Which House?"

His face changes. "Touché," he says, with an appreciative smile. He introduces himself: David, Lowell House.

It's known as "dropping the H-bomb." The moment you reveal that you went to Harvard, and the lengths to which you might go to avoid doing so. There are different philosophies. I've always thought it best to be direct. If you avoid answering, it both over-inflates the significance and suggests a value judgment about the person you're talking to.

I got into Harvard off the wait list, a fact I shared with none of my classmates. My mother thought the wait-listing had to do with my freshman and sophomore science grades, and maybe it did. I didn't tell her when my favorite teacher disclosed that a member of the admissions committee called her to inquire about me and whether I had interests and passions of my own or was just trying to emulate my mother. The acceptance call came a few weeks later.

My mother wanted to go to Radcliffe, but she didn't get in. I got to do what she did not. Debt was constantly on her mind, and she had to work throughout college and every summer, as did my father. They worked hard so I could know the freedom they craved. So I could become the type of privileged private-school kid they found so intimidating when they arrived at college.

Within minute one of our conversation, David mentions being on the *Lampoon*. Freshman year, I "comped" the *Lampoon*—

Harvard-speak for applied. This involved sitting cross-legged on the floor in an overheated room at the Lampoon Castle, waiting my turn for one of the comp directors—seated above me in a cracked leather armchair—to read my proffered humor pieces and dispense criticism. They rejected me via a note, delivered under my dorm room door in the middle of the night, which informed me that my jokes "failed to transcend referential humor."

"I was on *The Crimson*," I tell David. "Editorial board." I do not share that *The Crimson* was my second choice, that I only joined after failing to get into the *Lampoon*.

"The enemy!" he says. *The Crimson* and *Lampoon* have a long-standing rivalry, and nobody writes for both. "What if somebody sees me talking to you?"

I take a deep sip of my drink and note the proximity of our bodies. We graduate to work talk. David tells me he is doing the comedy thing. "A little acting; mostly writing."

"Are you staffed?" I ask.

"For a hot second," he says, offering the name of a recently canceled NBC multicam.

"RIP," I say. "But hey, it'll be staffing season before you know it." I am, if not yet fluent, becoming conversational.

"I work in development at XBC," I tell him, compressing the liminal blob of temp life into a shape so solid, it feels almost disingenuous.

When David asks for my number, I am confident that he'll text. I feel smooth and fresh and powerful, typing my details into his phone, like a snake that has shed old skin.

———

THE STRAIGHTFORWARDNESS of David's attention is unfamiliar and appreciated. It provides a new frame of reference for my past nonrelationships. All the mind games and mutual manipulations. This is how it's supposed to be, I think, with new clarity. I should not have to be a perfect mix of sexy and sweet, standoffish and approachable. Somebody's interest in me should not be so tenuous that a single ill-timed text can shatter it. And if it does, then he, whoever he is, probably isn't worth my time.

I end up back at his apartment after the second date, on a Tuesday night, eight p.m. drinks at a bar in Los Feliz, the journey to which involves a freeway lane-change ballet complicated enough to require GPS assistance. I turn on NPR in hopes of catching up on the day's news, but the GPS voice keeps interrupting.

"We begin this hour with talk of a cease-fire in the—*use the left lane to stay on I-10 East*—with more casualties on both sides. Israel—*use the left two lanes to merge onto CA-110 North*—heavy artillery shelling from—*take US-101 North slash US-101 South exit toward Ventura slash I-5 South slash I-10 East slash CA-60 East*—In Berlin, a boar attack wounded—*use the right two lanes to merge onto US-101 North*—their obsession to find and consume food—*use the left two lanes to stay on US-101 North*."

I give up and switch to oldies.

At the bar, one glass of wine and I'm buzzed. I've barely eaten all day.

Afterward, at David's apartment, I pull myself up from the couch before any clothes come off. I'm not one for following rules, but it feels like the right thing to do. Before I walk out the door, he asks if I'm free on Friday. I say yes.

For our third date, David suggests drinks at a restaurant attached to a West Hollywood hotel. It's one of those self-consciously cool places, where doll-sized servings are carefully plated with swooshes of multicolored sauces and the cocktails include flavored foams.

It's a fancy choice on David's part. Another indication of his seriousness, or maybe just his desire to impress. Particularly notable given that he's in between writing gigs, tutoring private-school kids to pay the bills. I'm standing up front by the entrance, looking around for David, when a man approaches me.

"Hi," he says, smiling.

"Hi," I say back. He is middle-aged, white, nondescript. I'm fairly sure I don't know him.

"Are you Shadow?" he asks.

It takes me a moment to understand that Shadow is a name, and in that moment, confusion or blankness or both must flash across my face. I don't have a chance to say no before he jumps in with, "I am so, so sorry. Please excuse me." He hurries off.

I'm still processing when I find David in a chair facing the back of the room. He rises to give me a hug hello. "Something weird just—" I say as I take a seat across from him, but then I stop because there's that man again, and he's greeting a woman. "Oh my god. That's Shadow."

"What? Who?" David says, swiveling his head. The man is walking out of the lobby, a hand on the small of Shadow's back.

"That guy," I say, but it's too late now. I cross my legs. "I—I think I was just mistaken for a prostitute. Or escort, I guess? An expensive one, I hope."

"What? How? By who?" David asks. He's getting more worked up about this than I am. I'm not sure how I feel about it yet. I tell

David about the man. "You don't know for sure that she's a prostitute, though, right?" David says.

"I guess not," I say. "But her name is Shadow, the man had clearly never met her before, and when he realized I wasn't her, he was super embarrassed."

I only got a brief look at her, but that was enough to register some general similarities and significant differences. We are both fake blondes in tight black dresses. But Shadow's hair is blonder, her dress tighter and shorter, and her boobs are bigger and more prominently on display.

"That is so, so not okay!" David says. "That guy should—"

"Should what?"

"I don't know."

"Maybe I should take it as a compliment, right? That man thought I was attractive enough to make money for my body."

"You weren't bothered by it?"

"It's not that," I say. "It's more—" But I started speaking before thinking, and I suddenly find that I don't want to open the door to a discussion of body image and the male gaze and the chubby teen I used to be. "Complicated," I finish.

When the waiter comes, I order a dirty martini. "Going for the gin," David says, and I try to remember if I've mentioned liking gin.

"I'm in it for the spherified olive," I say.

"Oh yeah! I read about that. It sounds cool. It's like a gel ball—"

"It's a ball of liquid encapsulated by a thin gel layer formed by the chemical reaction between calcium chloride and sodium alginate," I say, interrupting him. My junior year of college, I took a class called Science and Cooking, which I thought would be an easy way to satisfy my science requirement. This was a ridiculous thing to think, given that I had never demonstrated aptitude for science or cooking. It turned out to be the most challenging, time-consuming course of my college career. But to my continual delight and surprise, I didn't just skate by—I excelled. I loved it. My final project was about the molecular ratios of spherification, and the professor nominated it for a university-wide science prize.

I could have played this differently. Could have waited for him to finish sharing his explanation of spherification. It's not quite mansplaining, what he's doing. He'd have no reason to guess that I'm an expert on this obscure subject. I could have said something less obnoxious, more casual, like "I actually know a lot about spherification." But I went with the most boastful option. I wanted to see how he'd react to it, this unabashed assertion of knowledge.

The look he gives me is one of unguarded admiration.

The martini arrives with both a spherified olive and a tradi-tional one. I lift the toothpick-speared real olive to my mouth and wrap my lips around it, maintaining eye contact with David throughout. I am too sober for this to not feel ridiculous, but I can see the desire in his eyes. I want to be the person he sees.

The sex could best be described as bland.

One night, I whisper, "I want you to take control," to see what he'll do with it. The answer is: not much. He looks down at me, silent, eyes wide. "Have your way with me," I add, lying beneath him, legs spread. This doesn't help.

He proceeds to fuck me missionary-style. After a minute or two, he pulls my legs up over his shoulders. My body feels like a folded tortilla. A sneer of concentration appears on his face as he pumps in and out with increasing urgency. I give up.

"I want you to come for me," I say.

I want to be in control. I want to be controlled. I want to control who controls me. I want to understand my wants and why I want them. I am only now beginning to suspect that all the time I've spent trying to make myself desirable has come at the expense of thinking about what I might myself desire.

———

LITTLE COMMENTS, tiny things, nothing really.

"You're a short skirt kind of girl, aren't you?" Zach says to me one day, and I freeze.

("Just throw it right back at him and call him an ill-fitting plaid shirt kind of guy," my mother advises later. But my reflexes aren't fast enough.)

"Would you say you're a softcore or a hardcore feminist?" Zach asks another day.

"Call me Andrea Dworkin, but I prefer not to think of my feminism in terms of porn," I say. I'm getting quicker on the comeback.

"Who's Andrea Dworkin?" Zach asks.

It occurs to me that I have never actually read Andrea Dworkin. I add *Read Andrea Dworkin* to my to-do list, under *contact lenses; hair; script coverage: sandman thriller, cryptozoologist procedural; figure out birth control.*

"The party was full of 617s," Zach tells Julian, an assistant known for his good looks, great hair, and love of surfing. They are standing in front of my desk. Julian and I have spoken only once, and barely, when Allyn took me on an introductory tour around the floor. He and Zach have a friendly and distinctly male rapport. No matter how socially savvy I become, I will never reach this last-name, high-five, bro-hug level.

"Not bad," Julian says. "Throw me an invite for the next one, dude."

"People from Boston?" I ask Zach.

"Oh no," he says. "You don't know the area code system? First number is for face, second is a zero-or-one binary—would you or wouldn't you—and third number is body. It's a classic."

Locker-room stuff. No big deal. I can handle it.

"What kind of porn do you like?" I ask David one night, about a month into dating.

"I don't," David says. "It's so fake and exploitative." He explains that he's seen a few videos that are different, more realistic, more tender. He likes those.

"What search term do you use?" I ask.

"'Romantic,'" he says. "Or sometimes there's a 'Popular with Women' category."

I try to watch one. The background music is ridiculous. The soft focus, dappled lighting. Arched backs, long kisses, everything in such slow motion.

Shouldn't I like this in him? Shouldn't I consider it a sign of respect?

Instead, I wish he'd said *amateur* or *threesome* or *oral* or *public*. *MILF* or *gangbang*. *Big ass* or *creampie*.

"Hold my head," I say. "Pull my hair. Tell me how much you want to fuck me."

"I love being inside you," he says. "You feel so good. You're so good."

He doesn't ask what porn I like, which is fine, because I don't know if I would answer honestly. *Forbidden, inappropriate.* Power dynamics subverted and perverted. Men driven by lust, doing what they shouldn't. Men losing control.

One night, David notices a bruise on my upper thigh and asks about it, running a finger around its perimeter.

"Anemia," I say. "I bruise easily."

I take more care to vary the injection sites and switch thighs more frequently.

———

THE TROUBLE WITH the office outfit game is that the more compliments I receive on a given clothing item, the less frequently I can wear it.

One day, Julian's boss, Billy, waves me into his office as I walk down the hall. "I just wanted to introduce myself," he says. "You've been doing a great job."

"Thanks," I say. "I'm trying! I'd love to contribute more to the department."

"You already are," he says. "You have great energy. I love those shoes."

I look down at the pointed-toe, cherry-red heels. Borrowed, like all my nicest things, from my mother.

Every few weeks, more shopping. When salespeople bring over

clothes for me to try, they usually guess size small, and they're often right. I always thought that if I could fit into a small, I'd be able to acknowledge that I was thin, that my weight problems were in the past. But now here I am, and there's my body, and the truth is, it looks mostly the same to me. My stomach is flatter, my arm muscles more pronounced, and that does feel good, but there are still trouble spots, cellulite dimples, fatty areas to camouflage. Part of me knows I should work on accepting my body as it is, but another part thinks that if I could just reach some critical milestone, body acceptance will be easier, and so why not shoot for that? I'm getting close. I must be close.

———

DAVID KEEPS ASKING questions I don't know how to answer.

What's your favorite color?

If you could travel anywhere in the world, where would you go?

Mountains or beach?

Cats or dogs?

Summer or winter?

"I don't know," I say.

"What do you mean?" he says.

"What do you mean what do I mean?"

He looks at me like one of us is underwater.

It would be easier to answer for my mother: pink, any tropical location with my brother and me, beach, dogs, and summer.

———

"IT'S NICE TO HAVE A BOYFRIEND, isn't it?" my mother says. My mother, who also always said that I should never rely on a man to make me feel happy or whole. "Nice to have someone to do things with. I never wanted to end up alone. Look at me. Nowhere to go, nobody to see." I'm sitting by her bedside. Darkened room, Sunday afternoon. At home, a pile of scripts I told Zach I'd read this weekend, thus far untouched.

"We haven't defined the relationship yet. I don't know that he's my boyfriend," I say.

"You will," she says.

"Can I open a window? Or at least raise the blinds?"

She offers an indifferent shrug, which I take as a yes. I slide off the bed and cross to the windows that span the better part of the western-facing wall. Pull the cord of the blinds all the way up. I open a window, feel the relief of fresh air, light streaming in. Midsixties, blue sky, line of palm trees in the distance. On a clear day like this, you can see all the way to the ocean. A straight shot to Heartbreak Hotel, thin blue strip of the Pacific beyond.

"You should date a lot while you're young," my mother says. "That way, you'll have a pool to return to if you end up middle-aged and divorced. My friends who remarried, they mostly ended up reconnecting with old flames, college sweethearts, that sort of thing. I didn't have nice boyfriends when I was young, or ever, really. I had no confidence. I thought I was ugly and fat and unlovable. So I moved all the way across the country for a man who didn't especially want to get married."

How many times we have had this conversation, a looping record, subtle riffs. "You're not ugly or fat or unlovable," I say.

She laughs. "Now I'm just old. That's worse. It's too late for me."

"No, it's not."

"Oh please. You think the sixty-year-old men in this town are looking to date women their own age?"

My mother dated some in the first few years after the divorce. After she left my father. This was no secret, that she had done the leaving. "I would never say a bad word about your father or ask you to pick sides," she told me, "but that man is incapable of loving anyone but himself."

None of the men who came after my father lasted long. I resented her dating, but then again, I was a child. I didn't want a strange man condescending to me at the dinner table or sharing her bed or taking my place as my mother's cocktail-party date, never mind the fact that I found those parties exhausting and boring and I was invariably the only person under forty. I didn't like the idea of her having needs that I alone couldn't satisfy.

What I wouldn't give now, though, for her to have, if not a boyfriend or a partner, at least other people in her life with whom she enjoys spending time.

When my parents were married, they were very social, and they entertained often. I have warm memories of their dinner parties—the twinkle, the sophistication, the sweating silver ice bucket on the bar, toys crammed shut in the cabinets underneath. The click of heels on hardwood floors and the fizzy feeling of descending the stairs in my party dress.

After the divorce, there was a gradual emptying, a slow drift from shore. I can't pinpoint a specific moment when my mother's social world began to contract, but by the end of high school, every time we had people over for dinner—which was not often—it felt like we were playing at real life, pretending that our home was always like this, lights on and kitchen fragrant, as opposed to curtains drawn and dinner delivered.

I didn't know what other homes were like, whether there were other modes of being. I only knew my mother had two speeds: on or off. Her periods of depression grew longer, darker, and imbued with a magnetic force against which I felt powerless. "It's the Nana genes," she often said. "We have the Nana genes."

Growing up, I told my mother I loved her all the time. Compulsively. Dozens of times per day. Too much, she told me finally. "I know you love me," she said. But other times I would find her crying in bed, saying nobody had ever loved her.

"It's beautiful out," I say now, facing the window, away from her. A weak offering. If I look directly into the glare of her pain, it will blind me.

"Another shitty day in paradise," she says.

FOUR

DAVID CAN'T COME WITH A CONDOM ON AND THE pill makes me bloated and irritable, so I have decided to get an IUD. Enough of my friends have raved about theirs—no cramps, no periods, it lasts five years, and so on. I'm sold. I make an appointment for early on a Friday morning in December. The nurse assures me that I should be fine to go into work afterward.

I tell my mother about it over the phone the night before on my way home from work.

"Why would you do such a thing!" she says. You'd think I had announced an intended nipple piercing. "I wouldn't get one if I were you," she says. This is not the reaction I was expecting.

"Why not? They're supposed to be great."

"They're dangerous. I had a friend in law school who got one, and it perforated her uterus and destroyed her fertility."

"The technology is better," I say. "They're safe."

"I don't know about that."

"I do, though. I've done the research. I have friends who have them."

"Did Dr. Kim say this was a good idea? He couldn't have recommended it." My mother and I share a gynecologist. Dr. Kim both delivered me and gave me my first pap smear. It's a lot. Too much, perhaps.

"Dr. Kim says it's safe."

"Are you sure that's what he said? If I were you, I'd look into all the risks."

"Yes, I'm sure! And I literally just said that's what I've done."

"Don't jump on me. Why are you yelling at me? I'm trying to be helpful. I wouldn't want you to lose your fertility; I'm only thinking about what's best for you. I haven't seen you all week, now you call and tell me you're too busy for me this weekend and might be destroying your body, and I worry. Is that so terrible? To love you, to care about your future? To want you to know the joy of having children, the greatest joy of my life . . ."

I end the call with a flurry of frustrated apologies. "I'm sorry, I'm sorry, please don't cry. Don't cry. There's nothing to cry about."

"There's everything to cry about."

Back at my apartment, I shove a hexagonal white pill as far up my vagina as it will go. The following morning, I take 800 milligrams of ibuprofen and drive my dilated cervix to the doctor's office, which is located between Balenciaga and Cartier on Rodeo Drive. As I slide my feet into the stirrups and edge my ass down to the end of the exam table, Dr. Kim asks after my mother. I inquire about Dr. Kim's daughter, who was a year ahead of me in school. All very normal small talk except for the fact that my legs are spread, vagina splayed, and Dr. Kim is on his way in with a speculum. I try to focus on the watercolor painting on the wall across from me. A landscape, mountains, smeared trees. It hurts. A piercing cramp, then another. Feels like what it is, I guess: something being shoved into my uterus.

"All done," Dr. Kim says. "The strings will soften over time."

Success, I text David.

I buy stick-on heating pads in the pharmacy around the corner, as the nurse recommends. But the pad is too big for my stupid low-cut underwear, so I have to paste it half on my panties, half on the inside of my jeans. As I get into the car, I contemplate calling in sick. Going home, curling into a ball. Then I check my email and see a note from Allyn—Gregory's assistant is out sick today. *Can you cover?*

This is what I've been waiting for. The chance to interact with Gregory, to demonstrate my competence. Allyn says Gregory thinks his current assistant is flaky and disorganized. My task, I understand, is to present myself as the opposite. And that starts with showing up. I take a little more ibuprofen and half a Klonopin, for good measure. Just to take the edge off.

By the time I get to the office, I'm feeling a little spacey, but that could be any number of things. Nerves. Ibuprofen on an empty stomach. Klonopin. Whatever. I make my way upstairs and pass Zach's cubicle en route to Gregory's office. "Good luck," he says. "You got this. And if you can't handle my phones today, that's cool, but if you can forward the line over to Gregory's desk, that'd be awesome. And drop a line if you hear anything about *Olympus?*" Zach's been jumpy this week, waiting for Gregory to read and weigh in on the latest pilot draft, which is neither terrible nor good. The network will decide which scripts to order to pilot in the next few weeks; *Olympus* is "in the mix," meaning it's not at the top of the list, but it's not quite dead yet, either.

"I'll do my best!" I say. No witty repartee in me this morning.

Gregory's office is along the senior executive corridor, which connects the front and back bullpens. These offices have the best views, looking out over New York Street. The assistant desks line the interior hallway, divided into pairs. Gregory's office is at one end, and his assistant's desk is a disaster zone. I never registered this before, not fully. To get between the front and back bullpen, I usually take the back hallway, which is lined by filing cabinets—less formidable than a row of stressed senior assistants.

The desk is piled with papers, stacks upon stacks, the surface barely visible. A quick inventory reveals dozens of DVDs in paper sleeves, three mostly empty plastic water bottles, a bottle of Lysol spray, unopened mail, and several legal pads filled only with geometric doodles. Two sticky notes hang off the bottom of the computer monitor. One reads EXPENSE REPORT. The other: THERAPY!

I see no computer log-in information, no Desk Bible.

Every assistant I've covered for so far has left one, some more comprehensive than others. They are a guide to your job and your boss. Some have multiple authors, compiled over several assistant generations. Passwords, preferences, things to avoid. Half of the notes in Allyn's Desk Bible are incomprehensible, but the other half are useful.

It's nearly ten; Gregory will be here any minute. The red voice-mail light on the top of the phone is illuminated. I press the power button on the computer monitor, which brings me to the log-in screen. My stomach contracts, pain radiating from my uterus. I sit down in the desk chair, press a hand against my lower belly, and glance around the desk again. It has to be here. It's probably right in front of me. I take a breath.

I turn to my left, to the desk belonging to Julian. We still haven't really interacted, but he occasionally acknowledges me with an upward-nod hello, which is what he offers now. He's wearing his headset; I'm not sure if he's currently listening in on a call or that's just his default. I gesture at the desk, the computer monitor, and the phone, channeling my confusion into my facial expression as clearly as I can. He gives me something between a smirk and a smile and turns back to his dual-monitor setup.

And now here comes Gregory, leather messenger bag over his shoulder, coffee cup in hand. I've heard he's difficult, high maintenance, a bad manager. But the late-thirties guy who greets me this morning and thanks me for "jumping in" is nothing but polite. As he opens the door to his office, he makes a joke about his assistant's mess, says he hopes I can find what I need, but to let him know if I have any issues.

"I'm sure I'll be fine," I say weakly.

"Any voicemail?" he asks.

"Oh, yes, just a sec," I say. Passwords. Where could she keep the passwords? I riffle more desperately through the piles of papers around the keyboard. Wedged between scripts, I find a single sheet, **IMPORTANT INFO** bolded at the top. Brief flash of relief, smothered when I discover it's only a list of Gregory's food and drink preferences.

Water: Fiji, room temperature.

Lunch: When he says "just a salad," he means a La Scala roast chicken chopped with no cheese, extra garbanzos, add pepperoncinis.

No passwords.

I'm out of ideas. I look over to Julian. "Hey, Julian?" I say. He appears not to hear me.

"You can just tell me who left word, no need to worry about the phone sheet," Gregory calls out from his office.

"Okay," I call back. Then, to Julian, "Quick question?" I make a concerted effort to dial up the volume of my voice. "Sorry to interrupt, but do you know where she keeps the log-in info?"

"Oh sure, you should've just asked," he says, plucking a sheet from the front folder of a standing file on his desk and holding it out to me. I grab for it, equal parts grateful and incredulous. No time to dwell on the question of how long he would have waited, watching me flail. I scramble to log in to the computer while checking voicemails, a misguided attempt at multitasking that results in mistyped passwords and numbers. *Press four to repeat the message.* Four. Four. Four again. "Yo, it's Andrew, give me a shout," some guy says, as if he's the only Andrew around.

One of the strangest things about covering for someone is the full access to their life, their identity. I can read their email, communicate as them. I have to, in fact. That is the job. Even if I wanted to respect their privacy, I couldn't. Information I need—about meetings, materials, whatever—is often intermingled with more personal communication. So I learn that, as Allyn mentioned, Gregory's assistant is indeed looking for another job. Is unhappy with Gregory. *He's driving me crazy,* she wrote to someone yesterday.

"Holiday party's at three, right?" Gregory calls out. "Want to make sure I don't have anything bumping up against that."

This is the first I've heard about a holiday party. Because I'm a temp, I'm not on any official email lists. I don't get invited to things, don't know about them unless someone tells me. Sure enough, there it is, on Gregory's calendar and in his assistant's cluttered inbox. *Holiday party,* from three to four p.m. on Soundstage 26. Seems like a remarkably unfestive scheduling choice, but what do I know?

I am not dressed for a holiday party. I am dressed for comfort, in a white button-down with armpit stains underneath an oversized sweater. I have a heating pad pasted to my lower belly. I couldn't have known or planned better, but still, I am frustrated.

On his way to a meeting, Gregory asks for a specific script. He stands in front of my desk as I stare, overwhelmed, at the stacks of papers surrounding me. There must be forty scripts here. I don't want to admit I can't find it before I've even looked, but the odds seem slim. I start flipping through piles at random, feeling the building pressure of his impatience.

"You know what, forget it," he says as I make it to the bottom of the fourth pile and find, just in time, the script in question. As I hand it to him, I say, "Ideally, there would be a better system than this," gesturing around me, making the split-second decision to throw his assistant under the bus. I'm not proud of it, but it's immediately clear that it was the right move.

"You're telling me," he says. "I don't know how she lives like this."

Zach comes over for a midday pep talk. "How are you doing?" he asks. "You seem a little nervous. It's important not to seem nervous. Gregory doesn't like that."

"How could I not be nervous? Look at this mess."

My stomach hurts. Badly enough that I want to double over, press a pillow against my lower belly, all sorts of things I cannot do here and now. But other than that, everything is basically fine until the early afternoon. Gregory is eating lunch in his office and watching a new cut of an off-cycle pilot called *Unsung* that just finished reshoots. He has asked that I only interrupt him if it's something important. I'm about to head to the bathroom to replace my heating pad when the phone rings.

"Gregory Grey's office!"

"It's Veronica. I'm here with Robert."

I was worried about my ability to judge what counts as something important and am, at the very least, relieved by the lack of ambiguity. I instant message Gregory, and when he doesn't immediately respond, I knock on his door. "Veronica and Robert on the phone," I say.

"Both of them? Together?" His facial expression the human equivalent of bugged-out cartoon eyes. I nod. Back at my desk, I put my headset on and press mute. This is my first time listening in on a call like this; the most important person Zach receives calls from is Gregory.

Veronica and Robert have both watched the pilot. It's a soap about a young undocumented immigrant from Guatemala living in Los Angeles, working as a nanny for a wealthy family while secretly harboring dreams of musical stardom. I haven't seen this new cut, but I read the script—I have been reading everything I can get my hands on—and it's the most compelling pilot I've encountered in a while. It was written by the daughter of Guatemalan immigrants, and it has a depth and authenticity that I'm coming to understand is unfortunately unusual around here.

"Gregory," Robert says, voice booming through the phone. "What happened to Bianca?"

"What do you mean?" Gregory asks.

Veronica laughs, a sharp sound. "Don't tell me you didn't notice. Did she eat a whole farm between August and now?"

"She's pregnant," Gregory says. "The actress."

"She's *what?*" Veronica says.

"Yeah, I only just found out myself," Gregory says. This is a lie. I heard him discussing it with Zach last week, how it would impact a potential production schedule.

"How could this have happened?" Veronica says.

"I can explain how it happened . . ." Robert says.

"Thank you, yes, I have two myself. That won't be necessary."

"I'd say let's can her and reshoot altogether, but we've already sunk so much money into this," Robert says. "But fuck it, if we have to do it, we have to do it. She's our lead."

"Right, so I've thought about that—" Gregory begins.

"You knew about this?" Veronica says.

"No, no, I mean I'm thinking about it right now, and the only thing I'm wondering is, will we run into issues with employment law? Firing someone for being pregnant . . ."

"Not for being pregnant. For looking pregnant. The character is supposed to be young and hot and not with child. This girl on screen is not the girl we cast. She looks like a blowfish," Veronica says.

"Hey now," Robert says. "I bet plenty of men would still take a blowie from her. Right, Gregory? Wouldn't you?"

Gregory laughs, but it sounds forced. "I'd have to get my wife's permission first!"

"You know what I always say: If you don't want to fuck her, why cast her?" Robert says.

"I can check with Business Affairs," Gregory says. "But if we pick this up for fall, we could push production until summer, and she will have given birth by then."

"But will she have her body back by then?" Veronica says. "There should be something in these casting contracts about appearance. Maybe we can get her on breach of contract."

"I'll ask BA, let you know what they say."

Gregory comes out of his office, shaking his head. "Fuck me," he says. "Fuck everyone."

At least Gregory responded in a semi-reasonable way, though. That means something. That has to mean something.

Just before three p.m., the entire department gathers to walk to the holiday party. Given that these people are forever running late for meetings and phone calls, I'm surprised by their punctuality. I don't know for sure if I'm invited, and Gregory heads for the elevator without saying anything one way or the other. But then Allyn comes by to collect me. I feel a surge of appreciation for her inclusivity, such a striking contrast from Julian's behavior this morning. She has started inviting me to drinks with assistants from various studios and agencies, and she always introduces me as an assistant, not a temp. We walk together, trailing behind the rest of the group. I tell her, in brief, about the call I listened in on.

"Anorexic cunt," Allyn says. I don't have it in me to go into the politics of *cunt* right now. My cramps are back, and they're bad. *Breathe deeply. Just breathe.* People live with pain worse than this every day.

The soundstage is sweltering, under-decorated, and under-catered. The only drink offerings are hot chocolate and water, with assorted liqueurs to spike the hot chocolate. Food is limited to one table of baked goods. The few clusters of high-top tables look silly in such a large space, and there are no chairs. In the front, two women from Publicity stand behind a folding table, handing out orange raffle tickets. We are instructed to write our names and office extension numbers on half and drop it in the big glass vase on the table.

"The prizes are good," Allyn not-quite-whispers in my ear, "but this is also how they take attendance. Veronica reads out the winners, and if she calls your name but you left early . . ." She trails off.

I know better by now than to ask "Then what?" The answer: it would be a bad look.

I feel sweat gathering at my hairline, trickling down the nape of my neck. Under my arms, my breasts. I'm sure my cheeks are flushed. If only I could take off my sweater. But I can't. The underarm stains, they're bad. I checked in the bathroom mirror earlier.

The spiked hot chocolate was a mistake. Too heavy on the Kahlúa. If only there were somewhere to sit. Allyn is pointing out people I don't know. I'm not sure how much longer I can stand here before giving in and excusing myself. I am too overwhelmed to think of a good lie. But I should not talk about my vagina in the workplace. I will not talk about my vagina in the workplace.

"I got an IUD this morning," I confess to Allyn.

I have now talked about my vagina in the workplace.

"Oh my god, those are the worst. I get them all the time," Allyn says. "Do you need cranberry juice?"

"Oh! No. I mean, yes, UTIs suck. But IUD, not a UTI. Birth control."

"Right! Dyslexia brain fart. I've always wondered, how big are they? Do they just shove it up there?"

And so I explain, which somehow leads me to mime the action of inserting the T-shaped device up a vaginal canal with my hands. Allyn breaks into a big, performative smile and I pause. I turn around, and there is Robert, right behind me.

"Hello, ladies," he says, stepping forward and putting a hand on each of our shoulders. "I hope you're discussing something good."

I take in the room around me; it's loud, lots of noises echoing around the soundstage walls. Maybe he didn't hear. Maybe he did. Fuck me.

"Of course," Allyn says.

"Always," I say.

"Do tell," Robert says. Hands still on our shoulders. I look to Allyn, but she is frozen.

"We were talking about *Unsung*," I say. It is suddenly the only project I can think of by name.

"Oh yeah? You watched the cut? What do you think of it?"

Again I turn to Allyn, giving her the opportunity to answer first. She does not take it.

"I think the writing is sharp and there isn't anything like it on air. It's a big opportunity," I say. Robert nods but doesn't speak. Is he waiting for more? What more can I say? I haven't even seen the cut; it came in this morning. "And I think a lead who actually looks like a real woman and not an emaciated stick could reso-nate with a lot of viewers. The average American woman is five foot four and one hundred and seventy pounds, after all. Not that Bianca is anywhere near that."

Fuck everyone.

"I agree," Allyn says. "I completely agree."

"Five-four and one seventy, huh? Is that so," Robert says. I don't know where those numbers came from or if they are accurate. "Looking around here, you'd never know!" He laughs. "I should keep circulating. Enjoy." A lift of his hot chocolate and he is off.

"Nice rebound," Allyn says.

"Was that very embarrassing or only kind of embarrassing?" I ask.

"Not very, I don't think."

"I lectured the chairman on body positivity. I can't believe I did that."

"I can't either." She looks over at Robert, who is now talking to a group of men wearing what I have to believe are accidentally matching checked shirts. "Do you know him? He seemed super familiar with you," she says.

"I've met with him," I admit. She is waiting for more, so I add, "He's a friend of my mother's."

"Aha," she says. "Now it makes sense."

"What does?"

"This job you got. We've never had a floating temp before. Don't get me wrong, it's useful, but it's super random. But if it came from Robert, it makes more sense," she says. "Don't worry, I won't tell people, if you don't want."

"Thanks. It's not a secret. I just don't want people to treat me differently. Not that Robert and my mother are best friends or anything like that," I add. *Stop talking. Just stop talking.*

Veronica and Robert step up to the microphones positioned in front of a table full of prizes. The room silences. "Next year, if the ratings go up, I promise better catering!" Robert says. "How's that for incentive?"

That night, David brings ice cream over to my apartment. "All I've eaten today is unbuttered popcorn and one fish taco, so I'm ready to indulge," he says. "How are you feeling?"

"Like a disaster," I say. We sit on the couch and pass the cartons back and forth as I tell him about my day. In doing so, I discover that David is hearing a different story than the one I thought I was telling.

"The access you have, it's incredible," he says. "You see that, right? The chairman of XBC asked for your thoughts on a project in development, and you got to listen to a call with the people who make decisions about what ends up on air. You went to a party on the soundstage where some of the most famous shows of the past decade were shot. That's really cool."

"It is cool," I say, bringing a gloopy spoonful of mint chip to my mouth. "You're right." Of course he's right. Forest for trees. It's a useful reminder.

"Do you know how many people would kill to be in your position?"

David has been working on a pilot to use as a staffing sample. He has a manager, but his manager doesn't always call him back.

"I know," I say. "I do know that. But that doesn't mean I shouldn't be frustrated by the things I heard on that call, right?"

"No, I was only saying."

"Perspective, yeah. It's just disappointing. Maybe I should be equally upset about Robert's comments, but Veronica's hit me harder."

"Why do you think that is?"

"Because I was hoping for more from her. Sure, the 'if you wouldn't fuck her, why cast her' comment is gross, but it's the kind of thing men have been saying forever."

"That shouldn't excuse it."

"It doesn't. But it makes it less surprising and more like something you just have to live with, since it's so ubiquitous. Zach talks that way too. To be honest, I expected Gregory to do the same. It was a relief that he turned out to be uncomfortable with it."

"How do you know he was uncomfortable?"

"He was super awkward when Robert made the crack about blow jobs. He said he'd need his wife's permission, and he laughed, but it sounded forced. He was trying not to engage."

"But he did engage. Even if you think he did it awkwardly. And no offense, but probably worth remembering that you could be projecting what you want to see in him. It's in your best interest for Gregory to be the good guy in the scenario, since he's the one you could be working for."

"Fine, fair point. But it would be absurd to expect him to call Robert out on it or anything like that. Robert is his boss's boss. I wouldn't have been surprised if he played along even more than he did. But Veronica. I'd heard talk, and I chalked it up to the usual office sexism. What powerful woman hasn't been called a bitch, right? But she really is a bitch. Not a woman's woman, as my mother would say. Probably my mistake for assuming she would be."

"That's interesting," David says.

"What is?"

"You expect the best from women and the worst from men."

"That seems overly reductive."

"Am I wrong, though?"

This conversation has become more agitating than cathartic. I am tired and full and now annoyed at David, who hasn't said or done anything wrong. I am relieved when I hear a rattling in the front door and Gemma bursts in, reeking of palo santo, a cardboard box in her arms.

"I come bearing gifts," she says, setting the box down on the coffee table and removing a glossy brochure from the top. She kneels on the floor and begins rummaging through the box. "These are for chakral healing." She looks up at me, then David, assessing. She passes David an orange stone streaked with white. "Citrine, for the solar plexus chakra," she says, glancing at the brochure.

"How do I . . . use it?" David asks.

"I can't answer that for you. It's a very personal experience, how you interact with the vibrations. But for citrine, we recommend starting with the affirmation 'my life is filled with positivity and abundance.'"

"Positivity and abundance? Who wants those?" David says, but the joke falls flat.

"If you don't approach energy medicine with an open heart, it won't work," Gemma warns. She hands me a light blue stone. "Blue lace agate for the throat chakra." I turn it over in my palm, cool and smooth.

"What's the affirmation?" I ask.

"'I release fear of judgment and gently speak my truth.'"

"I'm still thinking about that phone call," David tells me in bed that night as I surface for a seventh-inning blow-job stretch. "Does anyone really call it a blowie?"

"What if we don't talk about work in bed? I think I'd be into that as a kind of blanket rule," I say, running a finger up the underside of his cock, trying to be cute about it.

He gasps and nods. His cock twitches. I feel like a snake charmer. The sigh as I wrap my lips around him, the way he thrusts his hips toward me.

"This is the best head of my life," he says, which is what he usually says. "How did you get so good at this?"

I have a weak gag reflex: bad for bulimia, great for blow jobs. In lieu of an answer, I offer a moan.

———

GREGORY'S ASSISTANT gives notice at the start of January.

"Luckily, Gregory's open to both girl and guy assistants. He doesn't have a clear preference," Allyn tells me. We are standing at her desk, unpacking plastic containers of chopped salads, sorting lunch orders. She explains that some executives prefer one or the other—Julian's boss, Billy, for example, only ever hires guys.

"That's literally gender discrimination," I say.

"It's not like a rule, it's just some people get along better with men or women," she says.

"But we're not private, personal assistants, right? This is theoretically an apprenticeship system. You have to be an assistant to become an executive. So if you're an executive and you only hire male assistants, you inhibit women's opportunities to get their foot in the door, which then limits their advancement, which propagates the gender imbalance among executives."

"No, but some executives prefer female assistants, so it balances out."

"But say there are two female execs and five male execs. If both the women hire female assistants and all the men hire male assistants, it's still unequal."

"But it's not just women who prefer female assistants. A bunch of men do too!" Allyn says, and I laugh.

"That's a different problem!"

"What do you mean?"

"Why do the men prefer female assistants? Do you think they feel more comfortable asking women to do stupid personal tasks for them?"

"I never thought about it like that," she says, lifting one clear plastic container up for inspection. "Do you see olives in here? I said no olives. Doesn't that look like an olive?" She points to what is definitely a black olive, buried in shredded romaine. "Oh! And Gregory went to Harvard. You know that, right? Make sure to tell him you did too. He'll like that."

Allyn is right. Gregory does like that. During my interview, he says he can tell already that I'm like him: an OCD and organized Harvard type, not the all-over-the-place creative type. I smile and nod, though I am not, in fact, organized, and I don't have OCD. People like to use "OCD" as shorthand for "type A." A humblebrag. Like saying your greatest weakness is working too hard. I know that I don't have OCD because I actually did as a child, and it wasn't cute. Compulsive praying, cleaning, counting, reciting historical dates. You want to know the Chinese dynasties in chronological order? I'm your girl. An attempt at control, and so on. Then depression took over, and then I was so overmedicated that it took all my energy to maintain a veneer of organization. The compulsive behaviors petered out, leaving only anxiety in their wake. I found a combination of antidepressants and mood stabilizers that worked well enough.

I would like to be organized in a healthy way. But the closest I come right now is giving off the impression of organization. What I have is a good memory. It served me well academically, but I've learned to be careful about it interpersonally. Turns out people don't remember everything they've ever told you and find it creepy if you do. Go figure. In the office, though, I can use it to my advantage. "My assistant remembers everything," I've heard Zach tell people on the phone. "I have to be careful around her!" Occasionally he calls me his external hard drive.

So I do not correct Gregory. I allow him to think I am just like him because I know this is what he needs to think to offer me the job, which, just a few days later, he does.

The early days on Gregory's desk are thrilling and bewildering. He is exceedingly polite at first, a bit formal, even. *Just wait*, Allyn warns, *he'll get anal soon*. Once my status changes from temp to permanent, once my email signature reads *Office of Gregory Grey*, people begin to learn my name, to reach out and ask me to get drinks. I realize that most people are only being nice to me because of who I work for, that when agents call and try to charm me, it's because they're hoping I'll remember this while scheduling meetings. I know all these things and try not to take the attention too personally or make too much of it, but still, it feels so much better than being ignored. In my early months, when floating and on Zach's desk, some execs didn't even look me in the eye. When I move to Gregory's desk, those same executives come up to introduce themselves to me, as if they've never seen me before. Veronica Ross nods at me for the first time while walking at a fast clip down the hall for a meeting. It's like being recast in a better part, going from Extra to Guest Star: no more real, but a more fun role.

FIVE

I'M SITTING ON THE TOILET PEEING WHEN MY HEAD-set beeps. I've had to pee for an hour, but Gregory has been in the car, stuck in traffic and rolling calls on his way back from lunch.

I weigh the risks. Second beep. I'm wearing a skirt, and I have Purell at my desk. I stand up, wipe, and click the earpiece. "Gregory Grey's office!" I say, rushing out of the restroom before the toilet's automatic flush begins.

"Hi, Nick calling from Eyrie Einhorn's office," the voice in my ear says. Eyrie's a big-deal agent. "I have a favor to ask. Eyrie's coming for a pitch today, and she needs to know how many steps it'll be from her parking spot to the conference room. Footsteps, not stairs," the assistant says. "I'm sorry. I know."

I send an intern down to the garage to walk and count. There was a time when I couldn't have issued this assignment without laughing. But at this point, I can do it with almost a straight face. "Small steps," I call after her. "Eyrie has a short stride."

The fluorescent lights in the hallway are bright and there aren't any windows, but sometimes Gregory will comment on the sunset and I'll go into his office and look out at the pink-and-purple sky above New York Street. "Beautiful," I'll say, looking at the time. Gregory is probably late for a meeting.

"Why am I always late?" he'll ask. "We need to work on this. It's your job to make sure I know what time it is. How am I supposed to know what time it is?"

It is my job not to point out the watch on his wrist, the clock on the wall, the digital displays on his phone and computer screen.

I don't love sitting next to Julian, who continues to be sort of the worst. He'd say we're friends, and so would I, because that's how it works here, which is also the worst.

My first week on Gregory's desk, Julian invited me to lunch, sushi at the place in the mini mall where everyone goes. It's nothing special, and the parking is lousy, but it's close, and as an assistant, leaving the lot in the first place is daring. Over lunch, Julian regaled me with his résumé and professional strengths. "I'm really good at booking travel and getting reservations," he said. He paused to let me appreciate this. "Those are skills worth developing," he said, swirling wasabi into his soy sauce with a chopstick. "It can be challenging at first."

He advised me to order some smart-looking books on Amazon and arrange them on the end of my desk. "Don't worry, nobody will ever stop long enough to ask you actual questions about them," he reassured me.

"Why not just bring in the books you're actually reading?" I asked, with my sweetest smile.

When I first started at the network, I'd listen with amazement to executives bloviating on phone calls, cultivating a superficial feeling of intimacy and trust with the person on the other end, spinning words into sentences that contained the illusion of meaning but very little actual content. I couldn't imagine pulling it off myself. I feared I lacked the charm as well as the duplicity, and it seemed just, well, wrong. But look at me now.

"We're really excited about that project," I say, when what I mean is, "I've vaguely heard of it."

"I love him" means "I've met him" and "She's great" means "Her name rings a bell."

In the mornings, I check my individuality at the door, by the fingerprint scanner where I input the last five digits of my social security number, then press my thumb into the scanning pad. When in doubt, I always speak in the plural.

I am a good assistant, it turns out. A great one, even. I am accustomed to considering another person's comfort a precondition for my own. I have a knack for anticipating Gregory's needs as well as the ways in which his self-centeredness might upset others in the department. I am here, I am listening, I understand your frustration, I say. I am an always-smiling intermediary.

"You're a mind reader," Gregory tells me.

I'm doing well and learning fast, and the success brings with it a certain satisfaction, a sense of belonging. I never imagined I might take such pleasure from being part of a system. This system, in particular, one I never expected to fully accept me. I have little time—and even less energy—for sustained introspection. My mind is occupied by short-term problem-solving.

I roll calls, drop calls, log calls on a phone sheet that never ends. I meet people. I avoid meeting people. I learn to play drinks chicken. I read scripts. I write up coverage and send it out to the department. *This is compelling for an intergalactic political soap*, I write.

As many days a week as I can manage, I drag myself out of bed before six in the morning so I can make it to hot yoga or spinning, depending on my mood and how much my body aches. I work toward that place past exhaustion, where my vision smears and glows like the inside of my eyelids after looking at a bright light. If I keep pushing past the burn, through the so-hot-that-I'm-cold feeling, I find it, just for a moment: freedom.

Then the lights come on and I stumble back into the world, back to the banalities of my morning routine, checking emails at stoplights even though I know I shouldn't because I want a sense of what kind of disaster to expect from the day.

———

I THINK I'M HAPPY. Everything is going as it's supposed to. I have a job that people would kill for, right at the pulsing heart of Hollywood. Sure, it's sometimes awful, but I'm paying my dues. This is how it works. I have a boyfriend who is nice and cares about me. I have healthier, more meaningful friendships than I did the last time I was in LA, even if yes, it is true that Gemma is my only nonindustry friend, and lately, all she wants to discuss are chakras and spiritual energy. "Are you practicing self-care?" she asks when I return home bleary-eyed, bearing scripts and leftover lunch salad. I have my own space, away from my mother. I am thinner than I've ever been in my life. I've finally stopped the injections. Susana is proud of me for this, although the truth is it's mainly because my weight loss plateaued and I was light-headed all the time.

"But how do you feel?" Susana asks over the phone.

"I don't know," I say. "How am I supposed to figure out how I feel?" On the other end of the line, Susana is quiet. "That's a real question," I add.

I talk to Susana twice a month. Every other Tuesday morning, I drive to work early, park on a nearby side street, and connect my phone to the car's Bluetooth system for a phone appointment. I still appreciate her presence and feedback, but it's harder over the phone. She feels so far away. I realize that I should probably find a therapist in Los Angeles, but I'm reluctant. Susana knows me so well; I don't want to have to start over.

I've been having more trouble sleeping, though. Susana increases my Ambien dosage. It helps.

———

I SEE MY FATHER once in a while, dinner or a weekend brunch every few weeks, and he seems fine with this frequency. We have pleasant though not very intimate conversations, and I try not to keep track of how few questions he asks about my life. Our interactions have always been tinged with formality, oriented around thoughts and ideas, not feelings. He doesn't tell me about his personal life or ask about mine. I try to believe that I have made peace with this, but I wonder, sometimes, about the difference between acceptance and resignation.

I see my mother less often than she would like, both because I am trying to set boundaries and because my free time is increasingly limited. She is starting to feel ignored. She is worried I don't care about her or want to spend time with her. I know this because she tells me. My brother, who is now a sophomore at USC, spends every weekend with my mother and often multiple nights during the week as well. I have tried, unsuccessfully, to tell her this isn't healthy or normal, and to encourage him to spend more time at school, with friends. But he doesn't want to hear it from me; our relationship has always been strained, potential goodwill eroded by years of mutual resentment. He says his classmates are stupid and that if he doesn't visit, she might not get out of bed all weekend—even with him there, she sometimes doesn't—and if I actually cared, I would visit more, I would not abandon him as I have.

I call a couple times a week, usually when I am in the car, leaving the office at night. I work eleven-hour days, not counting the at-home script coverage and constant emailing. I am exhausted. I tell her this; I downplay my social life, most of which is work-adjacent anyway. I sense that she's keeping a running tally of things I prefer to spending time with her. I want to say that it's not healthy for adult children to spend most of their free time with their parents, but I know that I can't, that it would be useless. Not to mention the obstacle of her unwillingness to go anywhere, do anything, or have a conversation unrelated to her misery and frustration.

"How nice for you," she says when I mention plans with someone. "I'm just at home alone. And my headaches have been awful; I'm in such pain."

"I'm so sorry about that."

When I say I've had a long day or a busy week, she says I wouldn't believe how hard she's been working, what a stressful week she's had.

"It's not a competition," I say.

"I didn't say it was," she says. "All I'm asking for is a little kindness and compassion. Even an 'I'm sorry you're in pain, Mom' would be nice."

"That's what I said! I literally just said exactly that."

"I didn't hear it," she says.

"How about we make a weekly date?" I say. Boundaries. "Maybe Sunday afternoons?"

"That's just a few hours," she says.

I explain that I wish I had more free time, but I don't, and I also need to take care of all the things I can't do during the week, like laundry, grocery shopping, and cleaning.

"I could hire you a cleaning lady," she says.

"I appreciate the offer," I say. "But I'm trying to be at least somewhat self-sufficient."

"And I admire that. But you don't have to be. When I was your age, I was alone in the world, and it was so hard. You aren't. You have me."

"I know," I say. "Thank you."

"I don't want to be an obligation, some chore you're checking off the list," she says.

"You're not."

"I only want you to spend time with me if it's something you want to do. Not as a favor to me."

"I want to spend time with you. Of course I do."

I hang up feeling angry, and frustrated with myself for my anger. Why can't I give her what she wants without feeling pain? Why does this have to be so hard?

On Sunday morning, I call and ask if I can bring anything over when I visit.

"Klonopin and pot," she says.

I was thinking along the lines of lunch.

"What kind?" I ask.

"Flower. Sativa. Triple Jack if they have it, otherwise whatever the top of the line is."

"And is there a prescription you want me to pick up? For the Klonopin?" I ask. One of the boundaries I've tried and failed to set is not sharing prescription medications.

"Oh, no, I'm out. But you must have some, don't you? Can't you just bring me some of yours?"

"I have a few extra," I say. "Not that many. But I'll bring them." Not a big deal, I tell myself. Not worth triggering her anger over this.

There are medical dispensaries all over the city now, and obtaining a medical card requires little more than thirty-five dollars in cash and claims of an ailment—pick a pain, any pain. I got mine at a storefront on Melrose called 420 Doctors, a walk-in-only operation sandwiched between a tattoo parlor and an improv comedy theater. The waiting room was furnished with two plastic chairs and a small TV playing nature documentaries. I came armed with a tote bag full of psychopharmaceuticals by way of medical justification, but that proved unnecessary.

Allyn brought edibles home to her family for Christmas; they took them together Christmas Eve. It was amazing, Allyn said. Everyone was so nice to each other for a change.

To have parents who get stoned is apparently now borderline normal, borderline cool, depending on the audience. "My mother smokes so much weed," I told Allyn recently. Testing the waters. She was leaning over my desk chair, trying to fix the development grid formatting, which Gregory had messed up. "I'm sorry. I made all the changes he asked for, but then he went into it late last night and made more, and now here we are."

"Such a fucking micromanager," she said, clicking away with

my computer mouse, resizing columns. "Your mom sounds cool. Do you guys smoke together?"

"Sometimes," I said. It's new, telling people about this. I've only started doing it now that there's less stigma attached. And I am only telling a partial truth.

I caught my mother smoking for the first time when I was ten. Taking a hit from a small pipe early in the morning on a school day. I was terrified. The lessons in school were clear: Drugs are bad. Smoking kills. Only losers do drugs. Not respectable, competent, high-achieving people like my mother.

My mother said she was smoking because things were difficult with Nana then. She made it sound like something new and temporary. Nana's fifth husband had recently died, leaving Nana on her own in Florida. She called my mother all the time, complaining of new medical ailments. Her head, her back, her stomach, her legs. Her loneliness, her abandonment. Acid rain, burning holes in my mother's resolve. Hence the pot, she said. To help her deal with the stress.

This was years before she disclosed that both she and my father spent much of my childhood stoned. That the older woman who sold beaded jewelry out of her apartment in Venice, whom my mother brought me to visit regularly, was her dealer.

My mother didn't tell me to keep her marijuana use a secret. I came to that conclusion on my own. Occasionally, I would hear her allude to it in conversation with friends, and I would feel concerned about her cavalier attitude. How could she not worry about people judging her? Why didn't she understand what people might think?

It seemed to me that she smoked more and more as I grew up,

but it might just have been that once I knew about it, she made less of an effort to hide it. I got upset about the weed spread all over her bathroom counter. "If you don't want to see it, you shouldn't use my bathroom," she told me.

Other people might not get away with smoking as much pot as she did and does, but she has a prodigious tolerance. She can take a few hits and then write an airtight legal brief. The pot helps her participate in the world, blunting the sharp edge of her emotional and physical pain. There's a tipping point, though, where slightly stoned becomes very stoned, and she often fails to notice the distinction in herself. She gets slow, forgetful, repetitive. This is the version of her I worry about.

"You can refuse to get in the car with her if she's stoned," Nadine told me when I was a teenager. "That is absolutely something you can do. It's a safety issue."

I tried, I failed. She only got mad. And if I didn't get in her car, how was I supposed to go anywhere?

I didn't smoke until my junior year of high school. Up to that point, I abstained as a matter of principle. Then I tried and loved it. It felt like a revelation. The way it eased my anxiety and slowed my thoughts. I upheld certain boundaries for a while. I wouldn't smoke her pot, and I wouldn't smoke with her. She threw away a stash she found in my bathroom once, toward the end of high school. Said it smelled cheap. That if I was going to smoke, I should smoke the good stuff. "Where did that come from?" she asked me.

"One of the second-year associates at your law firm," I told her.

She laughed. "Giving drugs to a minor, now there's a great idea," she said.

During college, I discovered that the trick to being around her while she was stoned was to get stoned myself. High, we could spend peaceful, conflict-free time together. We could enjoy each other's company. Could eat cake for dinner and watch TV and laugh and I could pretend everything was okay enough. But that was during the void of college breaks, when I had nothing else to do with my time.

I worry about her, but what can I do? If I want to be allowed autonomy, I have to allow her the same, right? Her life, her choices, and so on. I do periodic online searches for studies on the risks of long-term marijuana use. The results are largely inconclusive.

So here I am at the weed store—this one has a chandelier and a waterfall feature; they're getting fancier—asking for top-shelf sativa. The "budtender" uncaps a large glass canister and holds it out for me to smell.

"Smells good," I say, which is what I always say. Most of it smells the same to me. I ask for half an ounce.

My brother's car is in the driveway when I arrive. I let myself in. "Hello?" I call. The only greeting I receive is from Abraham the pug, who comes waddling down the stairs, snorting with enthusiasm. Up, then, to my mother's bedroom. My brother's door is shut.

I find her in bed, under the covers. Pill bottles and empty cans of diet soda on her nightstand. There is something about simply walking in the room that makes me seize up. A hopeless, boxed-in feeling. "Hi," I say softly. "How are you feeling?"

She opens her eyes. "Bad," she says. "It's been bad." She asks me to shut her door. She doesn't want my brother to see her like this. "He gets so worried," she says. "He needs me. He doesn't have anybody else. Not like you. You have lots of friends. You'd be fine if I died."

"Please don't talk like that," I say.

"It's the truth," she says. I pass her the Klonopin, a few pills I put in an old antidepressant bottle.

"You're not dying," I say.

"Not today."

"Is there something I don't know about?"

"I'm just getting older. You have to think about these things. Could you pack me a bowl? The pipe's in the bathroom."

I do as instructed, grinding the sticky buds directly onto the bathroom counter and packing it in tightly to the reservoir that protrudes from the neck of the glass bong. I fill the bong with several inches of cold water and bring it, along with a long candle-lighter, back to my mother's bedside. She sits up gingerly. I hold a flame to the bowl as she inhales. The neck of the bong grows thick with smoke. If it were me, I'd give in and remove the bowl at this point, let some air in, but she keeps going. A long exhale. "Thank you," she says. She passes me the bong, still lit, a single tendril of smoke swirling thinly up from the blackened weed. I hesitate.

It's only noon. I don't want to fumble the rest of the day. But I know the boxed-in feeling will only get worse. Though I wish I had a better idea of how to cope, to feel secure, to stop feeling so much, I don't, and in this moment, a short-term solution is the best I can hope for. I accept the bong and lean my head down over it. Deep inhale, and with the exhale, a stomach-wrenching cough.

She pats a spot next to her on the bed. "Come sit," she says. "It's so nice having you here." She adds a pillow to the stack behind her head, propping herself upright. "What a week I've had," she says, color returning to her face and voice.

"What happened?" I ask, pleasantly softened. I kick off my shoes and climb up next to her.

"You know Detective Newman from *Justice Served*? Blake Peterson?"

"Of course," I say. "He's friends with Gregory, actually. Came in for a meeting this week. Kind of a jerk."

"What did he do?"

"Nothing significant, just a stupid hassle." I always offer Gregory's guests something to drink, part of the standard welcome shtick. "Can I offer you some water or coffee or . . ." I usually say, leaving the question open. And sometimes someone will use that opening to ask for a Diet Coke, or sparkling water, or, once in a while, tea. Most people know to just say yes to the water. Not Blake Peterson. Blake Peterson, sitting spread-legged on Gregory's couch at four in the afternoon, said, "You know what I really want?" with a wink and a glint in his smile that told me I was supposed to play along.

"I don't," I said. "Want to give me a hint?"

"I'd love a grilled cheese. And tomato soup, if you can wrangle it."

Gregory just smiled and said, "If anyone can find it, it's her," which was presumably a compliment but really just meant I had to drop everything and run around the studio lot in search of an afternoon grilled cheese. It turned out to be doable, thanks to a friendly grill chef at the commissary, but the tomato soup was a lost cause.

"Did he know who you were?" my mother asks, reaching for the bong.

"He knows I'm Gregory's assistant," I say. She takes another pull, then passes me the bong.

"But did he know that you're my daughter?"

"Of course not," I say after I exhale. "How would he know that?" I'm not sure where this is going or if I want to find out.

She shakes her head. "What was he there to see Gregory about?"

"I don't know," I say. "Why?"

"That man has been my issue of the week," my mother says.

"Why?" I repeat. Dread settles in, a familiar trapped-in-the-passenger-seat feeling.

"This is all privileged, okay?" she tells me. "You can't tell anyone." I nod. "Blake Peterson had a problem with a production assistant."

"A sex problem?"

"A rape problem."

"Oh god."

"'Oh god' is right. Apparently he's known for having wild parties at his house in Malibu. This production assistant—young girl, about your age—became friendly with him on set. He invited her to a party, and people reportedly saw her looking happy enough flirting with him by the pool, but after that, things went too far, or farther than she wanted them to go."

"And?"

"And the next week, the girl reported it to the showrunner, who tried to keep her quiet, offered to move her to post-production so she wouldn't be around Blake every day, but the girl was insistent, so the showrunner reported it to XBC's HR, and HR gave the general counsel's office a heads-up, and the GC called Robert, who called me."

"To do what?" I ask.

"To help. Robert knows this is my expertise, he called me and said, 'Listen, we have this young girl here, and she's very upset by what happened and wants to file a formal complaint; would you mind talking with her, as a favor to me?'"

This is the kind of case my mother used to take all the time, what she misses in her corporate life. Maybe this is good for her, I think, trying to push past my frustration at the proximity to my own work life. Would she be filing suit against Blake or the network? And if the network, why would Robert . . . Something is off here. "Talking with her. To offer representation?" I ask.

"To explain how this whole process works. What she can expect if she goes forward, files a formal complaint."

"I'm confused," I say, though I fear I'm not. "How is that a favor to Robert?"

"I told him I would be absolutely honest with her, and I was. She seemed like a nice girl, very shaken up. I told her what I tell every woman who comes to my office with a story like hers. That she doesn't have to be a hero, that her first duty is to herself, and she has to decide what's best for her."

I've been sitting in a cross-legged position; my right leg is now numb and tingling. I unfold my legs and shake them out. My mother has said all this before. It's the context, not the words. Like looking at a photo negative, at once familiar and jarring. "Hadn't she?" I ask. "She reported it. She wanted to file a complaint."

My mother leans over to her bedside and lifts one can of diet soda then another until she finds one that's not empty. She takes a deep, calm sip. "But she didn't know what it would involve. So I talked her through it. I explained that if she files a complaint, the network's lawyers will come after her, hard, to try to discredit her. They'll put a private investigator on her, if they haven't already.

Any skeletons in her closet? Exposed. All the people she's had sex with in the past. If she's ever been to therapy, taken any medications. Anything to make her seem unstable, unreliable. All her privacy, gone. And if anyone has ever seen her flirting with Blake Peterson, if she texted with him, anything like that, it will come out."

"But he still raped her. None of that excuses it." I slide off the bed and stand up.

"Course not. What's the matter?"

"Just pins and needles," I say, walking around the perimeter of the room. "But he raped her. The therapy, flirting . . . You've always said that stuff's irrelevant and sexist, right?"

"Of course. But this is how it always works. The network's lawyers will dig up as much dirt as they can. She'll need to get a lawyer, and I said I would give her names, but I wanted her to understand the most likely outcomes, because many women have no idea. They're hurt, they're mad, they want to file a report, as they have every right to do. But they often don't understand how much worse it could become, and they suffer more as a result."

"If they lose the case?"

"If they even bring a case in the first place. Her career in Hollywood will be over—any other showrunner who googles her and finds all this, you think they'll want to touch her with a ten-foot pole? And she has the additional complication of the rapist being a beloved celebrity. Remember what happened with Kobe?"

"Yeah. The girl backed out at the end, right?"

"She was terrified for her life. Her name was leaked, tons of death threats. The charges themselves were never dropped. There was plenty of evidence—blood, bruising, friends she told right after. But this poor girl had been through enough; she was too scared to testify. It's an awful position to be in. Traumatized for life, and your rapist gets to go on being a hero."

"None of that's fair."

"Of course it's not fair."

I am struggling to metabolize this information, and the marijuana isn't making it any easier. "So you told the girl all this to . . . get her to drop the case?"

I struggle to say the words. I don't want to be accusatory, don't want to trigger her anger. My mother would never do that. Except, did she? What if she did?

"No!" She pushes the duvet off and pads into the bathroom with the bong. I follow her and sit down on the edge of the tub as she gets to work emptying the charred remains into the trash and grinding up fresh weed. "I told her so that she could make an informed decision."

"But you don't regret speaking up about your rape, right? Did you tell her that?" I ask.

"I did, but I also told her how that decision ended up shaping my entire adult life, my career. And mine was stranger rape, the rarest kind. And he was armed. Aggravated rape, they call it. And still I got death threats, rape threats, for years. It was terrifying. And this was before the age of social media."

"So what did the girl decide? What's she going to do?"

"I think she's going to settle. I told her that the network would offer a settlement, two or three million, maybe, to avoid going the route of a formal complaint. And that it would come with stipulations—nondisclosure, nondisparagement—which is unfortunate, but the way the system's set up right now, it's the only way they ever agree to give money. I gave her some lawyer names, if she wants to have a lawyer negotiate for her, and I explained how the contingency system works. I gave her all the information I could."

I understand what my mother is saying. The truth of it. That rape victims are treated horribly in the court of public opinion, to say nothing of criminal court. That no woman should be forced to martyr herself. That it's important to know what you're in for. But the lesson I always drew was to fight anyway, to fight not in spite of that but because of it. Safe battles won't win a war.

"Doesn't everything you told her make a pretty strong case for settling and staying silent?"

"Maybe so."

"That's what Robert wants? That's why he called you?"

"Of course he doesn't want a big legal battle, but the network has the money. They'll squash this if they need to. The point is that these are the realities of the world we live in. It's not the world I wish we had, but it's the one we've got. I've been fighting for so long, and I've seen these cases go wrong so many times, and it's heartbreaking."

"So we're just supposed to give up and accept the system? If even people like you are encouraging that, how will anything ever change?"

"It would take something truly huge to see change. Something like all women banding together. And I do mean all women, which is what makes it so unlikely. Even if, say, the entire media—the columnists, talking heads, you name it— changed the angles of their stories, rose up in defense of women who accuse men of assault or harassment, do you think that would actually change anything?"

"Maybe?"

"Of course not! It would just pay lip service to change. It would allow people to feel good about themselves, like they're on the right side of the story. And maybe a few men would go down, some of the worst offenders, but that sure as shit doesn't lead to structural change. You're naive if you think there wouldn't be a backlash."

"What kind of backlash?"

"Men in power refusing to hire or mentor women because they'll say they're concerned about being wrongly accused of harassment, for a start. They'll try to flip the script, paint the women as manipulators and aggressors. And even if the media is on the side of the women, the media is not America. And let me tell you, not only do men in this country behave terribly toward women, women are awful to other women, too. Here, can you come help me with this lighter? I'm having trouble." She clicks and clicks, but there's a safety lock on, it isn't working. I hop off the tub and go over to help. She lowers her head and inhales.

"Take this case, for example," she continues. "Look at the women. Not the victim, the other women. The showrunner, she's a woman, and her first instinct was to bury this. Because she's trying to protect her show. She doesn't want to lose her own job, and she knows that Blake, rapist or not, is key to the show's success. And then Veronica Ross. I did a call with Robert and Veronica to give them some advice. I told them to take this case seriously, and to be very careful. I recommended they do a full investigation into Blake as well as the workplace culture at *Justice Served*. Veronica tried to brush the whole thing off. Said it sounded like this girl wanted to fuck Blake, that it was just a bit of fun gone too far."

"What did you say to that?"

"I asked what part of anal rape sounds like a bit of fun gone too far."

"She's terrible," I say.

"A lot of people are terrible," my mother says, dumping the ashed weed into the trash can under the sink.

"So what? We just let them win? That's the opposite of everything you've always said." This conversation feels like reading a familiar map upside down. Same landmarks, different destination.

"I don't know. All I can tell you is that I've been fighting this battle for thirty years, and in that time, very little has changed. I have to live with the reality of that every single day. That my life's work has been meaningless."

These words land with an unexpected force. She slumps back to bed, but I hang behind for a moment. I'm used to the usual narratives about her loneliness and depression and most important work being behind her. But that her work was important, her contributions significant: this was never in question. An overwhelming thought, that a path paved over decades could turn out to be a circle.

I take another hit for fortification before trailing back to her bedside to reassure her that her life's work wasn't meaningless and isn't over. I don't know what else to say.

Before I leave that evening, she reminds me that everything

she has told me is privileged information that she shouldn't have shared, and if I tell anyone about it, she could get in big trouble.

I tell her I understand.

I drive across town to my apartment in a daze, too distracted to even attempt the freeway. As I chug down Wilshire, the slowest of the east-west surface streets, I try to make sense of the situation. I had hoped sobriety would engender clarity, but it doesn't, not really.

It's not that I'm shocked by the allegations. It's disappointing, yes, and I feel terrible for the PA involved, but I wouldn't be surprised to hear of sexual misconduct from basically any man short of Barack Obama. Not surprising either that Robert and Veronica would want to bury it. It's my mother's participation that gets me, and how calm and reasonable she sounded explaining her role.

To present herself to this girl as an ally with expertise in this field, offering objective information to empower the girl's decision-making, when in fact she was there as a favor to Robert, is obviously disingenuous. But what she said about the scrutiny, the suffering, the way this can mold and mangle your whole life— that's all true.

I remember when the Kobe rape case broke. I was thirteen. The city abuzz, hometown hero accused. I watched my mother on TV, vociferous in her defense of the victim, uncompromising even in the face of aggressive criticism. At home, a different tone: that poor girl, this is going to turn out terribly for her, she told me from the start. She explained to me what would happen. She was right about all of it.

Everything feels slightly different in the office the following day, rotated by a few degrees. Selfishly, I am frustrated that my mother is now involved in my workplace, and at a much higher level than me. I know I don't really have a right to this frustration since she's the one who got me this job in the first place. Not this job, I remind myself. She got me the temp job, she helped put me in a position to impress Gregory. But he's the one who hired me, and he hired me because I worked hard, because I have proven myself. I tell myself these things, and I try to believe them, but it's hard not to feel that any steps I've taken toward independence are tenuous at best, illusory at worst.

I search Gregory's calendar for Blake's name and find that he has attended—or at least planned to attend—four of Blake's parties in the past year and a half. Throughout the day, I am distracted by thoughts about whether Gregory was at the party where this girl was raped, how much he knows. Why Blake wanted to meet with him last week, whether that was just a coincidence. When Veronica walks past my desk, I still sit up straight and smile brightly, though I hate myself for doing it.

After work, I meet David for dinner at a restaurant famous for its brussels sprouts. Every cocktail on the menu has at least one vegetal ingredient. I want very badly to tell him about the whole Blake Peterson situation, but I know I can't. Instead, I tell him only about my mother asking me to buy weed for her and bring her some of my Klonopin. He is so appalled by it that I find myself taking my mother's side. At this point, all that is the least of my concerns.

"That's so inappropriate of her," he says. "Asking you to buy drugs for her! And forcing you to share a personal prescription for a controlled substance."

"Weed is barely a drug," I say, taking a sip of my beetroot negroni. "It's not a huge deal." The cocktail tastes almost good.

"What do you mean?" he says. He spears a brussels sprout from the cast-iron skillet dominating the center of the table. "Aren't you telling me about it because it upset you? Are you suddenly fine with it?"

"That's not—" I say. "I just—" I say. "I guess what I mean is, I have issues with my mom's inability to regulate her emotions without weed or pills and how she doesn't respect boundaries and expects me to come running whenever she calls, but this wasn't malicious. It doesn't even rank on the list of most upsetting things my mother has done."

"I'm sorry to hear that," he says, setting the forked brussels sprout down on his plate, uneaten, his voice heavy with feeling. I was frustrated by his incredulousness, and now I am annoyed by his earnestness.

When I was younger, when—however briefly—I allowed myself to entertain fantasies about what it might be like to have a boyfriend, I imagined someone sensitive and caring. Someone who would make me feel seen and valued and respected. But did I think about a relationship only in terms of what I might receive from it? What about the other person? What about who they might be?

Here David is, right in front of me, and the more he likes me, the more ambivalent I feel about him. He is always available. He responds to my texts quickly, and he's full of ideas for dates and activities but, oh, you're exhausted and you'd rather stay in? That's fine too; he'll bring ice cream. David had a relatively happy child-hood. He has stable, supportive, still-married parents, the kind who both ask questions about his life and remember the answers.

These are good things, right? Shouldn't I want someone stable, someone who knows healthy love?

One night, at his apartment, David tells me that he read an article about failed marriages between high-powered female executives and freelance creative-type men, and he knows it's silly, but it made him a little worried.

"Failed *marriages?*" I say. We only met four months ago.

Two of the bookshelves in his bedroom contain food—pasta, grains, avocados. There's a mini fridge in his closet. "My roommate's a food thief," he explains. He tells a lot of stories about his roommate's food habits. "You wouldn't believe how much fried chicken my roommate ate," he says.

"Really? I wouldn't believe it?" I hate the edge in my voice. I'm not this person. Since when have I become this person?

He texts me: *My roommate cooked four jumbo hot dogs for breakfast, but then he only ate two.*

I wish I could tell my eighteen-year-old self: This is it. This is what's behind the locked doors of the Lampoon Castle.

I read the text out loud to Gemma. "He just wants to talk to you," she says.

"That's the most interesting thing he could think of?" I say.

But who am I to talk? How much time and energy do I devote to anticipating what Gregory might want for lunch on any given day? He is now so accustomed to my conscientiousness that he expects me to correctly guess what he's in the mood to eat without consulting him.

Maybe David is just following my lead. Maybe I tell too many food stories.

I don't want to be the most interesting thing in David's life.

My mother says that, in the early heady days of a relationship, if you really like a person, every little thing they do is touching. And if you just don't like them enough, every little thing will annoy you.

I don't sleep very well or for long enough when I'm sharing the bed, and I don't like how many of his hairs I find everywhere in my apartment.

These things shouldn't matter. Why do they matter; why do I care? Look how nice he is. The way he looks at me.

SIX

THE ACUTE AGITATION I FELT IN THE WAKE OF learning about Blake Peterson gradually fades. It's not like there's anything I personally can do. I'm not even supposed to know about it. I try not to imagine Gregory at Blake's parties or Blake sitting on Gregory's couch telling him about this vindictive girl who threw herself on him.

I focus on the facts: Gregory has never behaved inappropriately toward me. I don't need to feel conflicted about working for him. To my knowledge, he hasn't done anything wrong. At least I don't work for Veronica. Or Robert, even. I ask my mother over the phone if this has changed her friendship with Robert, and she says no. He's trying to do right by the victim, as best he can.

"He's one of the good ones," my mother reminds me. I'm in the car, en route to an aerial yoga class Allyn's been raving about. "When we met back in Boston, he was still working in local TV. We'd run into each other at galas and parties where I went to sing for my supper, to convince rich people to support victims' rights. My least favorite part of the job. Robert schmoozed with the society types, but he wasn't one of them. Jewish son of a lobsterman. He knows from being an outsider. We saw that in each other. You know his sister was raped? By her husband, just about the hardest thing to prosecute at the time. When I was growing up, it was legal for a husband to rape his wife. Probably seems crazy to you now, but that's how bad things were. I helped Robert with his sister's case, that's how we became close, and that's why he called me this time, because he trusts I won't steer him wrong."

I decide to accept this explanation. I see no viable alternative.

———

"PRETTY GIRLS SHOULD assume that every straight man they know would fuck them if given the opportunity," Julian says to me one day at lunch over sandwiches from the cafeteria, where the daily special always has at least one ingredient that seems out of place. (Today: barbecue chicken with onion, tomato, radishes, and arugula.)

"Regardless of the ramifications?" I say.

"Well, that makes it trickier. Maybe not. But I think it's safe to say that even if they can't or shouldn't have sex with you, they probably want to. Girls always act so shocked when I say that. But come on. Are you really surprised?" he asks.

"I guess not."

"See! So you have thought about it."

"In specific situations, sure. But not in a sweeping generalization kind of way."

"Why not?"

My phone buzzes, faceup on the table. I glance down. It's Zach, complaining about the time shift of this afternoon's team meeting. He knows I am only doing the bidding of a man who couldn't care less about anyone else's schedule, but he has been testy lately, frustrated by his lack of autonomy within the department as well as the downgrade of having to answer his own phone calls again. I slide the phone into my pocket. Time to go back up.

"Because then it would be impossible to live in the world," I say.

I go over to David's apartment after work. When I tell him about the conversation with Julian, he shakes his head and laughs at me. "Of course he wants to have sex with you!" David says. "How could you not come to that conclusion?"

"I don't know," I say, cactusing my arms in the air.

"When was the last time you insisted on believing that someone's intentions were innocent and it turned out to actually be the case?" he asks. "I see that face you're making. I think you're not as oblivious as you claim to be."

I smile and climb on top of him. I've given up on the "no work talk in bed" rule. The boundaries are too amorphous; my whole life is work-adjacent. New rule: no work talk during penetration. Foreplay's fair game. That night, David fucks me with more urgency and energy than usual, and I'm able to stay in the moment and enjoy it until, midthrust, he moans about loving my vagina. I've always hated that word. It feels simultaneously clinical and mushy. *Pussy* is better, but it's stupid and porny. All the other options are nonstarters: *cunt*, *twat*, *slit*, *snatch*. They just get worse and worse. *Beaver. Muffin.*

Internalized misogyny, Gemma says. She spends her weekends going to cuddle parties and orgasmic meditation workshops. When she invites me to join, I say I'm busy; to admit my disinterest would invite a conversation about sexual repression that I'd rather avoid. She encourages me to do Kegels to strengthen my root chakra.

———

ONE NIGHT, GREGORY decides last minute not to go to a big party at Universal Studios and offers me his tickets, which I eagerly accept. It's an industry-famous party, for which they shut down part of the amusement park to the public.

I bring David and have a great time. A giddiness and lightness that I haven't felt in a while, or have been too tired to feel in a while. Free drinks and games and rides with no lines and leaving the office before eight p.m. I see some assistants I know, from XBC and elsewhere, and we all wave hello and smile before continuing on our way, the setting sprawling and activities numerous enough to release pressure to network.

I feel flush with affection and gratitude for David. Look how sweetly he's trying to win a prize, though he's having such trouble getting the ring to land over the bottle. "I don't need a stuffed dinosaur," I say. "It's okay."

Later, in line for donuts the size of my head, he turns to me. "This might sound crazy, but . . ." he says.

"What?"

He shakes his head. "No, you'll think I'm crazy."

"You won't know unless you try me," I say.

But I know. Somehow, I know. It's in the way he's looking at me.

I shouldn't prod him. Because if I prod him and he says it, then I'll have to respond. Maybe it's perverse curiosity, or simple desire for confirmation. Like how when someone says, "This smells terrible," people always want to smell it for themselves.

"I read an article," he says.

"A whole article?"

"Never mind."

"Sorry, I'm being mean. Go on, really."

The couple in front of us receives their donut, which is pink-frosted and sprinkled and comes in a pie box with a clear plastic top, that's how big it is. What are we supposed to do with a donut that size? I'm not sure who wanted the donut, how we ended up in this line.

"I read an article about how to know if you're in love. What things you should know about a person before you can be sure it's love."

I ask: "Things you should know?" Also: "With sprinkles or not?"

"I'm sprinkles agnostic," he says. "To make sure it's not just physical desire or lust but something deeper. There was a whole list of questions, and I went through and realized I think I do know the answers to them . . ."

It's our turn, and the conversation is put on pause while we sort out donut logistics. I accept the box, which weighs more than I was expecting. "What were the questions?" I ask, following David over to a nearby table.

"It was things like who are her closest friends, favorite relatives, least favorite relatives, hobbies, ambitions. What's the best thing that's ever happened to her and what's the worst—"

"What do you think is the worst thing that's ever happened to me?"

He is quiet for a moment, thinking, and then he says, "I think when your parents got divorced, that was really difficult for you. Divorce is really hard on children."

I laugh, but it's that edgy, cold kind of laugh that's all exhale, no inhale. For a moment, I want to throw my drink at him. Instead, I gulp down the rest of it. I feel a sharp stab of loneliness and frustration.

It's not his fault. He can't know what I haven't told him. I have tried so hard to be cheerful and charming, to wring humorous anecdotes out of a cloth drenched in pain. Still, I wanted him to understand that there were probably wounds I hadn't yet shared.

Another thought, tickling: If I can't think of a singular worst thing, does that mean nothing was actually that bad? And if so, why all those nights spent crying in bed, gulping for air?

David volunteers that the article also advised about when is a good or bad time to tell someone you love them for the first time, and the article said not to do it when you're drunk or right after sex.

"That sounds like good advice," I say. "So now, for example, would probably not be a very good time."

"Because of the drinking," he says.

"Right."

David tells me he loves me a few nights later, right before sex. Technically still following the rules, he jokes. I'm on top of him, straddling him, and the words just seem to pop out, as if he coughed and now here they are, forming a fog between us. I feel both touched and uncomfortable.

I don't say, "No you don't. You barely know me."

I don't say, "Thank you."

I don't say anything.

I lean down and kiss him. His mouth is firm, unyielding. I pull back, look at his face, and grope through my mind for a possible response.

"That means a lot to me," I say. I watch his face fall.

"I was hoping," he says.

I backtrack, sidetrack, try to make it okay. I thought he under-stood where I was coming from, I could swear he said something that night at the amusement park about it being okay if I'm not there yet. He knows this is my first real "adult" relationship. He knows I have never been in love. I listened, and I took him at his word, though maybe I shouldn't have. Because of course he couldn't help but hope, right? But it still seems so foreign, so improbable, that someone might care about me this much, that someone might want me to love them.

I roll off him, onto my side, head propped up by an elbow, and run my fingers down his chest. I gentle my words. I don't want him to be upset; I don't want to hurt him. I want to be true to myself, though, too. It's such a new approach for me that I don't know how and where to draw the lines, to strike a balance.

"I think I might be falling in love with you" is what I land on. It's the best I can do.

In every relationship, my mother often says, there is always one person who loves the other more. And it's better, safer, to be the per-son who is loved more.

But how much more?

My phone rings just past six in the morning, a few minutes before my scheduled alarm. It's Gregory. "How's it going?" he asks. It's a conversational quirk of his. He opens every call with it, no matter how recently we last spoke.

"It's, uh, fine. What's going on?" I sit up in bed, as if he might somehow be able to see through the phone—or hear from my voice—that I am lying down. Next to me, David cracks an eye open. I mouth Gregory's name.

"I need your help with something."

"Of course."

"There are bees in my bedroom. What do I do?"

"I'm sorry, what?"

"Crawling up and down the window and the curtains. A lot of them, not just a few. Why are they there?"

"I don't know why there are bees in your bedroom," I say. I'm repeating the whole sentence for David's benefit, so he can follow along, so I can turn this into a bit of absurdist comedy as opposed to baffling reality. "Where are you now?" I ask Gregory.

"I'm in bed still. I opened my eyes and there they were. I can't move."

I think, but only for a quick moment, about the strangeness of Gregory waking up, seeing bees, and immediately thinking, "I have to call my assistant." I refrain from asking the obvious, which is "Where's your wife?" Gregory rarely discusses his personal life with me, a boundary I know not to take for granted.

"Why can't you move?" I ask.

"If I move, they might sting. I could be allergic to bees."

"Could be?"

"I've never been stung before. It's entirely possible I'm allergic and I wouldn't know. I don't think you appreciate how many bees are in here right now."

"I believe you, I do; I'm sure it's a lot."

"Are you going to help me or not? This is an emergency!"

I look around David's bedroom, the bookshelves of food, a towel discarded on the floor next to the dresser with drawers that don't quite close, Harvard beer stein full of coins on top.

"Here's what we're going to do," I say, trying to imagine him in a bedroom I've never seen. "You're going to get out of bed very slowly and calmly, and you'll stay on the line with me, so if they sting and you have an allergic reaction, I'll be able to hear and can send help. You're going to go to the closet, get the clothes you need for the day, then leave your bedroom and close the door so they can't get out, and I'll call an exterminator."

"What about the bottom of the door? They could get through."

"Roll up a towel and put it there."

"You're sure this will work?"

"Positive," I lie. I've learned that, in this job, expressing uncertainty is rarely a good thing.

I start laughing as soon as I hang up. I look over to David, hoping to find mirth that mirrors my own, but his face is solemn.

"That's insane," he says. "I mean it. It's crazy some of the things he asks you to do. Not to mention a waste of your talent and skills."

I just wanted him to laugh with me. "What are my skills?" I ask.

"Your intelligence and creativity. You know what I mean. Do you think all this is appropriate?"

"Of course not! But what's the alternative? This is how this industry works. And there are so many bosses who are worse. Yesterday I heard about a producer who threw a printer at his assistant because she made some scheduling mistake. But it was one of those huge laser printers, so it was really heavy and he couldn't throw it very far and it landed on the floor a few feet away. And his assistant just looked up from her computer and said, 'Oh, was that for me?'"

"That's terrible."

"Of course it's terrible! But isn't it kind of a perfect response?"

"The assistant should report him to HR."

"That's a death wish."

———

OCCASIONALLY, I WONDER what constitutes appropriate workplace behavior. If everyone views something as appropriate for a given workplace, does that make it so?

One afternoon, a nurse comes to give vitamin injections, an initiative organized by a casting executive. "I just need one cheek," the nurse—a buff man whose business cards feature a photo of him flexing and advertise testosterone in addition to vitamin B—tells me, pointing to my ass. Across from me, Allyn and two casting executives sit on the couch, getting IV vitamin drips.

"Isn't he the best?" Allyn says as I move to unbutton and unzip my jeans. I bend forward as instructed, only now noticing that the door is open. Across the bullpen, Julian is leading a group of people to the conference room. If they turn and look this way, they will see me bent over a desk in a corner office with my pants down.

A new feminist manifesto encouraging young women in the workplace to speak out and own their ambition has skyrocketed to the top of the bestseller lists. Veronica invites the author, who is a friend of hers, to speak at an expanded staff meeting. These meetings are open only to executives, which means most of the young women in this workplace can't attend. I ask Gregory if an exception might be made. "If it were up to me, absolutely. But it's Veronica's call," he says. "I wish I could send you in my place!"

Every so often, I search Blake Peterson's name on Google and Twitter, but nothing unusual comes up. It has been two months since my mother told me about what I now think of as "the incident." Blake has been written out of the last five episodes of this season of *Justice Served*. She says the network is sending him on vacation, telling him to lie low while the settlement is negotiated. I don't know what to make of it or how to feel, aside from general discomfort and frustration that I can't discuss it with anyone.

I try to hold on to the belief that I can play a part without becoming it. That I need to play the game in order to change the rules.

We're approaching the end of pilot season and midway through staffing season, which is when producers and executives plan writers rooms for the new pilots, contingent on receiving series orders in May. David has been hustling, and he's landed a few meetings. "My manager says they loved me," he reports after one of them, and I don't have the heart to remind him how little that means. *Love* is a neutral word in this industry.

I have learned to speak the language. I am no longer bumped by the jargon of it all. I know what it means to do a deep dive, take a big swing, hang a lamp on it, or do a Hail Mary pass. A script described as *soft* or *quiet* is probably about women. *Broad* is generally boring. A meeting, even if confirmed, is considered tentative until and unless reconfirmed the day before. Lunches are not to be confirmed until the morning of and are always at one p.m. Gregory often tells me that I'm doing an excellent job. The secret is remembering that even if it's not my fault, it's still my problem. It's being available and saying yes and not complaining when asked to drop everything to run to the Century City Apple Store for a replacement phone case because Gregory thinks his smells intolerably of pasta sauce. ("Smell. Arrabiata, from dinner last night.") It's being grateful that I'm not asked to cover up extramarital affairs or build dioramas for a child's school assignment or pose as my boss for eight hours of traffic school or figure out how to expense thousands of dollars of astrology consultations, the frustrations of which I've heard about from other assistants during recent drinks.

"She makes the prettiest grids," Gregory tells Zach one day when Zach pops into his office with a question. An inartful adjective for an Excel spreadsheet, but a compliment's a compliment, and I'll take what I can get. Gregory waves the updated pilot production calendar I've just handed him. "Did you teach her this?" he asks.

"Zach taught me everything I know," I say, which is both no longer true and exactly what Zach wants to hear.

At the end of pilot season, Julian gets a title bump to Coordinator and starts excluding me from email threads, claiming it's coordinators-only business, a power-hoarding move as transparent as it is frustrating. Though I'm the most junior assistant, because my boss outranks his, he has to defer to me on scheduling matters and comply with all requests I (per Gregory) make of him (for Billy). The same is true for Allyn, whose boss ranks beneath Billy, but she doesn't hold it against me; she knows we are only pawns. She loops me in sometimes, and when she doesn't, I assume it to be an accidental as opposed to deliberate oversight. A department head's assistant is expected to be well informed, but more often than not, I find myself at a loss, frantically messaging Julian and Allyn in hopes that one of them will provide the information I need in time to avoid sounding like an idiot. The two of them have begun concealing information from each other, too, and Julian is unsubtle about his efforts to encroach on Allyn's responsibilities. It's a bad setup all around.

"Hasn't he ever heard that a rising tide lifts all boats?" I grumble to Allyn one day.

She asks what that means. "Wow," she says. "That's a great phrase. Is it a feminist thing?"

My mother says I should ask for a title bump too. Over manicures at Tracy's Nails, one of the only places she can reliably be convinced to get out of bed to go, she advises me on how to present the situation to Gregory. She doesn't understand why I'm so shy about this. I've never been shy. Why now?

"I've only been on his desk for five months," I say. "What do you think, which of these pinks?"

"Those both look the same to me. And so what if you're newer? I'm sure you're doing just as good a job as Julian, right?"

"But that's not what matters. It's about putting in time, not proving competence."

"That's silly," my mother says. "Make it about Gregory. You're an extension of him. He wants you to be well informed, wants people to be able to call you for information—he's smart, he'll get it. Do you want your toes done, too?"

"I don't know, I think my toes are fine," I say. My toes are not fine. I've been tearing my toenails off, is the truth.

"You sure? If you're going to wear open-toe shoes to work, you should get them done. It's almost summer, you might want to wear sandals."

———

IN MID-MAY, the senior executives fly to New York for upfronts week, an advertiser-oriented carnival of events and parties. The assistants gather in Gregory's office to watch a live telecast of the XBC presentation. Robert gives the opening spiel, then introduces Veronica, who says she is thrilled to announce our *dynamic* fall slate. The returning shows you know and love—a quick montage— plus these exciting new series! Medical show, family sitcom, teen werewolf soap. *Olympus* didn't make it, but *Unsung* did—though for midseason, not fall. There's Bianca's face up on the presentation screen, the original actress. She has promised to get down to 115 pounds by the start of filming.

"Guess what I found out," Allyn not-quite-whispers to me. We're both standing in the doorway. "Veronica and I see the same sugarer."

"Sugarer," I repeat.

"You know, the woman who sugars you."

I imagine Allyn and Veronica being dusted with confection-ers' sugar, legs spread like a sliced cake. "I'm going to need more details," I say.

Allyn explains that sugaring is like waxing, only different, because it's supposed to be better, because it tears the hair out at the root, or in a different direction than waxing, plus it's organic and lasts longer. And it's gluten-free, too.

"But you're not eating the sugar."

"Of course not!"

"So why does gluten-free matter?"

"Your skin can be gluten intolerant. It's just better for you. Anyway, I was talking with my lady about work, and she said she has another client who works at XBC named Veronica. Small world, right?"

"I wonder if she'll tell Veronica about you next time," I say.

Allyn does a performative shiver. "I wonder what she gets done. Brazilian, landing strip, bikini?"

"I'm going to guess landing strip," I say, but it's an arbitrary guess. "High maintenance, but she might consider it more mature than a Brazilian."

Allyn nods. I don't ask what her own grooming preferences are, though I'm vaguely curious, in the way that I'm vaguely curious about all women's pubic hair choices. As a child, when I showered with my mother, I would examine the differences between our bodies. The prominence of her nipples, the curve and dip of her lower belly. The water dripping down off her pubic hair, droplet by droplet. I admired it all. My mother said that when I grew up, I would have hair there too.

Now I lie on the waxing table and butterfly my legs and say, "Take it all off." One waxer suggests coconut oil, another offers ice packs. A third, my favorite, provides numbing spray.

It hurts, and I never feel more like a pawn of the patriarchy than when I am lying there, legs spread, waiting for the pain, but I feel cleaner and more attractive like this. Except for immediately afterward, when I often look at myself in the mirror and think, "That looks like plucked chicken skin" and "What the fuck am I doing here?" David probably doesn't care. Not that I've asked him.

"Does sugaring hurt less than waxing?" I ask Allyn. A phone rings, tandem chimes from the hall and the office next door.

"Julian, that's you," I say. He nods from the couch but makes no move to get up. Bad assistant behavior, but since the higher-ups are at the presentation, he has leeway.

"Oh yes," Allyn says. "Absolutely. I'll give you my lady's name." She tilts her head and considers my face. "Have you ever thought about a lash lift?" she asks.

The more I attend to my body, the more areas for improvement I discover. It's a game of fucking whack-a-mole.

SEVEN

SUMMER BRINGS EXPLOSIVE REVELATIONS ABOUT government surveillance overreach, the legalization of gay marriage in California, and the looming threat of my mother's sixtieth birthday.

"How do you want to celebrate?" I ask her. It's a Sunday morning and we are sitting in the kitchen at her house with delivery omelets in plastic containers in front of us. I bring a disappointing forkful to my mouth. "Do you want to have a party? A nice dinner? What sounds good to you?"

"Nothing," she says, as expected.

"We could go to a spa? Get a massage?"

"Massages make me sad."

"How about a small party? Just a few friends?"

"Do you remember, I let you throw my fiftieth birthday party, but you didn't send out invitations early enough and almost nobody came. It was so depressing."

"I was thirteen."

"It's my fault, I shouldn't have let you plan the party. But you were so insistent, and I never learned how to put myself first."

"I'm trying to put you first now," I say. "But I need you to tell me what you want."

"There's nothing I want," she says, pushing the plastic container away from her. She's had one bite of toast, that's it. "Nothing left for me but work, never-ending work."

She climbs down off the stool and leaves the kitchen. I hear her feet on the stairs, stomping up to her bedroom. She wants me to follow, and I will, but I need a moment first. I take a big, dry bite of toast, then another. I eat four slices of toast in the span of two minutes, maybe three. I wasn't even hungry.

I find her sitting up in bed, answering an email on her iPad, pounding her index fingers into the on-screen keyboard, muttering as she types.

"Work?" I say. An obvious lesson here about work and life, but what if the work is fulfilling? Is it worth it, then?

"These numbskulls totally fucked up a motion and the client is pissed and threatening to fire us, and now I have to rewrite a whole brief by tomorrow," she says, frustration but also a certain kind of triumph in her voice. She might not admit to it, but she derives satisfaction from being the sharp-eyed eagle called in for the kill, fixer of even the most bungled situation. The only one who can and will save the day.

I don't want to talk about my mother with David, even though I know he would listen. I want to want it, to want him, so badly. Instead, I find myself being short with him, snappy. Frustrated by every little thing he does, every activity he suggests. He spends most of his days alone in his apartment or with the teenagers he tutors. I am his primary social outlet. But by the end of the work-day, I am invariably depleted.

I suspect there is something unhealthy about my aversion to his consistent affection. That I would probably be more into him if he were aloof, if he had less room for me in his life. If he forced me to plead my case.

Or maybe there's another lesson here. I always thought of a stable, secure relationship as a pipe dream, meaning if I ever found one, I would need to hold on tight. I thought there was something broken inside me that meant I didn't and wouldn't attract love the way other people did. That on some level, the only person who would ever love me truly and completely was my mother.

But if that's not true, if I am both as lovable and as broken as most other people in the world, maybe that means I have the ability to choose, not just to be chosen. Maybe I can and should feel capable of holding out for someone whom I love too.

I break up with David at my apartment on a Friday night, the week before my mother's birthday. Shortly after he arrives; it feels cruel to watch a movie first, to have a long conversation about our weeks and draw it out any longer. He cries. He says it's not fair how it takes two people to make a relationship but only one person to break it. He wishes I had told him I was unhappy. We could have talked about it, we could have worked through it, he says.

I don't know how to explain that I didn't know I was unhappy. I only know that I don't want to keep doing this. I tell him it doesn't have to do with him.

"Of course it has to do with me. If you loved me enough, you'd want to be with me."

"Maybe I just don't have the bandwidth for that right now," I say. "I feel spread pretty thin." A steady stream of clichés pouring from my mouth.

When he leaves that evening, I feel relieved and lonely. But I felt lonely when I was with him too.

I call my mother while staring at the underwhelming contents of my refrigerator. She doesn't pick up, and I find that this, too, is a relief. I dialed reflexively, out of a sense of obligation. Driven by a compulsion to divulge everything of import in my life combined with concern for her well-being.

But I don't owe her an immediate update, I realize. And nor should I feel burdened by the need to check in with her so frequently. *You are allowed to claim space for yourself. You are allowed to claim space for yourself.* I keep repeating it like a broken self-help tape, as if that's the key to believing it.

I spend the weekend mostly at home, mostly alone. Gemma has been dating a couple that lives in Venice, a complicated setup that I feel prudish asking questions about. She spends most of her time at their place, so I often have the apartment to myself. I do my laundry and reorganize my closet and get stoned and take long, scalding showers, allowing the water to pelt down until my skin splotches pink.

My brother is of little help with birthday planning. He has always gotten off easy when it comes to this sort of thing. The baby. *Be nice to your brother; things don't come as easily to him as they do to you,* my parents told me growing up. I heard this a lot: that things came easily to me. I didn't want to shatter the illusion. But I sometimes wanted my effort to be appreciated.

Gregory is in rare form at work the following week. Veronica eviscerates his presentation of our most promising new projects during a Monday-morning meeting, which puts him in a vicious mood. Even Julian takes pity on me. "You have to stop saying sorry so much," he advises. "Never say you're sorry if something isn't your fault. As soon as you say sorry, you take on responsibility for it, whatever it is, even if you couldn't have had anything to do with it. Say 'That sucks' or 'How shitty,' whatever you want. Just don't apologize."

My mother's birthday is Thursday, and I can tell it's going to be bad from the moment I walk in the door. "How nice of you to come," she says from the living room couch, where she sits with Abraham on her lap, my brother on an armchair across from her, face grim.

"Of course I'm here," I say.

"Not of course. I haven't seen you in weeks."

"Week," I say. "One week."

"It's been longer."

"I don't want to play this game." I almost say I'm sorry, but I stop myself.

She unboxes the trendy sneakers I have brought her and wags one in the air. "What is this?" she says.

"New Zealand wool," I say.

"Everybody knows only old ladies wear white shoes," she says. "Are you trying to be cruel?"

"They're not for old ladies. They're fashionable."

"Says who?"

I look to my brother for backup, but he won't make eye contact. "My coworkers? The internet?"

The evening reaches a crescendo when she accuses me of not

loving anyone but myself and I explode. "Don't you get it? I don't know how to love anyone but you!" I shout.

My brother calls me a bitch and I drive home in tears.

———

I SPEND A GREAT DEAL of the following month marching in place behind my desk with as much discretion as I can muster. Eyrie Einhorn has sold Gregory on the importance of taking ten thousand steps a day, as a result of which he has purchased a top-of-the-line Fitbit (expensed by me as a "research cost"). Every morning, he unstraps the device and deposits it in his outbox tray. My job is to retrieve it, upload the previous day's totals to a spread-sheet, print the spreadsheet, and put it, along with the Fitbit, in his inbox.

After the third time he admonishes me for his failure to meet his daily step quota, I take matters into my own hands. Every day, while he is in a meeting or on a notes call, I buckle his Fit-bit onto my wrist, pull the sleeve of my desk sweater down over it, and I walk. Briskly and with purpose, so that nobody will question me. I walk around the perimeter of the floor, then four flights down the outdoor stairwell to the ground-floor cafeteria, then back up the indoor stairs. Then back around the floor once more. And then I spend as long as necessary pretending to orga-nize the files in the cabinets behind my desk, walking slowly in place as I do. In this way, I give each of Gregory's days a boost of about two thousand steps. It's a crude solution, but so much of my job seems to be about coming up with crude solutions to ridiculous problems.

The tension between Allyn and Julian is worsening. Julian's

attempts to supplant Allyn as the nexus of inter-network gossip has exacerbated Allyn's tendencies toward hastiness and indiscretion, making her the top suspect when there's a leak from within. In order to beat Julian with a scoop, she often presses send without checking details, offering Julian an easy way to upstage her by Replying All with corrections. Both of them have been complaining about each other to Zach, who in turn complains about them to me in a way that makes it clear he enjoys playing both sides.

I don't know how much Gregory has picked up on—very little, presumably, since indifference to the political dynamics of his team is one of his weak points—or how much I should tell him. I could turn to Zach for guidance. He'd love that. He liked me better when I was green and full of questions. After I moved to Gregory's desk, he expected me to be his ears on the inside and to take pains not to fuck with his schedule the way Gregory's previous assistant did. I accommodate him when I can, but I don't bend over backward to do it; I know he wouldn't do that for me. Zach would be delighted to discuss my desire for a title bump and just as delighted to then gossip about the conversation with others. It's too easy to imagine. *Who does she think she is, expecting a promotion so soon?*

My mother's voice in my head: *Just go in and ask for it. If you don't advocate for yourself, who will?*

I wish I could call her for advice, but things have been rough since her birthday. The less time I spend with her, the more vicious her calls and emails become. She threatens to cut me off completely, to make me pay her back for the financial support she has given me over the years. She says she is going to take over my bank accounts and that I owe her all my savings. She says I don't think about her at all. But the truth is, I think about her constantly. When I am not with her, when I am deciding not to visit her after work at the end of a long day because I need time to myself, when I don't call her on my drive to or from the office because I'm nervous she'll be in a bad mood and it will throw me off, when I count the number of days since my last call or visit. Every personal decision I make involves her.

My brother has been home all summer. I wish I knew how to talk to him, how to tell him that he, too, deserves a life. But he is furious with me. Strings of angry text messages any time I say I have plans. *You think I ever have plans? You think I'm having fun?*

A vicious cycle, but I'm holding firm. The more extreme her behavior, the greater my resolve. "It feels important. A line in the sand kind of thing," I tell Gemma as we roll up our mats after a Sunday-afternoon yoga class. The teacher, a lithe brunette who also leads guided meditations through Gemma's company's "holistic wellness" app, comes over to offer a personal namaste.

"Beautiful class," Gemma tells the teacher, and I nod in agreement, though I didn't understand half her comments. *Move your elbows so your third eye rests on the mat. You are not your thoughts, and you are not your feelings. The hips are the garage of the body.* I figure it's like religion. You don't have to believe everything to get something out of it. I feel like a wrung-out towel, but in a good way, sweaty and subdued.

We deposit our mats in the trunk of my car and walk to the coffee shop next door for turmeric lattes. A hot beverage is the last thing I want, but Gemma insists it's a must-try. "That's meaningful growth," Gemma tells me as we hover with our mugs, waiting for a table. "I used to harbor so much anger and resentment toward my mothers for the ways they failed me as parents in childhood. I kept wishing they'd be kinder to me, and then I finally understood. It's my job to be kind to me, not anyone else's."

"Yeah," I say, the serenity of her voice compelling automatic agreement. "There, look!" I point to a table, and we descend. Only once we're seated do I reconsider. "Wait. It's definitely your job to be kind to yourself, but that doesn't mean other people don't have an obligation to be kind too," I say.

She shakes her head slowly. "Generosity," she explains, "is doing something for someone else as long as it doesn't conflict with what you want."

"No, that's convenience. Generosity is doing something for someone else even if it conflicts with what you want."

"No, it's not, because then you might resent them for it."

"Then you're not being generous. Generosity is doing something for someone else, even if it's not what you want, and not resenting them for it."

"That's what I used to think," Gemma says. She lifts her mug with both hands and takes a sip.

I let it drop. I look down into my mug, milky foam swirled into the amber liquid. I lift it and sip. It's terrible. I should have gotten the iced coffee that I wanted.

That evening, while I'm reading in bed, struggling through a pilot about sexy witches who time travel from seventeenth-century Salem to modern-day Boston, some Hillel lines come to mind, unearthed from a dusty cabinet of Hebrew school memories: *If I am not for myself, who will be for me? But if I am only for myself, who am I? And if not now, when?*

I text the lines to Gemma.

Beautiful, she replies.

The next day, I send Gregory an email asking for a check-in. He says yes, of course, anytime, and proceeds to ignore the times I set, and reset, on his calendar. *Can we push? I'm slammed*, he says once, twice, three times. Friday evening, after seven, he finally calls my name into the hallway and asks if now works for a chat. Julian hears this and swivels his head my way. I lock my computer screen, try to slow my breathing, and call back, "Sure!"

I close the door behind me and pull a chair up to the desk and remind myself that Julian would have no qualms about beginning this conversation, and I shouldn't either. *Act as if.*

"What's up?" Gregory says.

I explain the situation with as much tact and diplomacy as I can.

"I feel like you're beating around the bush here," Gregory says. "Why not just say what you mean, which is that she's being a bitch and he's being a bigger bitch and why won't these two bitches get along?"

"If I said that, then you'd think, 'Who's *this* bitch coming in here and complaining?'"

He laughs, pushes his chair back from his desk, and creates a web with his hands to cradle the back of his head. A position of relaxation and belonging if ever there were one.

I launch into my ask. I speak slowly and carefully. Behind Gregory, out the windows, the sun is setting, streaks of salmon in the sky above New York Street. I take pains to maintain eye contact as I explain how it will benefit him for me to be better informed, and how this requires a title bump. This is not an outlandish request, especially since I'm not requesting a salary increase. This would be a promotion in name only.

He says yes. He says it makes sense to him, and he can't imagine there will be an issue. He'll call Diane in HR now, and if they don't connect tonight, they certainly will Monday morning.

The rush, the release, the good kind of light-headedness. I open the door and go back to my desk, and when Julian shoots me a look—a wide-open, hungry-for-information look—I flash a smile and say, "Want any help putting together the Weekend Read?"

EIGHT

ONE AFTERNOON IN SEPTEMBER, TWO GREEN BOXES appear on my desk. They are bottle sized, wrapped with green ribbon and a bow on top. I assume that they are for Gregory, so rarely does anything arrive for me. But no, there's my name, and Julian's. Inside, a sweet note from Warner Bros. thanking us for all our work and scheduling accommodation this pitch season.

Julian perks up, pulls an earbud out of his ear when I say that it's for us, not our bosses. "What'd they send?" he asks.

"A bottle of red wine and a bottle of bourbon," I say.

"Do you have a preference?" Julian asks.

"Slight preference for bourbon, but I'm okay with either," I say.

"I'd prefer the bourbon. I'm not a big wine guy."

"Okay," I say. *Fuck you*, I think. Then: *Stop*. I'm being unfair. He doesn't know I don't really like red wine. I had my chance to say no, and I didn't because I was trying to be polite. Which is on me. But also gender norms.

Later that day, on my way back from a Fitbit walk around the office, I see Gregory standing in front of Julian's desk, chatting. I'm out of Julian's sight line but close enough to hear Gregory say, "Who are those from?"

"A thank-you from the Warner Brothers team," Julian says.

"Wow, nice. Good going, man. Making an impression." He offers Julian a high five over the top of the cubicle partition.

When I get closer, I see that Julian has put both the wine and the bourbon on the edge of his own desk, right near the carefully spread display of *New Yorkers* that I know he hasn't read.

I remove the bottle of wine from his desk and put it on the edge of mine, mirroring his setup. He watches me but says nothing.

Does he think I can't tell what he's doing? Or does he not care? I'm unsure which would be worse.

I don't like being alone with my indignation. I could tell Allyn, who will understand the nuances without forcing me to confront my pettiness, but, though she's currently frustrated with Julian, they are friends, and she is famously indiscreet. Competition aside, there is an easy, innocuous flirtatiousness between them that belies a kind of mutual understanding. Whereas when Julian and I talk, it feels strangely forced, as if we are on different planes and struggling to find somewhere to meet in the middle.

The next evening, a Tuesday, the fourth floor empties out until it's just Julian and me left. *Unsung* is in production on episode 103, and we are waiting for the day's footage—what's known as "dailies"—to be uploaded so that we can comb through and find the best takes of each scene to splice together into "selects," which will be sent first to our bosses and then, with their approval, on to Veronica, demonstrating—hopefully—how well everything is progressing. There have been a number of production-related issues thus far, and we've brought on a new showrunner, Lia Morales, to turn things around. All of which means that Gregory and Veronica are paying closer attention to these dailies than they might otherwise.

When I first started cutting dailies, I felt immobilized by uncertainty. Finally given an opportunity to make a decision and

I couldn't stop worrying about choosing wrong. What did I know about cinematography, about camera angles? What if Veronica watched the selects and called Gregory to ream him because I chose a particularly shitty take without realizing it? What would my defense be? "In my defense, I don't know what I'm doing"?

"It's not a huge deal. I just choose whichever take looks best to me," Julian told me.

I wanted to ask what made him so sure of his own judgment, but I refrained.

Usually Allyn, Julian, and I take turns on dailies, but tonight, because I am trying to prove my mettle as a coordinator and also because I am trying to be the bigger person and get back on Julian's good side—he's been testy ever since I got the title bump—I offer to stay late and help him, to make the work go a little faster. And after a little while, he takes me up on it. I suspect he didn't accept until he ran a cost-benefit analysis, trying to figure out if I could spin this to my advantage, to make myself look good with the bosses. The answer is no. If Julian sends the email, which he will, nobody will even know that I was here.

By nine p.m., only a fraction of the footage we're waiting on has been uploaded.

"Want a drink?" Julian asks. I swivel my seat to face him. "We might as well," he says.

"Sure," I say. He peels the foil off the top of the bourbon bottle from Warner Bros. and I go into Gregory's office to get two glasses from his well-stocked, though infrequently used, bar cart.

Glug of the bottle, a generous pour.

We review the footage as it comes in, taking turns, scene by scene.

Another drink, and then another.

I run down the hall to the filing cabinets and come back with an armful of snacks for us: an assortment, a child's vending-machine dream come true. A chuckle builds into contagious laughter as I share a discovery with Julian: one of the interns not only organized the salty and sweet snack drawers—a task I feel badly about doling out, though not badly enough to make the time to do it myself—but also took the initiative to create a third snack drawer, labeled HEALTHY SNACKS.

"It's filled with the least office-appropriate snack food ever," I say. "Guess."

"Whole peanuts?" he says.

"Close!" I say, skipping away down the hall. As I return, two things occur to me: I'm drunk. And I'm having fun. I haven't had fun in a while. "Sunflower seeds!"

"No!" Julian bangs his hands on his desk. "That's amazing!"

I float in and out of focus on the dailies. Julian and I devise a drinking game: take a sip every time the actor playing Bianca's employer slips into her native British accent by mistake. Once I finish my batch, I go over to Julian's desk and stand behind him to see what he's watching. He pulls out the earbud plug so we can both listen. Bianca is going to a kickboxing class to learn self-defense, to fight the agoraphobia and paranoia catalyzed by her mother's murder.

"Kickboxing won't really help her on the self-defense front," I say.

"Duh," Julian says.

I tell him about the self-defense classes I took in high school. I extol the virtues of practicing in an adrenalized state.

I am sitting on top of his desk, legs hanging down over the filing cabinet. "Glass?" he says, and I hand him mine, which is empty save for a glistening copper film at the bottom. I probably don't need another drink, but what the hell. "Can I ask you a question?" Julian says.

"I don't know, can you?"

"Fuck you. For real."

"Of course."

"And you promise not to get upset?"

"Sure, as long as it's not an upsetting question."

"You don't actually think self-defense classes make women capable of stopping would-be rapists, right? Isn't it dangerous to give them a false sense of strength when the truth is, if a man wants to rape a woman, there's nothing the woman can do to stop him?"

"Are you fucking kidding me?"

"Will you at least hear me out first?"

"Fine."

"Are you honestly telling me that if a man held you at knifepoint, you could take him? You have to agree that if a man is dead set on raping a woman, a woman can't stop him, and if she tries, she'll probably get hurt even more."

I set my glass down on the desk next to my thigh. It lands with a louder thud than I intended. "Finished?" I ask. He gives me a "floor is yours" gesture. "Holy balls." I wish I were less drunk, but there is something strangely sobering about this moment and the clarification of my focus. "Okay, so that's the wrong framing. We should be stopping men from raping, not critiquing women on how they respond to attack."

"Not only men. There are women who—"

"Statistically insignificant and it's my turn," I say. "We have to teach boys to respect women and fight against deeply ingrained misogyny, because when men rape, it's more about power than sex—no, still my turn—but until that day comes, yeah, I think there's value in taking full-impact self-defense courses like I did."

"You don't think it creates a false sense of security?"

"Do you have any idea how often I feel safe when I'm out in public by myself? Basically never. Women live their lives braced for attack, constantly weighing the risks of our decisions—is it too dark on this side of the street, is that man following me, am I alone in this parking garage. I didn't learn to 'take' a man holding me at knifepoint, we didn't do weapons scenarios, but we learned strategies for dealing with different kinds of unwanted attention. There are so many kinds of men who are dangerous, not just strangers with knives. Like, what do you do if a drunk and belligerent man approaches you on the street? How do you try to calm him down, prevent him from getting any closer, and prepare yourself to fight back if he doesn't listen? You're supposed to hand over anything they ask for—wallet, keys, purse. The only thing worth fighting for is yourself. It's about avoiding physical confrontation if and when at all possible."

"So they're not giving you an inflated sense of your own strength, telling you to fight back and risk getting hurt." He leans in, bottle in hand, to add a splash of bourbon to my glass. His forearm brushes my thigh.

"The goal is to avoid fighting, but worst-case scenario, if you can't, you should be prepared. That's why our practice fights were so intense. They'd try to scare us, because if you're fully adrenalized, the moves become muscle memory, and in the moment you won't freeze up trying to remember what to do."

"But say the guy is much bigger and stronger than you. You really think you could stop him? Wouldn't it be better to just lie there and let him do it and then leave as opposed to provoking him to hurt you more?"

"Holy shit!"

"Shh, you're shouting."

"There's nobody here!"

"There might be somebody."

"Then they're welcome to come join in on the fun—"

"I'm not trying to upset you."

My cheeks are hot. I pause, take a breath. I feel as though I'm bobbing for phrases inside my mind. A kind of mental game of Hungry Hungry Hippos, gulping down as many marbles as I can and then coughing them back out.

"There are a million factors beyond physical ability that would complicate things, but in terms of physical strength, social factors aside, if this is a guy who isn't armed, then yeah, I do."

"Seriously?"

"And in different scenarios, too. Approached from the front, from behind, in a closed space like an elevator, even in bed with the guy on top of you. Or the hypothetical me."

"A guy who's on top of you?" Julian says. "I don't believe that."

"Well, you should."

"I believe that you believe you could."

"Fuck you."

"You wish."

"What?"

He smiles. "Kidding." A fizz of energy between us.

I take a gulp of bourbon. Warm, but it no longer burns.

"I could take you," I say. "Easy." I hear an echo of my words, as if they came from someone else.

Julian stands. We're at eye level now—me sitting on his desk, legs dangling, him facing me, just in front of my legs. "Really?" he says. An eyebrow raises. He's standing so close. "You think so?"

I nod. "I'd show you, but I don't want to hurt you."

"Can you show me without hurting me?"

"Maybe. I could try."

I don't think there's anyone else around, but just in case, we go into Gregory's office and close the door. Push the coffee table with its carefully curated spread of magazines against the wall to make room on the floor, where a stylist-selected geometric rug covers the building's industrial gray carpeting.

Julian and I face each other. With my heels on, I'd be just a few inches shorter than him. But I ditched my shoes under my desk a while ago.

"So," Julian says. "What do I do now?"

I lie down on my back and tell him to straddle me.

When I rest my head on the floor, something happens. A feeling of suction inside my skull, followed by scrambled motion, a doubling of vision. I look up and try to focus, to remember what the correct placement is for the Double Whammy, which involves hooking my legs around his shoulders and using my lower body strength to send him flying on his back while propelling myself up to a seat. It's the most show-offy of the self-defense moves. Maybe I should just shove him off the usual way, by digging my feet into the floor and throwing him to the side. But I need a modicum of stillness for that, and the floor feels like it's moving.

The weight of his body, pressing on my hips, heavy. He leans forward, closer. A hand on my lower belly; I suck in, almost auto-matically. The heat of it. I didn't tell him to do this. My body reacts, a sharp jolt, but my mouth is stuck. That hand doesn't mean anything, I decide. But there is his other hand, moving higher, higher.

Incontrovertible: his palm on my right breast, grabbing. A thin bralette, silk shirt, almost no barrier. His hand a claw, mauling, then grabbing hold of my nipple between thumb and forefinger. I look up at his face, but nothing is in focus.

Warmth, pressure, then panic. A whirring sound inside my head.

It takes so long to get my mouth to work. "No," I say. "For real. No."

His other hand, struggling with the button of my jeans. He gives up, shoves his hand down my pants, inside my underwear. A jagged sigh. "You're so wet," he says.

I don't mean to be; I don't want to be. "Stop," I say, but I can't make my legs move.

He doesn't stop. He keeps going. His hands and mouth, slime and heat and pressure.

"Don't," I say, but he does anyway.

It only ends when I throw up on him. I retch, and he recoils.

"Jesus," he says. As if I've ruined the fun.

He runs to the bathroom. I crawl over to the couch and pull myself up onto it, focusing first on a square of the rug, and then at the actress on the cover of *The Hollywood Reporter*, staring hard until her face disintegrates.

With difficulty, I hoist myself to a stand and make it to the door, which I slam shut. The sound reverberates in my ears. I drag the trash can back to the couch and collapse.

More vomit, spattering against the plastic lining of the trash can, orange flecked with kale, foul smelling, but I keep it close. Heaving and heaving until it's just bile, clear and burning.

Julian is back at his desk. I walk past without looking at him. "You good?" he calls after me, but he stays seated, he doesn't follow. I don't respond.

I take an Uber home. My stomach lurches with every bump and stop in traffic. I try closing my eyes, then looking out the window. On the car radio, a pop station counts down the top songs of the day. A former child star turned provocateur compares herself to a wrecking ball. Next comes an anthem about rejecting silence and letting the world hear you roar, and then a soulful repudiation of the material trappings of pop royalty. The peppy ode to blurred lines that follows sends me over the edge.

"Can you . . . the radio?" I manage.

Finally, silence.

The apartment is empty when I arrive home. I am relieved to not need to explain my state, my evening. The prospect of forming words is overwhelming.

I wake up sick the next morning. My limbs leaden and achy, pajamas drenched in sweat. I stumble out of bed to pee in the predawn light and buckle to the floor. A piercing pain in my head. This can't be a hangover. This is unlike any hangover I have ever encountered.

I can't go to work like this. It takes all my strength to make it to the bathroom and back to bed. I struggle over to the other side in search of a dry patch of sheet. Reach out, grasp for my phone.

Sitting up hurts. Everything hurts. One eye open, head on pillow, phone extended in front of me, I struggle through the necessary emails. My absence will trigger a round of assistant musical chairs, since Gregory doesn't trust interns on his desk. I had Allyn cover for me once, while I ran an errand, and she bungled so much—canceling meetings Gregory wanted to attend, confirming ones he didn't—that he said never again. Julian will have to cover my desk and get an intern to cover his, which will annoy him. He'll also have access to my email and the ability to correspond as me for the day, an unavoidable intimacy that feels, in this moment, like a further violation.

The thing I want, more than anything, is to call my mother. To wrap my arms around her, to feel her cool hand on my forehead, to say: *I love you. I'm sorry. I understand.*

And: *Tell me what to do. Please.*

I always thought that if anything like this happened to me, I'd go straight to her. But it strikes me now that I had also been imagining an unimpeachable situation. One like hers—the stranger, the parking garage—even though I knew that stranger rape is the least common form. And I had been imagining my mother at her best.

Hot shame coursing through my veins. I was brought up to believe that there is no such thing as a woman "asking for it." That all assault is real assault. And I still believe that. So why is there a *but* ringing in my head?

A self-defense demonstration. Of all the fucking things.

It's not my fault. It's not. I know that. I said no and he didn't listen. He was drunk too, but that doesn't excuse him. I am not at fault.

It's not your fault it's not your fault it's not your fault.

In the course of these repetitions, I realize that I believe it. But so what? So what if I know it's not my fault? How much good does that do?

I consider the options. I think about what my mother told Blake Peterson's victim. How, when the story was relayed to me, I felt frustrated with the girl for backing down, for allowing her silence to be bought.

Newly astonishing: not the weakness of backing down but the strength of getting as far as she did. How many times she must have told her story before she made it to my mother. The horrifying, shameful repetition. How much worse her assault was. And sure, not a competition, but compared to anal rape by a beloved celebrity, an unwanted finger from a peer seems like nothing.

So easy to imagine what Julian might say. That it was consensual, that it was part of a joke, a game. *She wanted it. You wouldn't believe how wet she was.*

I spend all day in bed, incapable of focusing on anything, even TV. I drift between sleep and wakefulness, the latter worse. The loneliness of being trapped in my body, contemplating how much I take the absence of pain for granted in everyday life. How all-consuming its presence can be.

Julian is not my boss. He doesn't have power over me. Why should he get to have power over me?

If I don't tell anyone, I can contain it. Refuse to give it—or him—significance. Erase it, and, ultimately, prevail.

NINE

WHEN I GET BACK TO WORK ON THURSDAY, JULIAN is already at his desk, headset on. "Recovered?" he says, with a wink.

I want to scream. To take my fake nails to his face and claw his eyes, his cheeks. Instead, I stare. I say nothing.

It's the knowing look on his face. The hard edge of his wink. The memory of his voice, his ragged satisfaction: *You're so wet.* It's how confident he is that I won't tell.

I feel his eyes on me, even when they are not. As I watch him saunter down the hall, run a hand through his famously great hair, wave good morning to Zach, I wonder: Is it possible he thinks I wanted it? Is it possible he didn't hear me say no? But for the demonstration, he was supposed to stay still. He was supposed to follow my instructions. He was supposed to listen.

That evening, when I go to retrieve my car from the spot it has occupied since Tuesday morning, I quite literally hit a wall. Car in drive instead of reverse, I slam into the concrete wall in front of me. The force of the impact startles me awake, my body shaking as I jerk the gearshift into reverse and inch backward a few feet before returning the car to park.

Pull yourself together. But my heart is galloping, picking up speed. I grope through my purse for a Klonopin. No water, so I deposit the pill as far back on my tongue as I can and swallow it dry. Chalky taste going down, saliva chaser. *Breathe, breathe.* I can't. The panic spreads outward, my fingers tingle. I turn the car off.

I have to tell my mother about Julian, I decide. The next day, I drive to her house after work. But when I arrive, the house is dark and she is angry. She stands in her walk-in closet, tearing clothes off hangers, throwing items onto the floor. A cotton nightdress hangs loosely off her bordering-on-too-thin frame. Fury on her face. Howard hasn't sent in her Percocet refill yet; she's out of pills.

"How could he do this to me? He knows what pain I'm in!"

"Since when do you take Percocet?" I ask. "What is it for?"

"For my headaches. It works; it's the only thing that works." She pulls a black sequined blazer off a hanger and thrusts it at me. "Here, you take it, I don't need it. Nobody invites me anywhere anymore, I have no friends. All I do is give, and they take and take, but what about me? What about little me?" She drops to her knees in the middle of the clothes. "Take it," she says. "Take it all!"

"I don't—"

"Don't you think it's nice? It's Chanel. Vintage."

"It's very nice."

"So take it. What do I need with it? I have nothing to look forward to. My small, small life. Look at me, look at what I've become." She goes on like this, in ricocheting tangents. Limited connective logic, but the emotional thrust is consistent: she is miserable, nobody loves her, nobody appreciates all the hard work she does. She asks me to look in her bathroom, see if there's Klonopin hiding anywhere. I uncover a bottle at the back of a drawer, five pills rattling inside. I bring it to her, along with the half-empty can of diet soda by her bed. She shakes three pills out onto her palm and swallows them with a swig of soda.

When she begins to pull herself to a stand, I reach a hand out to help her. She waves dismissively and says, "Take the jacket and go!"

"I don't want the jacket!" Now I'm shouting, too.

"You don't want the jacket? Are you too good for secondhand? Is that it?"

"That's not it."

"Just leave me be. I bet you're only here because you want something. What do you want?"

"I'm here because I care about you," I say, even though she's right. I do want something. Her help. I came because I wanted her to put her arms around me and tell me it will be okay, I will be okay. The thought of the hug I want but can't have sets me off, tears streaming.

"What do you have to cry about?" she says, stomping off to the bathroom.

I hear the click of the lighter. I don't follow her.

I could stay until she calms down.

Maybe I should stay.

I can't stay.

I check to make sure the cordless house phone by her bed is charged before going downstairs and splashing water on my face in the front hall bathroom, my reflection puffy and red, but who cares. Retreat to my car, where I cry in silence, engine off. Force out a text to my brother, asking if he knows about the Percocet, telling him that she's having a rough day and just took at least a double dose of Klonopin, maybe triple. Quickly, the admonitions come. Why can't I stay with her? Why can't I do something for someone else for once?

A stupid pity party I'm having here. *I was sexually assaulted*, I could say. *I was assaulted on Tuesday and I'm really struggling.*

I type out the words. Look at them on the screen.

I'm sick, I write. *I'm sorry.*

———

THE PRESSURIZED SPACE of the cubicle, the tension I feel simply sitting at my desk.

Julian still isn't adding me to the emails I need to be on.

"It's my fault," he says. "I forget."

"Okay," I say slowly. Waiting for him to progress to the next step, to promise action. When he doesn't, I add, "So will you do it now?"

"I'm busy now. But I'll try to remember when I have a chance."

"What can I do to help, to make it easier?"

"Really nothing. Just keep reminding me when I forget."

I begin to wonder if there are openings at other networks or studios. But there's no way I could get a Coordinator title anywhere else. There would be questions coming from all sides. Impossible to leave without burning bridges.

There are empty hours at home. I clean the apartment and feel briefly accomplished, but then I have to live in it. So many different ways for people to contact me; the silence of my phone feels even more brutal for it. An urge to call my mother, a deep longing followed by pain because I don't know which version of her will answer and I'm scared to find out.

Gemma and I barely interact. She is still dating the couple in Venice and spends most of her limited time at home meditating, often in the living room, cross-legged on a round floor cushion, a crystal resting in each upturned palm. She says withstanding distractions is part of the practice and there's no need for me to tiptoe around on her account, but I do anyway. I've been feeling wary around her since our generosity discussion, reluctant to uncover more discomfiting insights.

I go to work drinks. I join Allyn at soul-crushing networking events full of hungry assistants collecting business cards. I update my photos on dating apps. I swipe left and right, try and fail to muster enthusiasm for the messages coming in from disembodied faces and names, people whose interest doesn't feel real or compel me to respond because I know that I'm not real to them, either. It's all placeholders and possibilities. Which should maybe be exciting but isn't.

A fuzzy, gray blankness. A mental ticker of how many days it has been since I've seen my mother. The feeling of extra stomach flesh folding over when I sit down—no matter how much I exercise, how much weight I have lost, it's still there, taunting me. Recollections of things I shouldn't have eaten. Frustration with my weakness.

Most disconcerting is my own disinterest. Insidious, an infection that has spread unchecked. The government is shut down in a standoff over the Affordable Care Act. I force myself to read the news and am embarrassed by my lack of curiosity.

My anxiety dreams are terrifying in their tedium. Lunches I have failed to confirm, conference rooms I forgot to book, phone numbers I can't seem to dial in time, my fingers heavy, immovable weights. But I prefer those dreams to the ones about Julian. Sometimes, he will appear in the middle of a dream, taking the place of a different person, someone I'm attracted to. A sudden shifting identity. Sometimes I am trapped, sometimes I am falling. These dreams, I try not to remember.

I dream about my mother, too: jumping into a pool as a child, into her arms. I wake up thinking about the silky feel of her limbs in the water, the security of her embrace. The skin on the inside of her elbow, the way I used to stroke it for comfort. The sound of her laughter, the dazzle of her smile.

My father, hovering around the edges with the remote reassurance of a cool, darkened room. He has always lived on a different plane from his surroundings, preferring the company of books to people. As did I, when I was a kid, but I chalked that up to not having met the right people yet. When I was young, he gave me one of his favorite books from childhood, an activity handbook called *How to Do Nothing with Nobody All Alone by Yourself.*

These are things you can do by yourself, the first page read. *You don't need any help from your mother or your father or anybody. The rule about this book is there's no hollering for help.*

I had high hopes for it. But then, on the second page, the book asked me to obtain an empty spool, either from my mother or, if she didn't have one the right size, the neighborhood tailor shop, which I was supposed to walk to by myself.

At the time, I wasn't allowed to cross the street alone, and there was no neighborhood tailor shop. I asked my mother if she happened to have a spool. "When was that published?" she asked.

I should take up a hobby, maybe. Learn to do something, anything. Find pleasure in my own company. But that takes energy, and I often feel like I'm half asleep, the world filtering into my mind through heavy cotton padding.

I haven't heard from my father in several weeks. He knows so little about my life, only what I share, unprompted. *This is the part where you say hi, how are you?* I've typed into my phone, only to then delete it. If I have to tell him to ask, I won't want to answer.

I spend too much time staring at my naked body in the mirror, quite literally navel-gazing. The Greeks had a word for it: *omphaloskepsis*. I take a photo of my reflection, then crop off the head. I stare at it until it seems strange. Me, not me.

My earliest memory is of being stripped. Two years old, in preschool at Temple Israel of Hollywood. Lying helpless on the lemon-yellow mats they unfolded in front of the plastic-kitchen play area. I hated that they were changing me where anyone could see.

I shared this story with Gemma at one point, but she said that two was too young for explicit memories. So I didn't tell her about the demented fantasies that followed me into elementary school. The strange thrill of imagining my teachers forced to strip and walk around the room naked while I watched, clothed.

Many men have seen and touched my body. It's no big deal. It's just a body. Everybody has one.

I make a list:

Three Chrises, two Alexes, and two Sams. A Matthew, a Mark,

and a Luke, but no John—yet. Jordan and Jeff, Daniel and Eric. Dustin or Justin, I can't remember which. David.

Now Julian, almost.

What does *almost* mean? Means it could have been worse. Shouldn't that make me feel better?

Something fucked-up: I wish I had seen his penis.

Days pass. Weeks. The worst part about it, of course, is that he is right there, next to me in the office. I will not smile or joke or do anything to appease. I speak to him only when necessary, as cool and distant as I can be from ten feet away. He is polite, careful. The bourbon bottle is gone. We go on.

TEN

I N NOVEMBER, ZACH TAKES A JOB AT NETFLIX, LEAV-
ing a low-level executive position open in our department. Both
Allyn and Julian are vying for it, and by virtue of being Gregory's
assistant, I am stuck in the midst of their machinations. I set meetings for each of them with Gregory, as requested, though I do Julian
no favors with my scheduling. I am relieved to be at a remove, not
competing with the two of them. Gregory is also meeting with
external candidates. He doesn't explain when he forwards email
threads and tells me to set up meetings, but I can do the math.

One afternoon, Allyn asks me to walk with her to the dry
cleaners on the lot. I don't have any dry cleaning, I tell her. Which
is true, but the other truth is that I don't feel like being pumped for
gossip. She asks me to keep her company, and I haven't been outside
all day, so I say yes. As we leave the building, Allyn says, "So I had
the meeting today."

Typical Allyn, zero details. "What meeting and with whom?"
I ask. I tap my phone awake. Three missed calls from my mother.

"With Robert. Didn't I tell you?"

"No," I say. "I don't think so, at least." I've been spacey recently.
My memory's off; everything's off.

"I reached out to ask if he had any time to meet for career advice,
to talk about the Manager opening," she says. "That was okay to do,
right?"

"Of course," I say. Why is she asking me?

"I know it's all way below his pay grade, but I remembered that you met with him, and he ended up creating that whole position for you, so I thought it might be worth a shot?"

"Sure," I say. I scroll through my call log to see how far apart the calls were. Three in a row. No voicemail. I text my brother: *Are you at home with her?* As I close out of Messages, a push notification from Tinder arrives. I've been swiping a little, though without enthusiasm. *New Match*, the notification reads. I tap and am brought not to my matches but to the main screen, a stack of new men to judge. First in the pile: Julian. Standing with a surfboard on the beach, wetsuit half unzipped to reveal his abs. Shaken, I shove the phone as deep into my jean pocket as it will go. Which, these being women's jeans, is not far.

Allyn has been silent for a moment, which is unlike her, so I look up. Did she see Julian's profile on my screen, the panic on my face? But no, she's not even looking my way. "That's what I thought," she says, glancing briefly in my direction. "Maybe it was stupid." There's something about her voice, or maybe it's her facial expression. I'm having trouble focusing.

"Why do you say that? How did it go?" I ask. Of course Julian is dating. He's twenty-six and single, why wouldn't he be on the apps? He must get a lot of play, too. The way he looks. His job, his smile. And the surfboard—nearly overkill.

"I think it was good," Allyn says. "He said I'd be a good fit for the Manager job. He said he'd push for me."

"That's great!" I say. That would mean Julian's not getting the job. A small mercy.

"Can I ask—" Allyn says, then stops. Which is strange; rarely does she give any kind of preamble to a question.

We're about to pass the commissary. Up in front of us is a series of tents with signs announcing an "Eco Fair." Pop music and smiling people handing out reusable tote bags emblazoned with our network logo. I don't need another tote bag, but it's being presented with such enthusiasm. I accept, and Allyn does the same.

"What was your meeting like? Was there anything . . . weird?" Her voice drops off at the end.

"What kind of weird?" I ask.

In front of us now, blocking our route to the dry cleaners, is what looks like a strange petting zoo. Three dogs, several rabbits, a small goat, and a large duck. A bearded redhead in a khaki bucket hat shoves a flyer in front of us. "All of these animals are available for adoption today!" he says.

"Including the duck?" I say.

"Absolutely! Are you interested?"

"How do we get across here?" Allyn asks.

"Has there been interest in the duck?" I ask, trying to imagine who on this studio lot would want a duck.

"We're trying to get to the dry cleaners," Allyn says.

"Can we just cross through?" I ask.

Bucket-hat guy is clearly about to say no, but then he shifts his attention from me to Allyn and I can see the change in his face, the draw of her beauty. "Sure, sure," he says, opening the waist-high fence for us.

My phone is buzzing, my mother calling again, and the goat is quick at my heels, trying to follow us out of the pen, not listening to the guy trying to summon her back—"Here, Peaches, come to me, Peaches, I have raisins, your favorite"—and Allyn is speaking, but I have no idea what she's talking about. There's too much going on.

"—a trust exercise?" she says.

"What?" I say. "What about a trust exercise?"

"So he didn't do that with you?" she says.

I'm lost.

"Sorry about Peaches! She gets excited," Bucket Hat calls after us. "I'll be here all afternoon! Come back, visit us, get to know Daffy!"

"What happened in your meeting?" I ask Allyn. "Did something weird happen?"

"Well. I don't know if—"

My phone again. "I'm so sorry, my mother is calling for the fifth time. Do you mind if I—"

"Oh no, of course, go ahead—"

I press answer but not quite in time. "Oh well, I'm sure she'll call again. Anyway. Sorry. You were saying?"

By now we have arrived at the dry cleaners. "No worries. It's nothing," she says. I've missed something, but the moment has passed. If it's a big deal, she'll bring it up again. I don't want to pry.

"Allyn's trying to schedule a meeting with Robert," Julian tells me the following day. Fishing to see what I know. I don't take the bait.

"Oh yeah?" I say.

"Do you know if she got on his calendar?" he continues, not buying my denial.

"I don't."

He shakes his head and pushes his chair back with a little too much force, rolling himself into the filing cabinet behind him with a soft bang. "I can't get his assistant to email me back!"

A quick, bitter flash of satisfaction at this, that there is something Julian wants but can't have. I haven't opened Tinder since the previous afternoon. I am trying not to think about Julian's dating life. No good can come of it. It's not like I can write a one-star review. There was no emergency with my mother. She was just having trouble turning her computer on. The screen brightness was toggled all the way down; the computer was on the whole time.

I know before being told, before the final decision is made, even, that neither Julian nor Allyn is getting the promotion. I can tell from the way Gregory speaks to them when they pass in the hall, an awkward stiffness in his voice. A new executive is hired, an outside candidate. Allyn says it was a diversity hire, a comment that I tell her she might not want to repeat to anyone else. Both Allyn and Julian begin to talk about looking for other jobs, but there are almost no exec openings around town. Allyn is unwilling to take a new job that's on-desk, says she'd rather wait it out at the network, that she has a feeling it's just a matter of timing and politics. I wonder what Robert said to her in their meeting to warrant this optimism, but I don't know how to ask without sounding like an asshole.

In December, Julian takes a job at Lia Morales's production company. It's on-desk, but he's been promised that if he puts in a year, he'll get promoted. I am envious—Lia Morales is exactly the kind of producer I would like to work for, ambitious and known for cultivating new talents. I haven't met her, but when I listen in on *Unsung* calls, I'm consistently impressed by her deft rebuttals of stupid network notes. Working for Lia, Julian will get to be more closely involved with *Unsung*. I try not to think less of Lia for being taken in by Julian's charms. I tell myself that Julian leaving will solve my problems, or the most important ones, at least. That the atmosphere at the network will be better. That I will feel like I can breathe once I no longer have to see his face every day. That I will be able to move forward.

ELEVEN

RÉSUMÉS POUR IN FOR JULIAN'S REPLACEMENT. Allyn recommends an agency assistant named Nick. I know him, it turns out. In the Hollywood sense of the word. Meaning: I have spent more time on the phone with him in the past six months than I have with any of my actual friends. He is Eyrie Einhorn's assistant, and, having done his mandatory year at an agency, he's ready to move up to a network gig.

"He's really smart," Allyn tells Gregory, standing in the doorway to his office.

Gregory comes out into the hall. He nods slowly. "Smart's good." He turns to me. "Do you know him? Do you agree?" I can tell from Gregory's face and the syrupy indulgence in his voice that Allyn calling someone smart doesn't mean much to Gregory. Allyn is still smiling. I hate him for it, for what he's doing.

"He's a lot like you," Allyn tells me. "Into books and politics and things." I might once have considered this too broad to indicate anything, but my standards have changed.

"I don't know him personally, but he's very competent," I tell Gregory. I mean this as high praise, and I know Gregory will receive it as such.

The first thing I say to Nick when I meet him in person is "I blame you totally and completely for the step-counting hell I'm currently living in."

He holds his palm up to his chest. "From the bottom of my heart, I'm sorry."

He's tall, friendly-faced, and a few years older than me. Before working for Eyrie, he was a journalist, a freelance TV and culture critic who decided he wanted to be on the making side of things.

On his first day, Allyn and I take him to lunch—sushi in the mini mall, standard. The dynamic is beautifully different than it was with Julian. Usually, it takes me a while to suss people out, to figure out which part is performance and which is real. But Nick I like right away, and I find myself wanting him to like me.

"What was Julian like?" Nick asks me as he dumps Julian's cubicle detritus into a trash can.

"He has great hair," I say.

"Say no more."

I am responsible for teaching Nick the systems and processes of the network, just as Allyn and Zach once taught me. The responsibility falls to me without much discussion. I sit right next to him, and I know how most things work around here. It surprises me, that realization. How far I've come, how fully integrated I am into this department, this company where I used to feel lost and foolish and out of step.

This has its downsides, though, which I confront when I explain certain things to Nick. Processes that make no sense. "This is how you submit reports for departmental expenses," I tell him. "You print out the American Express statement, and then at the bottom, you write the word 'approved' followed by a signature."

"Whose signature?"

"Nobody's. We don't know who's actually supposed to do the

approving, so make the signature illegible. Then you email this address and say, 'Please see attached for my approved expense report for this month.' And that's it."

"That's it?"

"Believe me, when Allyn passed the job on to me and described it like this, I emailed to ask, but nobody ever responded."

"Copy that."

"For exec expenses, it's thirty dollars per person for lunch and sixty dollars for dinner, so make sure your numbers add up and the fake guests make sense. Occasionally Veronica will poke through and ask questions. I once got in trouble for putting an actor and both his agent husband and the director he cheated with at the same meal. Don't get me started on the three-hundred-dollar tab from an airport Chili's that I had to turn into a ten-person business lunch."

Nick asks the same questions I asked Allyn once upon a time. Before the effort of trying to effect change outweighed the effort of putting up with various inconveniences and I gave up. Decided to focus my attention elsewhere, understanding that my energy was not inexhaustible and needed to be carefully parceled.

Nick still has that optimism, the faith that logic will prevail if only you present it—build better systems and they will come. I feel a little embarrassed by what I suspect is, to a certain extent, my laziness and complacency, but it is also motivating.

When we split up assignments, I don't have to worry that he won't do his part, or that he will somehow overdo his share in a way that hurts me. He doesn't take credit for my work, and I don't take credit for his. These aren't such remarkable things—they should be the baseline for professional courtesy, I realize, but so far I have found that they are not, and so I am appreciative.

What's remarkable is how safe and supported I feel. How much of a difference it makes to have Nick by my side up to eleven hours a day, five days a week.

I've muted Julian on all my social media platforms, and when he reaches out to schedule meetings or notes calls for his new boss with anyone in our department, he goes through Allyn, not me.

The looks Nick and I exchange when jointly listening to conference calls, or when our bosses are having a conversation across from us. The eye lock. A shock, a sizzle, a moment so unfamiliar, I'm not sure how to process it.

One day, he notices me doing the awkward walking in place that I do while filing scripts. "Is that for the Fitbit?" he asks. I freeze. "We should do a handoff system. Any time one of us—you, me, Allyn—has to run an errand or go downstairs, we pick up the Fitbit on the way. That's how I did it at the agency, and it's a lot easier."

"You too?" I say.

"Of course," he says.

Our taste is similar too. This I discover when I read his coverage. His prose is articulate, his analyses thoughtful and fair. He becomes my sounding board, my partner in arms, and I trust him instinctively and completely. I come to rely on him having the same reaction to a given email, or script, or problematic comment overheard on a call. Allyn was right: Nick and I are alike. It's new and thrilling, this mutual recognition.

"Is he straight?" Susana asks me during a Tuesday-morning phone session.

When I saw Susana in person, every week, it was easier. She once compared me to an onion, needing to be peeled, layer by layer. With the distance, it feels like some of the layers have regrown. I want to tell her everything, but I don't know how. Instead, I find myself talking about smaller stuff. Workplace politics, bad dates.

"Yes, he's straight," I say. "Long-term girlfriend. Why do you ask?"

"I was just wondering, from the way you talk, if you might be interested."

"It's not like that," I say. "I don't think it's like that."

I haven't thought about Nick sexually. When I consider my affection for him, it feels emotional and intellectual, not physical. More mind than body.

Can't we just be friends? Wouldn't that be something new and good and valuable to experience?

But now the seed is planted.

Shortly thereafter, Nick and his girlfriend break up. Things weren't working, he explains. It was a long time coming. They were such different people, had really grown apart. Time to rip off the Band-Aid and all that.

"Do you think there's a chance it has anything to do with you?" Susana asks.

"Of course not," I say. "It couldn't possibly, right?"

I don't think about it actively. More of a low-grade humming. *What if what if what if.*

This year, I dress appropriately for the holiday party and organize a white elephant gift exchange for the department. I contribute a candy dispenser full of M&M's with Gregory's headshot on them. It's the most popular gift in the pile.

———

UNSUNG PREMIERES IN JANUARY, and it's a huge hit. In its second week, the live ratings go up, which is almost unheard of. Broadcast television's biggest challenge, in this day and age, is that people don't watch live television. Except here people are, and boy, are they watching.

Early every weekday morning, a company-wide email goes out with the Fast Nationals—the numbers on who watched what the night before, on our network as well as the others, according to whatever complicated system Nielsen has devised to extrapolate based on their sampling of Nielsen families. CBS often comes out on top, but that (according to us at XBC, at least) is because their viewers are old and they just turn on the TV after dinner and leave it on all night. XBC's audience skews younger, which is a point of pride and enticement with advertisers. But those same advertisers would also like bigger live viewing numbers, and when it comes to that, we've been struggling, the Fast Nationals a dreaded daily reminder. Even *Justice Served*'s numbers are down now that the episodes without Blake Peterson are airing.

But here is *Unsung*, a dark horse success story. Viewership is unprecedentedly high, particularly in the Hispanic community. Turns out those viewers like to see complex, compelling Hispanic characters on TV in more than just token roles. Who could've guessed?

The party line is that everyone knew *Unsung* would be a success, which isn't true. If the network were really banking on it, they would have put it in the fall lineup instead of launching it mid-season. The truth, or what used to be the truth, is that Veronica considered it too narrow. Translation: she wasn't sure white people would tune in, since there are so few white characters on the show.

The success is good for Gregory's spirits, and, in turn, good for mine. He's easier to work for when he's in a better mood, and this was a much-needed boost, given the underwhelming performance of our new fall shows. I'm trying not to resent Julian's proximity to the project—so easy to imagine him going out for drinks, waxing poetic about a project that he, too, often described as narrow and soft. Still, one hit show is not enough to keep a network afloat. The celebratory buzz sparked by the Fast Nationals soon gives way to the mundanity of everyday business.

It's midday on a Wednesday and I am struggling to get a notes call going when a text from my mother comes in: *Don't act like a spoiled selfish bitch then call to say you love me.*

Not now, I think.

I have a dozen people waiting on Gregory, who says he needs just a few more minutes to wrap up internals, during which the execs discuss and compile notes for their external notes call with the writers and producers. Pilot coverage is distributed among the development team, two execs per project, generally. Gregory isn't assigned to specific projects; he's supposed to take a more managerial role. Everyone would be happier with Gregory if he learned how to delegate. His insistence on being in the weeds on so many pilots makes my life an endless scheduling hell. He has been asking for "just a few more minutes" for the past twenty minutes.

Sometimes, Gregory hates it when I schedule internals and

externals back-to-back. "This is way too jam-packed!" he'll say. "No wonder I'm running late. I haven't had any time to breathe, let alone go to the bathroom."

Other times, he gets upset with me for *not* scheduling them back-to-back. "What are we waiting for? Let's get them on the phone!" he'll say.

It often has to do with how problematic the given material is and whether our team needs time to compile a document with the key trouble areas clearly outlined before delivering the notes. Gregory and the covering executives email their initial thoughts to each other as soon as they read, before meeting to discuss. If I were copied on these emails, I could do a better job of gauging timing and arranging the schedule. But I am not copied on them, ever. I've asked. Gregory told me that if he started looping me in, the other assistants would want to be looped in too, which would be *too much*. "You're smart. Use your best judgment," he said.

But I have no information. Best guesses only look like good judgment some of the time. And so, here I am, same as every day, fielding anxious instant messages from studio assistants, periodically jumping up from my desk to tap on Gregory's door. It's reached the point where I don't have to say anything; my presence in the doorway is enough.

I tap myself off mute. "Just one more minute," I say, voice full of false cheer, the veneer wearing thin.

The network always joins last. First on are the writers, then the producers, then the studio executives. Only when this whole crowd has gathered can and do I put Gregory et al. on the line.

Today, I get the notes call going a mere twenty-three minutes late. Or to put it another way: seven minutes from the end of the allotted time window and thirty-seven minutes before I have to begin the cycle again for another call. A brief relief, as I hear the Polycom ringing once, twice (why doesn't he pick up already? He's sitting right there; this is ridiculous), and then, finally, finally: "Hi, everybody. Gregory, Billy, and Andy here."

When he introduces the team like that, they sound like a boy band, in their matching dark-wash designer jeans and plaid button-downs. I mute my headset and pick up my cell phone.

Two more texts from my mother:

I know you don't really care about me

You can stop pretending

I groan audibly.

"What's up?" Nick asks.

Instead of answering, I simply pass him my phone. It's only after I've done it that I recognize the significance. I have never shown my mother's messages to anyone aside from Susana.

"Oof," Nick says. "Is this unusual?"

"I wish."

At lunch, Nick and I go downstairs for sandwiches and bring them out to the courtyard to eat. I find myself speaking openly about my mother. "There are a million interrelated issues," I say.

"Aren't there always," Nick says.

"Sometimes things are fine," I say. "Better than fine. She's kind and generous and supportive, and she says all the right things. But other times, this. I've been trying to carve out space for myself, create some independence."

"And she's not taking that well."

I am surprised by how good it feels to tell Nick about my mother. To hear the empathy in his voice. How easy it is too.

He tells me about his father, who was both an alcoholic and the principal of his New Jersey elementary school. We talk about parentification and secret-keeping and *The Drama of the Gifted Child*.

Things are not always bad with my mother. We do have good days, at the end of which I often feel wracked with guilt because look how much she has done for me, how lonely she is without me, how much my company means to her. Why do I feel the need to flail? Why not let her reel me in?

If only I could allow the waves of her emotions to wash over me as opposed to riding them myself. But this is easier said than done. And if she senses me being cool, keeping myself at a distance, she lashes out further. Like the texts I showed Nick. She was upset because I took two days to respond to a text, which I tried to make up for with a phone call. Never mind that she regularly fails to return my texts or calls and expects me to keep calling and calling until she picks up.

In a few days, this will pass. She will forget she ever sent such angry texts, she will call and entreat me to come shopping with her, or get my nails done, hair, who knows. If I am withholding, she will get mad. If I remind her of these unnecessarily cruel texts—if I point out that I have never sent her messages like this, and that if I did, she'd be unlikely to let me forget—she will say she was feeling lonely, or that she'd been in pain, or something of the sort. I am expected to understand and forgive. I feel like a ping-pong ball being thwacked back and forth across the table, my mother and Gregory at the paddles. Perpetually braced for contact.

TWELVE

TOWARD THE END OF FEBRUARY, I GET A CALL FROM Eyrie Einhorn's new assistant, who asks to set a meeting for Blake Peterson. I try to stay calm as I type out a message to Gregory, following the standard protocol of getting his permission before setting a meeting.

"Yeah, and loop in Veronica's office for scheduling. She's expecting it, and she needs to join," Gregory calls out from his desk. "Soon. This week if you can swing it."

"Who's that for?" Nick asks me. "Sounds high profile."

"Blake Peterson," I say. "Did you deal with him much when you worked for Eyrie?"

"Not all that often, fortunately."

"Was he difficult?"

"At least difficult-adjacent," Nick says. Then, lowering his voice: "He makes an agency assistant buy drugs for him."

"Seriously?"

"Seriously."

"Who?"

"He asked me to when I started. Eyrie's previous assistant handled it for him."

"Did Eyrie know?"

"Her line was that she didn't know anything. When I asked her about it, that's literally what she said. She held her hands up over her ears and said, 'I don't know anything about that.' Meaning, of course, 'Handle it and keep me out of it.'"

"So what did you do?"

"I didn't know what to do. It's not like I'm a purist, but I also wasn't thrilled about the idea of doing illegal stuff in my first industry job. Plus, I had just moved to LA, and I don't do anything harder than pot, so I didn't even begin to know where to get the stuff he wanted. I was talking about it with some other assistants over drinks, and one of them said she'd do it. She was a big fan of his. I felt bad passing along my dirty work, but clearly not bad enough to stop it."

"Jesus."

"Eyrie wasn't his point agent, though, so he didn't cross the desk that often. She's his person for new development and production ideas, and he wasn't doing much of that when I was there."

"Think this means he's trying to get into producing?"

"That'd be my guess."

I make a face.

"Not a fan?" Nick asks.

It's a quiet afternoon, but I look up above my cubicle divider and down the hall anyway, to make sure nobody's lingering nearby. "Keep a secret?" I say.

"Of course."

"I have solid info that he did something bad."

"How bad?"

"Bad bad."

"Sex bad or entitled-celebrity bad?"

"Make that a combo meal."

"Damn," Nick whispers. "Do people know?"

"Not people. It's secret, under NDA-level wraps. But Veronica knows."

There is something about even saying her name that makes me want to sit up straight and suck in my stomach.

"Is she as bad as she seems?" Nick asked me the other week.

"I really wanted to like her," I told him. "I did."

We were listening in via conference call to a meeting helmed by Veronica. Gregory was pitching some of our top off-cycle development projects. "Boring, boring, boring," Veronica kept saying. Gregory could barely get to the end of a sentence. "Give me something new, something fresh, something *undeniable*. Every pitch you hear, every project you buy, ask yourself: Is this undeniable?"

Afterward, Gregory summoned all the executives to his office to brainstorm about which projects on our slate seemed most *undeniable*. Ever since, he's been saying things like, "The premise is interesting, but is it undeniable?"

It goes without saying that Veronica is a horrible boss. We've all heard the story about the assistant who had to get her into Mexico without a passport—private plane, and nobody checked until they landed. And we heard the screams from down the hall when the new assistant ordered the wrong kind of hand soap for her private bathroom.

"Nature or nurture, do you think?" I've asked Nick. "Did power turn her into this?"

"Both. You know what they say, the abused assistant . . ."

"Becomes the abusive boss. But hard to imagine her as anyone's groveling assistant."

"Not groveling. Scheming. You've heard how she is with talent."

I don't know how people buy it. The simpering gloopiness of her voice. But everybody wants to believe a compliment, I guess.

"Veronica seems like someone who would cover up a murder without blinking," Nick says to me now. "To say nothing of rape."

"Nail on head," I say. We share a moment of extended eye contact, during which I feel a flush of panic and guilt. I told my mother I wouldn't say anything. And I haven't said anything. Is it my fault if Nick guessed?

"But what can we do about it?" I ask.

He nods, as if in acknowledgment of an intractable position, which is, I realize now, the reaction I was expecting but not hoping for. What if he said we have to tell someone, what would I do then? More nothing and just feel a little guilty? Or would his encouragement be enough—but enough for what, exactly? That's the problem. That's why I framed the question so rhetorically, so dejectedly.

"Sucks, doesn't it?" Nick says.

Nick probably thinks I know someone who was raped by Blake Peterson. How else would I know about it, if it's NDA-level secret? I can't clarify without revealing my mother's role, and that she shared privileged information with me. Though I've told Nick a lot about my mother, this is secret information of a different sort, the kind that could get her into real trouble.

It's bullshit that Blake Peterson gets to keep his reputation. But what am I supposed to do, refuse to schedule a meeting for him on behalf of a girl I don't know who has signed an agreement to stay silent? What would that accomplish? It's not as if Nick thinks there's something to be done either.

Itching at me as I run through these rationalizations is the reminder that there actually is someone I could speak about, a person who violated me, who continues through his workdays unscathed, reputation pristine. And I have no plans to do anything about that. But that's different. And I'm over it, mostly. Sure, fine, I haven't been able to orgasm in five months, and, though I am deeply lonely, I feel repulsed at the mere thought of being touched by a man. But I don't think about Julian all the time anymore. That's progress.

When Blake comes into the office for his meeting, he rises to greet me with a hug.

"My grilled cheese champion!" he says, and I try not to stiffen too much. I'm unnerved that he remembers me. This time, he only asks for a Diet Coke. I bring him back to the conference room and wait for Gregory and Veronica to arrive before I shut the door behind them and return to my desk. The last thing I hear is Veronica saying, "My love! We've really missed you around here."

Blake's newly formed production company and newly inked overall production deal with XBC are officially announced the following Friday. That night, Nick and I have plans for dinner, just the two of us, before Allyn's twenty-ninth-birthday drinks.

Black dress and heels and kale nachos and grilled octopus tacos and tequila, and it's not like I actually think anything is going to happen, but there's something different about facing each other for a sustained amount of time, as opposed to swiveling our heads to the side to trade looks but mostly looking straight ahead. Entire conversations conducted without eye contact over instant messenger. Something different about not being in my work clothes, about the buzz of alcohol. Smells of perfume and frying cheese as opposed to stale coffee and frustration.

We discuss work and also not work. We discuss Blake, a little.

How it doesn't matter that he's a shitty guy, as long as America loves him and he brings in money.

"It's just so easy, so obvious," Nick says. "That you shouldn't hook up with anyone you work with. Period, full stop. No matter what."

Period. Full stop.

"Even if there isn't a power imbalance?" I ask.

"Even then. Better not to muddy the waters. Don't you think?"

The clarity, the rigid adherence is striking.

I'm surprised to find that I am not as disappointed by it as I thought I might be.

The following day, I meet my mother for a hair appointment at a salon in Beverly Hills, just outside its tourist clusterfuck center. Pellegrino offered with a straw and a bubbling promise of transformation. Slippery-black-robed and seated in a chair, I face myself in the mirror. The stylist slides up behind me, runs her fingers through the ends of my hair. "So what are we doing?" she asks, and suddenly I feel like I might cry.

"I don't know," I say.

"The color's grown in well," she says.

My mother returns from the shampoo station and takes a seat next to me.

"You thinking lighter, darker, or about the same?" the stylist asks.

"You can do whatever you want," my mother says to me.

"I know," I say, voice clipped. My cheeks are hot. Coursing through me, an embarrassingly adolescent urge to rebel, to do something dramatic to my hair, to say fuck it and dye it dark or cut it short. But even as I consider it, I know that I won't do it. I don't want to do something that might make me less pretty, not after all the work I've put in, and this bleak understanding creates an additional layer of frustration, this time directed inward.

I dyed my hair dark brown once, in high school. When I came home and my mother saw me, the first thing she said was "You were so pretty as a blonde." Barely a month passed before I highlighted the brown away.

"What do you think would look best?" I ask the stylist. "What would be most flattering?"

We end up going blonder, my mother and I both.

We sit side by side under the heaters, our hair bleach-painted and Saran Wrapped. My mother chats away as if everything is fine between us, and I try my best to repress frustration with her lack of self-awareness. I have stopped discussing my emotions and personal life, limited though it is, with her. I'm not sure whether she has noticed.

I ask if she has heard about Blake and his new production company. She has not. I ask what happened with the settlement.

"It got signed," she says, after glancing around to confirm that nobody is within earshot. We are alone on this side of the salon. "The girl will get money, enough money that it'll make a real difference in her life, but doled out over an eighteen-month period, to ensure she upholds the terms of the agreement. And that's that."

"But Blake gets rewarded with more money! Even though Robert and Veronica know he's a rapist. They do know that, right? They believe the girl?"

"Well, yes and no. They know there were allegations, and the network agreed to settle them. But do I know what Veronica Ross tells herself about Blake? No. She might think this girl was crazy, desperate, any of the things people say about girls who cry rape."

"But Robert. You're friends with him. Doesn't this affect how you see him? Knowing he would do this?" I feel flushed, and not just from the heat radiating down from the helmet above me.

"Do what? Try to save his job?"

A pause as the stylist comes over, lifts the hood of the heater, and peels back a strip of Saran Wrap to check the color. "Just a few more minutes," she says to both of us. Once she has retreated to the other side of the salon, my mother continues. "If you require your friends to pass a purity test, you won't have many friends. Robert's trying to protect his business. Can you blame him? He built this network into what it is, and it's a rocky time for network television; he's trying to hold on to his job. And sometimes that means making uncomfortable business decisions. Is it what I would have done or advised? No. But these aren't my decisions to make."

"I wish I knew what Gregory knows," I say. I've been fixated on that this week, going as far as searching Blake's name in Gregory's inbox when he was out to lunch. I found nothing of note. I've spent time imagining conversations between Veronica and Gregory, Veronica disclosing or alluding to Blake's *alleged* misbehavior. Trying to guess how Gregory would respond.

"What does it matter?"

"Why do I care if my boss is knowingly protecting a rapist or not? Seriously?"

"Gregory has always been respectful to you, hasn't he?"

"In that way, yes."

"So fine. That's what matters. Judge him on that," she says.

But I've seen how deferential Gregory is to Veronica. I know he wouldn't put his career on the line for this, even if he thinks it's wrong. Maybe I shouldn't blame him. He's just trying to protect himself.

"Forget about Blake," my mother says. "Focus on you: What do you want?"

"You don't think it's bad of me to keep working there, knowing about this?"

She laughs. "Please. Of course not. Do you think other networks are better? They're worse. What are you supposed to do, martyr yourself on behalf of a PA you've never met? Who would that help? You just need to keep pushing forward. When you're in charge, you can change how things are done. But you have to get there first. What's the next step for you at work?"

I don't feel entirely comfortable with this answer, though it paves the path of least resistance. Uphill, but still. "Covering projects and attending pitches," I say. "That's the next step."

"Good. So focus on that."

As our heads bake and bleach seeps into our hair, my mother helps me practice what to say to Gregory to convince him that I'm ready to start hearing pitches.

"You just have to go in there and do it," she tells me. "If you don't think you deserve it, he won't either."

I don't know how to explain the transformation that happens when I leave my car and enter the office every day. How I become a little less certain, a little less of a person. It's like pin the tail on the donkey: being spun around and around and then, blindfold removed, trying to figure out which way is forward.

After a few days of rescheduling, I finally slip into Gregory's office and say what I practiced with as much confidence as I can muster. Gregory rearranges the row of pens on his desk and nods as I speak. "Sounds good," he says. "As long as there's room in the meeting and you make sure your desk is covered, fine by me. Have you seen my second green pen? I had two green pens here, and now one is gone. And my Purell. I'm running low on Purell."

"I ordered more of both. They just came in."

The look of gratitude he gives me for this, for the ways in which I have learned to accommodate his neuroses. I suspect this has endeared me to him as much—if not more—than any of my more substantive work.

When I first met with Robert, he advised that in order to prove myself and my intelligence and get past the administrative drudgery, I should find an area of expertise. I spent a lot of time worrying that I lacked expertise, but it seems I was overthinking it. My niches, as articulated by Gregory, are books and women. A lot to unpack there, but I box it for now. Gregory says to keep an eye on incoming pitches, though I may have to wait a beat until pitch season gets going and the volume picks up.

In the meantime, I dig for treasure in the Weekend Read, an ever-growing and oft neglected mountain of scripts. I unearth a pilot called *IPO* based on a book about young investment bankers in New York City, complete with sex, scandal, and a murder mystery. Hardly a perfect project, and predictable in a number of ways, but the dialogue is sharp, the characters are complex, and it folds in a surprisingly nuanced critique of capitalism. I send laudatory coverage out to the department. Nobody responds. Only once Nick seconds my endorsement does Billy chime in, saying, "Thanks for this, Nick, I'll check it out." No acknowledgment of me.

Billy reads, likes, and emails the team asking for a second read. I see his message just before bed, during a cursory post-alarm-setting, pre-sleep email refresh. Bedroom dark but for the blue light of my phone screen, I tap out a quick, impassioned note expanding on my initial coverage and press send.

I wake up the next morning full of linguistic regret. I should have kept it to one paragraph, and what was I thinking using the phrase "liminal space"? I wasn't trying to show off; I was just too tired to think of a less pretentious alternative. While stopped at red lights on my way to the office, I dash off another email.

Sorry, this is what happens when I email while drunk hahaha.

———

EYRIE EINHORN'S OFFICE reaches out to set a pitch meeting for a modern-day *House of Mirth* in Silicon Valley. *Bingo*, I think. Women *and* books. It might even be good. I'm excited until I notice that Blake Peterson is attached to produce. I consider sitting it out but reason that if I do, I'm the only one who suffers. So I email and ask to attend. A relief to learn Blake won't be there himself, just his development exec.

On the day of, I blow-dry my hair and wear a dress and heels. During, I listen attentively and take notes. The writer and producers treat me with respect, and it feels good. I make comments that reveal my familiarity with the source material. A dopamine rush to see the writer's surprise when I ask, "What's your Bellomont?" I inquire about plans for Lily's drug-dependency storyline. "Klonopin or Ambien?" I joke. The writer laughs. Everyone else looks at me like I'm the one on drugs, but it's fine, it's worth it.

"Either!" the writer says. "I'm open to network notes."

She directs the rest of the pitch to me, glancing only occasionally at the other executives in the room. It's a good pitch and sounds like a fun show. But there's no murder or superpowers and it's all about a

woman. Plenty of sex, but we can't air that. For reasons never sufficiently explained to me, some alchemical blend of FCC regulations
and internal broadcast standards, XBC prohibits overtly sexual content. Sounds of passion (heavy kissing and breathing) are permissible,
but sounds of intercourse (rhythmic moaning or grunting) are not.
Kissing is fine, but not with tongues. We can see characters on top
of each other, but they must be intertwined in a nondescript position
rather than a specific position of intercourse (i.e., missionary) and
there should be no simulated movements. *Overly graphic* violence is
also prohibited, but that's a standard vague enough to leave wiggle
room. Shoot-outs, chase scenes, knife fights, car bombs—these can
and do make it on air. But a woman in a bikini that doesn't cover the
entirety of her ass cheeks? Absolutely not.

By the time the writer describes the debauchery of Bellomont—a
Mendocino estate with cryptocurrency mining downstairs and an
orgy upstairs—I know there's no way we'll buy it.

After a pitch, it is customary to gather in the office of the highest-
ranking exec for a discussion of the project and whether to make an
offer. This is the first time I have been privy to such a conversation.

As soon as the door is closed, before the discussion begins,
Gregory turns to me and says, "First things first, can we talk about
how good you look today?"

I go to my mother's house for dinner that evening. I don't realize
how upset I am until I walk in the door. "I'm going to stop wearing dresses," I say. "And makeup. And stupid dry-clean-only silk
shirts that wrinkle as soon as you put them on. And heels!" I kick
the pumps off my feet, right then left. More momentum than I
realized; the right shoe hits the living room wall with a thump.

"What are you talking about?" my mother asks, walking down the stairs.

"Do you want these? I'm getting rid of them. I'm getting rid of all my clothes."

"Why would you do that?"

"I hate it. I hate it all." I slump down onto the couch.

"So fine, buy new clothes," she says, sitting down on a chair across from me.

"It's not just the clothes," I say.

"Then what is it?"

"Everything!" (*It's me*, I want to say.)

"Are you crying?"

"Am I not allowed to cry?"

"Please don't jump on me."

"I wasn't."

"Yes, you were."

"I sat in on my first pitch today."

"That's great! That sounds like a good day!"

"You didn't let me finish."

I keep going. I tell her about the pitch and what happened after, when everyone gathered in Gregory's office to discuss.

"That's it?" my mother says, with a laugh. "All that happened is that Gregory said you look good today? Who cares? The point is he's letting you attend pitches. And you *do* look good today."

"But that's not the point! I want to be listened to—"

"Aren't you? Gregory knows you're smart—"

"Sure, fine, he knows I'm smart, but he only values my opinion in a qualified way."

"That's not true—isn't he going to buy that project you found?"

"*IPO*? Yeah, I think so, but only because Billy likes it. And Billy only read it after Nick said to. And I lied about being drunk to explain why I hadn't dumbed down my coverage. How backward is that?"

"You didn't have to do that."

"Yes, I did. I did. Don't you get it? Everyone loved that this was my drunk-girl personality. But if I was like, 'Hey, yeah, I'm passionate about this project and have a decent vocabulary,' they'd think I was obnoxious." I'm out of breath, worked up. I've forgotten where I was going with this.

"But in the end, you won. They're buying it, aren't they? I'm sure if you asked Gregory, he'd say how much he values your opinion."

"Of course. And he probably really thinks he does, which makes it harder to address." I'm aware, even as I speak, that this isn't quite it. I'm expressing a pure, self-righteous indignation, but what's bubbling in me is murkier, swirled with a heaping dose of self-loathing.

The truth is, when Gregory told me I looked good, I liked it. It felt like an accomplishment. It felt almost as good as him agreeing to buy *IPO*. And what does that suggest about me and the person I've become? I say as much to my mother, who laughs.

"Why are you laughing? What's funny?"

"Why is it so terrible to care about how you look, to want to be complimented on it? Isn't that the point of it all—the exercise and healthy eating and beauty routines?"

"The empowered answer is supposed to be that I do all that because it makes me feel good. But I really do it because it makes me look good, and looking good makes me feel good, and that is so fucked-up!"

"Oh please. I have no patience for beautiful women saying it shouldn't matter how you look, it's all about how you feel. Easy for them to say, they already look good! I've always found that I feel my best when I look my best, and why should that be such a crime?"

"Because . . . because . . ." My thoughts are knotted; I don't know what string to pull on first. "Well, for one thing, because it takes almost all my time and energy to look this way. And I've been acting like it's a matter of being almost there, like if I just lose five more pounds, I could stop thinking about my appearance so much and could focus on more meaningful things, but the reality is that getting there requires all my thoughts and energy, and once I'm there, maintaining it requires almost as much. It's not freedom, it's a self-policed jail cell!"

What's stupid is how fucking obvious it is. It's so obvious. This is not an aha moment. I've known it all along, but I thought that I could and would be able to strike a balance, and when I didn't, I was quick to forgive myself, to say, *Oh, don't worry, you're focusing on your body right now; you'll find balance later.*

A full-time preoccupation: Boutique fitness. Fake nails, biweekly. Monthly waxing. Eyelash tinting. Accutane for bacne, a partial result, perhaps, of all the exercise. Expensive skin cream to counteract the extreme dryness and skin chapping from the Accutane. Jeans so tight, the seams leave indentations on my flesh. Painful heels and hand-wash-only thongs. Hair appointments every six to eight weeks, too expensive for me to afford, so I go with my mother, side by side, expensive fake blondes.

"Put it on my card," she says, and so I do, with some guilt, but not enough to stop me from going through with it. All in an attempt to fit through a door that always seemed a little too narrow.

All so people would like me. But do I like me? Because this

is me; here I am. I called an Edith Wharton novel "underlying material" today.

The problem is, though I want to make space for more meaningful concerns, I don't want to give up looking good. And why should I have to give up looking good, if looking good makes me feel good?

"I'm an active participant in my own oppression!" I say.

"Now you're being ridiculous," my mother says. "You think you'd be more liberated if you grew out your armpit hair and stopped wearing bras or deodorant?"

"Maybe."

"No way. Then you'd just be smelly and strange, and you'd be doing it to conform to someone else's vision of empowerment, which is participating in another kind of oppression, don't you think?"

"Do you know how much time I spend getting ready in the morning? The guys in the office, they wear the same thing every day. Plaid button-down shirts and jeans. They just get up and go. No decision fatigue."

"What's decision fatigue?"

"It's how the more decisions you make in a day, the worse your decision-making gets. It's why Obama, Mark Zuckerberg, they always wear the same thing. If the men can do it, why can't I?"

"You think men get ahead because they don't have to think about what to wear in the morning?"

"No. But in making myself exactly the kind of palatable woman that they want me to be, aren't I part of the problem?"

"And you're going to fight that by wearing plaid?"

"That's not what I mean."

"You're a beautiful girl. Enjoy it. There's nothing wrong with enjoying the way you look. Why would you want to make yourself less beautiful?"

"Are you saying I'd be less beautiful if I wore plaid shirts?" I ask. This is not the question I meant to ask.

"You want to take on fat as a feminist issue? Fine, go ahead, that's up to you. Or you can leave that to the less attractive women and enjoy your looks. God knows I wish I did. I look at photos of myself from when I was younger, and I think, 'I wasn't fat at all!' But my mother had me so mixed up, hating the way I looked—I tried so hard to shield you from that, to not do that to you."

I shake my head. My mother catches it. "What?" she asks.

"What do you mean, what?"

"You look mad."

"No."

"Okay."

"It's just—do you really think I grew up thinking I was pretty?"

"Didn't you?"

"Of course not!"

"But that's not my fault. Do you think that was my fault?"

"I didn't—I don't know whose fault it was! But, Mom. I went on a crash diet when I was ten. Who does that?"

"That was your idea. I only ever tried to support you." She starts crying now, big, heaving sobs, her shoulders hunched forward.

I want to go over and hug her, to wrap my arms around her body. It scares me, the fragility of her limbs, the thin, near-translucence of her skin.

I also want to scream. I want to purge my rage, let it flow like lava until I am drained, until she feels the heat and burn. I want to hurt.

"Do you really think people at work take you less seriously because of your looks?"

"No."

"See?"

"If anything, they like me more for looking good. That's the issue. They approve of me because I look a certain way, which means I have the money to spend to look this way, which means my parents have the money for me to spend to look this way, because I'm not making it on this salary. And I went to the right schools and know the right brands and restaurants and places to mention—and none of that has anything to do with *me*, with any knowledge I might have or contribution I could make. It's just luck. Luck that I was born into a certain privilege and grew up a certain way, and if I didn't, I'd never even have a chance, not in this industry, or in plenty of others, and that's such bullshit!"

"Why are you yelling at me?"

"I'm not."

"You're yelling."

"Sorry. It's just . . . I have all the things. I know I do. And I'm sitting here throwing myself a pity party and I hate myself for it because I have no right to complain, but the truth is, it's still really fucking hard, and I don't know if I can do it."

"Of course you can. You're doing it now."

"But it's destroying me."

"No, it's not. Look at you. You're not destroyed; you're thriving."

"This? This is thriving?" I stand up and walk over to the gilt-framed floor mirror that leans at an artful, room-expanding angle in the corner. I straighten up and suck in, reflexive mirror behavior. My red dress wrinkled, my eye makeup smeared, my exhaustion visible. But even so.

"See?" my mother says.

I nod. I see, through my eyes as well as hers. The privilege of potential, the rueful wisdom of hindsight. A cold flush of preemptive regret about opportunities not yet squandered.

I can do it. I'm doing it.

THIRTEEN

OVER THE COURSE OF THE NEXT FEW MONTHS, I make changes. Some days, I go to work with wet hair. Other days, no makeup. I wear flats more often, even sneakers once. I keep highlighting my hair and doing my nails, but I buy a couple plaid shirts. Symbolic and silly, but what a relief it is to just get up in the morning and go, as opposed to standing dead-eyed in front of my closet, wondering what items to combine and how much discomfort I can tolerate that day. Once in a while, I dress up. But only because I want to.

I take over the college internship program. When I separate out résumés for interviews, it so happens that nearly all of the ones in my "to consider" pile belong to women. The guys' cover letters and résumés aren't as strong. In an attempt to be fair, I throw in a few, but their interviews are underwhelming. When I realize that the first two to make it into the "yes" pile are white Jewish girls, I feel ashamed, and from then on, I make a point of interviewing and hiring more nonwhite candidates.

"Don't you think we should hire at least one guy, to be fair?" Allyn says.

"No," I say. "Look around. Do you see a shortage of dicks?"

I take the most capable intern under my wing and do things I wish had been done for me when I was starting out—that is to say,

I explain more than just who has fucked whom and who's a bitch to avoid.

I attend pitches and start going to drinks with young studio executives and agents—a step up from the assistant drinks game. I take great care with my notes on the story area, outline, and drafts for *IPO*, which Gregory has allowed me to co-cover alongside two other executives.

The frustrations continue. In spite of my attempts to act otherwise, I'm still Gregory's assistant, and I still spend most of my days playing calendar Tetris, a thankless game where the pieces keep moving and you can't press pause.

Sometimes, I return home from work or drinks under a cloud of loneliness, longing for someone, though I don't know who. I try to ignore the aches; I try to be patient. I try not to think about what if Nick and I didn't work together, what then? I tell myself that the friendship matters more, and I think I believe it.

I stop going to so many early-morning exercise classes; I give myself permission to sleep in. I start journaling more, and though the entries are often just logs of stupid frustrations, the process of writing them down dilutes the attendant emotions.

July 10: I can imagine my future self struggling to remember discrete incidents, the phrase "so-and-so being a dick" conjuring a big gray mass of frustration, the imprints of accumulated experiences as opposed to individual days and weeks, so, future self, to jog your memory: yesterday was the day Gregory kept repeating "I am literally going to fucking kill somebody" after we closed a deal on a third outer space show only for Veronica to announce that she's gone sour on space, and Veronica fired her second assistant for failing to

find a six-foot-long gummy worm in time for her daughter's twelfth
birthday party.

Some days, I am aware of a sensation I suspect to be numbness.
A poor substitute for calm, but it's a relief to not feel so much all
the time.

In August, I accompany my mother to her law firm's annual party
at a hotel in Beverly Hills that we—good, outraged liberals—are
supposed to be boycotting, since it's owned by the sultan of Bru-
nei, where homosexuality is punished by stoning, et cetera.

"Good luck finding anyone at the firm who cares enough about
that," my mother says as we drive east on Sunset, out of Brent-
wood. "They probably got a good deal on the event space."

"But you agree—"

"Of course I do. But I have to go to the party. They're doing a
toast to me tonight. Ten years at the firm. Can you believe it? Ten
years practicing corporate law." She sighs, and I sense her mood
turning.

I don't know what kind of response she wants. "That's a long
time," I say carefully.

She shakes her head and grips the steering wheel. "I never
wanted this. It's all for you."

"I appreciate that," I say. A familiar curdling in my stomach.
We have had this conversation so many times. Traffic is backed up.
It's been drizzling off and on today. When it rains in LA, which it
rarely does, everyone forgets how to drive. There's too much time
for this to devolve into tears before we reach the hotel. "I really do.
But please don't keep doing it just for me. If there's something else
you'd be happier doing . . ."

"It's too late for me," she says. "When I was in my twenties and thirties, I had so many dreams of what I might become. But your dad wanted to move to LA, he wasn't going to compromise, and I wanted children so badly, so I said yes. I thought I could stay connected to my friends back east, I had no idea how isolated I'd feel. And then there was you and your brother, and the divorce and the tuition . . . If you'd asked me thirty years ago who would be more successful today, Robert Baum or me, I would have said me. Hands down. I'd been through so much pain already, and I pulled through, not because I was smarter, but because I worked harder than anyone else. That was the only thing I knew I could do. I was lonely and miserable, and I didn't know if I would ever find love or have a family, but I never doubted my career. I really believed I could change the world. Or a piece of it, at least."

A burning flare of recognition, the wire between us pulled taut. It's easy to imagine myself saying the same in thirty years. I watch her face carefully, the furrowed eyebrows, downward curl of her mouth. Glistening in her eyes.

"Nobody tells you which choices are the ones that will matter. You don't notice the doors closing until it's too late. And now here I am, washed up and out of the game, and all I can do is make money for you and your brother so you don't have to make the same kind of decisions I did. So you can really do what you love."

"I don't know if I'm making the right choices," I say. "But I also don't feel like I have many choices right now."

"Not yet, but you will."

"Only if I keep playing by the rules. And then I wonder, at what point am I just fully complicit in a fucked-up system?" I look out the window as I speak, at the blur of green hedges obscuring obscenely priced houses from view.

"You're being too hard on yourself."

"I don't know, I think maybe I'm not being hard enough. What if I've already sacrificed my principles and now I'm just trying to make myself feel better about doing it? I send in deal memos for pitches from Blake Peterson's production company, and I smile and nod when Veronica claims in department meetings that she wants more projects with diversity and strong female characters but only ends up buying projects from white men she's worked with before. Nick and I talk about how wrong it all is, but what good does that do, aside from maybe mollifying our consciences, letting us feel like we're different, we're not like them, because if we had the power, we'd wield it differently. But in order to get the power, I have to make the people in power believe I deserve it, which means acting in ways they approve of, and that's how I end up becoming complicit."

"You haven't sacrificed your principles. You just haven't had a chance to act on them yet."

"But by the time I do, will it be too late? To act on my principles, I need power, but to get power, I need to abandon my principles. It's a trap. But if I say I don't want to participate in a sexist and racist and elitist system, then what? I just quit? Leave the industry?"

There's an accident up ahead. We pull to a stop behind a white Range Rover with a vanity plate that reads DEDNSDE. A little on the nose. That would be the network note.

"Be patient and keep doing what you're doing," my mother says. "Are you happy? That's all that matters. I'd do anything in the world to make you happy."

We maneuver around the accident, a mangled Porsche that drove straight into the driver's side of a Prius trying to cross at a lightless intersection. A cluster of people confer with two uniformed cops. No ambulances, at least.

"But there is something you can do," I say, softening. Maybe it's the darkness of the car or the softly waning light outside. The side-by-side intimacy without eye contact. "You can take care of you. Get out of bed, do things, see people, eat meals. Those are things you can do that would help me. It's hard for me to be happy when you're in so much pain."

"I can't help that," my mother says.

"You have to try," I say. "Please. Promise me you'll try."

I'm crying now. Usually she is the one to cry first.

"I've tried. Don't you think I've tried?" Now she joins me with the tears, hers bigger and louder, short breaths and heaving shoulders.

"I know you've tried. But you have to keep trying. Or try something different. Please. For you but also for me. That's a thing you really can do for me."

We're approaching the hotel now. She turns onto a quiet side street a few blocks away and pulls over. We sit in the dark, car in park, engine running. I take her hand in mine, an unexpected fragility to it.

"My mother took to bed and didn't get up for years," she says. "It was terrible. Nobody wants to spend time with a miserable, depressed mother. I get that more than anyone. I don't want to push you away the way my mother pushed me. Nothing I did was ever enough for her. Which made me want to do nothing at all. It felt like I had to choose: my life or hers. And so I chose mine, and

I ran, and for years, I didn't look back. But that's a terrible position to put a child in, and I hate the thought that you might have felt that way too. It destroys me. Because the last thing in the world I have ever wanted is to cause you pain."

This self-awareness strikes me blind. She has never taken responsibility in this way. In her stories, she is victim, martyr, or both. Long-suffering survivor. I thought I had given up wanting her to acknowledge and legitimize my pain. The destabilizing force of her words suggests otherwise. I feel sliced open, emotionally splayed. "Mom," I say. It's all I can manage.

"I hurt you, didn't I?" she hiccups. "Please forgive me. Please tell me you forgive me."

A momentary urge to say, *No, you didn't hurt me, please don't be upset, it's okay, I'm okay.* I push past it, I hold firm. "You did hurt me," I say. I pause, bracing for attack. Never before have I been this direct. I know that if not now, then someday, this will come back around as an exhibit in the ongoing trial of my misdeeds. But for the first time, I can tolerate the prospect. The honesty is worth it. I tell her she has hurt me, and also that I forgive her. That being her daughter is a privilege; she has taught me so much, helped me become who I am, who I am still becoming. And for all that, I am grateful, I say. And I mean it.

By the time we arrive, the party is in full swing. Tasteful flowers, soft lighting, affluent laughter, and barely there hello hugs. Squeeze of lime in my drink, cool crisp of tonic and bite of gin. This may not be the place my mother wants to be, but it is clear how appreciated and admired she is here, by partners, associates, and paralegals alike. She takes particular care to mentor young women associates, and as soon as we arrive, a group descends to say hello and to tell me how wonderful my mother has been to them.

I have heard this many times, from many women. Usually, it provokes a murky pride spiked with isolation and resentment. Now I am relieved to find no trace of those darker undercurrents. I feel pleasure and gratitude that my mother has been such a role model, and that she instilled in me the importance of paying it forward and building alliances. Threaded through, though I don't know what to make of it yet: a budding sense that my view of what that means might differ from hers.

Later that evening, sitting on my bed in a cocktail dress, newly magnanimous and loosened from gin, I text David. I want to know if I was too hasty in breaking up with him. If the problem was me, my inability to open up or accept the love he was offering. He responds right away. He's leaving a comedy show at The Pleasure Chest, a sex toy store in my neighborhood. I meet him at a bar nearby.

"You look amazing," he tells me. "How have you been?"

I tell him that it has been a tough year. That I've been consumed by work, that I've struggled to negotiate between my mother's and my boss's needs. That I think I'm making progress but I'm not entirely sure. David nods and nods, so understanding. He places a warm, familiar hand on the small of my back, and I do not recoil. In texting him tonight, I have given a sign that I want something—well, duh, sex and validation—but perhaps more than that. In my tidied-up story about how I've been, he may hear an explanation for the breakup and my subsequent silence. I don't want to mislead him. But I am two more gin and tonics in.

And so even though I know getting back together with him is not the answer, that I am not obligated to date someone just because they want to date me, even if they are perfectly nice and inoffensive, that I can and should hold out hope for a relationship that feels different, feels right, feels like love, whatever that is, I let him call a car to take us back to my apartment. In the back seat, I run a hand up his denim-clad thigh and thrill at the sharp intake of breath when I make my way to his crotch and feel him harden underneath my hand. I register, for the first time in a very long time, a jolt of desire. But by the time he is thrusting above me, face twisted with exertion, it is gone, and I close my eyes in what I hope looks like an overflow of feeling as opposed to a longing to exit my body.

In the morning, I wake with a headache and his erection pressed against my ass. I slide out of bed and into a robe and stumble to the kitchen, where I stand at the sink, drinking glass after glass of water until I feel bloated and ill, a deeper thirst still unquenched.

FOURTEEN

THE GROUND GIVES WAY ON A WEDNESDAY IN OCTO-
ber that begins as blandly as they usually do. Meetings to be
moved, coverage I've been trying and failing to make time to write,
an Outlook calendar that makes my eyes hurt. Most of our new fall
shows have, if not quite flopped, then—to spin it more positively—
not yet found an audience, and tensions are running high. I've just
finished making reservations for a lunch initially scheduled for six
months ago when the email goes out.

From: Veronica Ross

Subject: Thank you.

I understand immediately that it's bad news; everybody knows
that's what "thank you" with a period as opposed to an exclamation
mark means.

In the body of the email, Veronica announces her resignation.

The energy in the office changes immediately—a sudden silenc-
ing followed by purposeful strides back to desks, urgent patter of
keyboards, group chats quickly filling with fragments, nobody
speaking out loud.

Nick and I swivel our desk chairs to face each other and exchange
matching looks of shock-horror-excitement. Allyn sends a message
to our group chat: *Ding dong the witch is dead!*

The letter itself is diplomatic, of course. It suggests an amica-
ble, consensual parting of ways. Questions begin to circulate: Who

knew what when? How long has it been under wraps? And most importantly: Who's going to replace her?

The *why* isn't asked, not really. It's mostly assumed. This is how things go when ratings are lousy. The appearance of cleaning house. The network president takes the fall. Robert will claim responsibility for *Unsung*'s success and shift blame for the flops to Veronica.

The phone starts ringing. Executives, agents, assistants, hungry for information. Gregory is an obvious candidate to replace Veronica, and everyone knows it. He wants the job, badly. Everyone knows that, too.

When assistants from all over town, people I barely know—or, according to the Hollywood dictionary, in which anyone you have met once can be called a friend, some of my dear friends—appeal to me for gossip, I am not immune to the seduction. I find myself flirting and joking, keeping my answers vague enough that the callers will assume I am hiding something.

Gregory summons the whole department into his office for a team meeting. He tells us to stay calm, that everything is going to be fine. I catch his eye for a moment and he gives me a brief, nearly imperceptible nod, but it's enough.

There are rumors about department restructuring. Head count shifts. A potential opening for a lower-level executive.

This time, I pay attention.

Exactly one week after Veronica's resignation email, Robert makes an appearance on the fourth floor. Word spreads about his presence before I see him, via an all-caps instant message from Allyn. No time to respond. There he is, right in front of me.

"Hanging in there?" he says, tapping his fingers on the edge of my desk.

"Always," I say, with a bright shiny smile.

"Gregory in?"

"Yes. Let me just make sure he's—"

But Robert doesn't wait. He walks over to the closed door while I am still midsentence, raps briefly on it before opening. I hear Gregory say "Yeah?" after the knock—he almost certainly thinks it's me—and my arm muscles seize up. As a rule, Gregory doesn't like to be surprised.

Robert goes in, shuts the door behind him, and I turn wide-eyed to Nick.

"Do you think?" Nick says.

"I hope," I say.

He's in there for a while. Long enough that I have to push a notes meeting. Long enough that messages start popping up from people all over the floor, asking for information.

When finally Robert emerges, he pauses for a moment in front of my desk and says, "I hear you found a good one for us."

I gather myself quickly and say, "Yes! I really think it will be."

"That's the kind of initiative I like to see," he says. One more rap of the fingers and then he's off. I watch him leave, heart thudding, replaying my words in my head, wondering if I said the right things, if I sounded weird, if there was something else I should have said.

My months of digging through the Weekend Read finally paid off. I struck gold—a script not just passable but good, a project worth fighting for. It's called *The Color Line*, and it's a drama about police brutality in Philadelphia, focusing on the mother of an unarmed

Black boy killed by a cop on his own street. The writer is a Black woman from Philadelphia. The characters are multidimensional, the social critique nuanced. And the outrage over Michael Brown's murder in Ferguson is widespread enough that the higher-ups just might sign off on it. Horrible to consider it that way, but there it is.

We have a moral obligation, I wrote in an email to the department, to explore and depict the criminal justice system as it actually exists in this country. Which is not what we do, currently, with our lineup of shows like *Justice Served*, where the cops are good and the jury trials fair. Once in a while, an exception, a dirty cop or a trial gone wrong, but it only proves the rule.

If we are serious about wanting diverse programming, I continued, well past my usual self-enforced 250-word cutoff, this is the kind of diversity we need. Not a show written by a white man, directed by a white man, starring a beautiful, thin white woman and a bunch of other white dudes, with a Black actor thrown in as the mayor or chief of police.

I went on and on and pressed send without softening my wording.

It worked. Gregory read the script immediately, loved it, and reached out to the agents, who are asking for a pilot commitment, which means more money and therefore requires Veronica's blessing and budgetary sign-off. Both Gregory and I have been waiting anxiously for Veronica to read it, frustrated by a reticence now obviously attributable to her pending resignation. Her departure means Gregory has to go a step farther up the food chain, to Robert, for the go-ahead.

I'm touched that Gregory would take care to give me credit for the find. It's not like him.

If Gregory becomes President, it will impact me. The President's assistant—or assistants; it's possible he'd hire a second as well—traditionally plays a more exclusively administrative role and is less likely to be involved with specific projects. At this stage, it would be tantamount to a demotion for me.

If ever there were a perfect moment to promote me, it's now. I feel a certain frisson every time I drive onto the lot to work. These things take time, I remind myself. But that's in normal circumstances. And this isn't that. Veronica will be out by the end of the month—just two weeks away.

Allyn is full of speculation about who will run the department if Gregory gets the job and whether she'll get the new Manager slot.

"Where did you hear about the Manager opening?" I ask. "Is that real?"

She nods. "I had coffee with Robert," she says.

Coffee with Robert. I flag this. Maybe I should reach out to schedule coffee with him. If he met with Allyn again, surely he'd meet with me, too. Pretty transparent, but so it goes.

Allyn is fishing for more information, which she thinks I might have. On this front, at least, I can be honest: I know nothing.

I'm nervous to voice my hope. I am only twenty-four—that's very young, almost impossibly young, to be a network executive. Who am I to say I'm ready or capable? And what about Allyn, who is nearing thirty and has been gunning for a promotion for a long time now? I don't necessarily want to compete with her, but I also don't want to step back and wait my turn.

"Julian's getting promoted at Lia Morales's pod, did you hear?" Allyn tells me. "Boy wonder over there, but who's surprised."

"No," I say. "I hadn't heard." I have worked hard not to keep tabs on him. I feel a sudden choking, panicked sensation. Gulp it down, swallow it away.

I email Robert, cc'ing his first assistant, to set up a meeting. "We'll get this on the books ASAP," the assistant assures me, but he offers no dates.

"I want this," I tell Nick. "But I don't want to seem arrogant, like I'm getting ahead of myself."

"It's not being full of yourself to want to get off-desk. You've worked hard, why shouldn't you want it?"

We're in the archive closet, rooting through boxes of DVDs in search of two midseason episodes of a short-lived drama from four years ago, which Gregory has insisted he needs immediately, for reasons left unexplained.

"I don't know. Because I haven't put in enough time. Because I'm younger than Allyn, and is it rude for me to try to leapfrog over her? What I want, I think, is for someone to give me permission to want this."

Nick shakes his head. "You need to give yourself permission. You can't wait for someone else. That's the nice girl in the corner waiting for a boy to ask her to dance. And maybe she gets asked by the boy she wants, maybe she doesn't—she's given up agency." He stands on his tiptoes to reach a box on the highest shelf and pulls it out, dislodging a blanket of dust. The interns are supposed to keep the closet organized, but they obviously have not. Nothing is in order. This could take forever.

"Or maybe it's Regency-era England and she had very little agency to begin with," I say.

"Thank you, Miss Austen." He passes me the box and reaches for the one behind it. "I say go for it. I hereby endorse your campaign for Manager."

"Thank you," I say. "Really. Do you think I have to tell Allyn?"

"Now that's for you to decide." He lifts up a DVD in a paper sleeve. "Found one!" he says, triumphant.

I tell Allyn via instant message. *I think I'm going to throw my hat in the ring. For the manager job*, I write, like it's casual, like a coward.

> **Allyn:** *that's great!*
> **Me:** *Really? You're okay with that?*
> **Allyn:** *of course. you do you. it's smart bc even if you don't get it, you're letting Gregory know that you're ready for a step up. good long game*

It takes only two days for Gregory to find time to meet with me — by which I mean for me to make time in his schedule, and for him to agree that he doesn't have something more pressing to do during the allotted time.

I make my way into his office and try to project a confidence I don't quite feel. I'm wearing heels and the dress he complimented after that first pitch meeting. My hair is blow-dried. I have prepared a list of the various ways I am already filling the role of Manager, of what I could bring to the team, of thematic areas worth exploring for new shows. *If* you were to be in a different position, being your assistant would come with a very different set of responsibilities, I say.

I give him a moment, and he remains silent for long enough that it feels like confirmation.

"I've been meaning to talk to you about that," he says.

With this, I am off and running, pitching myself as confidently as I can, and he doesn't say anything definitive, but he does say that when possible he likes to promote from within. I've certainly proven I can do the job, and if it were up to him, he'd offer it to me today, but this being a bureaucracy, there's more to it than that.

This sounds at first great and then terrible—both an endorsement and a preemptive excuse.

"I'll keep you posted," he says, and then the phone rings and our meeting ends.

"This is good," Nick says. "It's very good."

Allyn seems unconcerned when I tell her the meeting went well. She says she's happy for me, that it's good for me to start announcing my readiness for promotion. "But you haven't met with Robert, right?" she asks.

"No," I say.

"Okay, good," she says. "I mean, not good, just okay. You know what I mean."

I make a mental note to follow up with Robert's assistant.

One week later, Gregory calls me into his office, tells me to shut the door.

When I return to my desk afterward, heart thumping, I try to keep my face as neutral as possible, but Nick can see through it, and the truth is, I want him to.

"Is it?" he asks.

I shake my head, then nod. "Not officially. In the works. Secret for now."

He claps. "That's amazing." Then, quieter, "Congratulations."

The timeline is unclear, but to use Gregory's jargon, "the ball is rolling." And knowing this gives me a sense of forward motion and rejuvenation, that fresh-faced, damp-hair, post-exercise feeling. I finally have some control—or I soon will—and this knowledge refills the coffers of my patience for the interim period. I can begin to plan for the future in a way that feels real. Can imagine a life in which I am more than an appendage.

FIFTEEN

THE XBC EXECUTIVE BUILDING HAS TWO SETS OF elevators: one leading from the mazelike parking structure up to the lobby, and the other from the lobby to the five floors of offices. In between, in the middle of the high-ceilinged lobby, stands the security desk, where guests check in and employees tap ID cards upon entrance. I usually shuffle through on autopilot, attention tuned to my phone's inbox, but one Tuesday in November, when the elevator doors open onto the lobby, I feel inexplicably unsettled. They say the human mind only processes 30 percent of what it sees. I look up, and there she is: my mother. Elbows on the security desk, watching the guard—Devon, this morning—who has the phone up to his ear.

"Mom!" I say.

"This your mom?" Devon says. I nod. He puts down the phone. "You can go on up, then," he says. "You've got a very nice daughter."

"Sometimes!" she says, and he laughs.

She follows me over to the right bank of elevators. There's one open and waiting; she follows me in.

"What are you doing here?" I ask.

"Work, what else. What floor is Robert again?"

"Five. Why—" I say, trailing off when I realize she is engrossed in her phone, no longer listening. "Mom? Is it Blake?"

She shakes her head vaguely, in a way that I think means no, but I can't be sure. "Later," she says.

"Are you okay?" I ask.

"Same as I always am."

I notice an unblended line of foundation along her jaw. I reach out and smudge it into her skin. The bell dings, elevator doors open. Fourth floor. This is me. "There's a little more," I say. "Just rub in, along there. Will you call me after?" I ask, though I suspect she'll forget.

I know without needing to be told that whatever's going on, it's Not Good, in a serious, capitalized kind of way. The most I can hope is that it won't affect me.

A crazy, selfish thought: She's here to get my promotion taken away from me. And she's going to do that by going straight to the top, to Robert. It makes no sense. She isn't even mad at me right now. But what, then, is it?

The most likely scenario involves Blake—something to do with the settlement, loose ends to address. Or maybe another woman has come forward. But she shook her head when I asked about Blake. Which means she either wasn't listening to my question or it really is something else.

I retrieve the key to Gregory's office from the tray on my desk and struggle to align it with the lock. I feel like I'm outside my body, piloting a video game character. I force myself through familiar motions rendered newly strange. Lights on, computer on. I can't complete these early-morning tasks quickly enough. I lean over Gregory's desk and log him in, waiting impatiently as the desktop screen pixelates into view. Open his email, scan the most recent subject lines. Nothing out of the ordinary.

I have a bad feeling that whatever is happening, it is bigger than Blake—and the Blake situation seemed plenty big. But that my mother dealt with mostly through conference calls. For this, she has shown up at the office, first thing in the morning. If it were a long-planned meeting, she would have told me about it.

I return to my desk and shakily log myself into my own computer. Nick has his headset on; he's rolling calls. I can't bear to wait until he's off the phone. I send an instant message telling him my mother is upstairs meeting with Robert.

He swivels around to face me. The eye contact brings me back into my body for a moment.

"Why?" he mouths.

Soundlessly, I reply, "No idea."

Though he can provide no answers, I feel a quiet reassurance in his presence. A reminder that, whatever happens next, Nick will be beside me, and not just physically, not just because he has to be. Of all the things I might need to worry about, he's not one of them.

The next hour passes slowly. I keep refreshing my personal email, tapping my cell phone awake to check for missed calls. At 11:15, once I sweep Gregory into a conference room for his first meeting of the day, I hurry into his office, close the door for privacy, and dial my mother. No answer, just two rings, then voicemail. Does that mean she's still in there, meeting with Robert? It's been two hours. I happen to know, from scheduling recent meetings for Gregory, that Robert's day is broken down into twenty-minute segments. I slump back to my desk and stare blankly at the computer screen.

"Are you okay?" the intern asks instead of her usual, "Need help with anything?" which gives me a sense of how well I'm masking my emotions.

I have a twelve o'clock pitch meeting. Generally, I look forward to pitches, but today, I don't want to be away from my email for that long. I fear something is going to happen, and I am going to miss it.

As it turns out, I'm right.

Just ten minutes into the pitch, through the glass door of the conference room, I see Gregory shoot past, a blur of blue plaid. Running. Gregory never runs.

The writer and producers are on the other side of the table, facing inward, oblivious. The writer is still in the beginning of the teaser, talking about the detective and the cartel she's trying to bust. Do any of them have names? Did he actually just say *Papi* and *Jesus*? This is never going to end.

Pay attention. You're going to have to ask questions, so you need to pay attention.

I've missed something. Suddenly everyone's out on a yacht in the marina. The detective's cover has been blown.

"The big boss orders his henchmen to tie her to cement blocks and throw her overboard, which they do. The camera follows her as she sinks down to the ocean floor, trapped and flailing. But then, just as we think it's all over for her . . . she opens her mouth. And breathes! She's a *mermaid*! End Act One."

If only I could check my phone without them noticing. Once upon a time, I would've killed to be in a pitch, any pitch, even a pitch about mermaids, which is only an "even" in my book. Gregory, for his part, is convinced that mermaids are going to be the next zombies.

"So most of the show takes place underwater?" I ask.

"We're envisioning about seventy-thirty."

"How do they speak? Underwater, I mean. Do they speak?"

The headline: **BLAKE PETERSON RAPED PROD ASST, XBC CHAIRMAN ROBERT BAUM COVERED IT UP, OUSTED PRES VERONICA ROSS ALLEGES.**

Allyn is waiting at my desk when I get out of the pitch. She wants details, wants to know what I know. I shake my head. I play overwhelmed, I play surprised.

A roaring in my ears. Deafening, almost too loud to hear myself speak as I pull the article up on my computer screen and scan quickly to see if my mother's name is mentioned. The answer is no. Not yet, at least.

This is bad, I think. This is very bad.

And then it gets worse.

A second headline: **VERONICA ROSS ACCUSES ROBERT BAUM OF SEXUAL HARASSMENT.**

I excuse myself to the bathroom and call my mother from inside a stall, staring hard at a water stain on the ceiling to focus my scattered nerves. Three times in a row, no answer.

Nick and I go down to get food for the executives. Everyone has canceled their lunches. "She's not picking up," I tell him in the elevator.

"Maybe she's—"

"But she was here to see *him*."

"But do you think she would—"

"Listen. Remember how I told you I knew something bad about Blake Peterson? She was my source. Robert did cover it up. So did Veronica." The words come tumbling out.

Nick nods, his face calm. He's truly unflappable. It's amazing.

"She met with the girl, discussed options, basically encouraged her to settle, as a favor to Robert. But that was different. It wasn't Robert being accused."

First floor, into the cafeteria, straight for the sushi line. Voices lowered. I watch Nick's face for signs of judgment, but his expression is neutral.

"Is it possible—?" Nick makes a circle gesture with his right hand.

"That she's helping Veronica? No way. She's been friends with Robert for a long time, and she thinks Veronica's a bitch, that she's part of the problem."

"She's not wrong."

"I know." Arms loaded with plastic sushi containers, we retrace our steps back up to the office. "I just don't know what to be nervous about," I say.

Back at my desk, I open my sushi container and am repulsed by the salmon's raw smell, the oily orange gleam. I can't bring myself to eat.

All afternoon and into the evening, I call, and she doesn't pick up.

I text, email, try the home line. Nothing.

In the office, it's like everyone's stoned. Response times are off, faces dazed.

I could go to her house after work, see if she's home. Send an email letting her know I'm going to come by, if that's okay—more statement than question. She likes it when she tells me not to come over and I do anyway. But this is different.

A twist of anticipation and dread as I drive west. I'm well past the 405 when it occurs to me: What if she's not home? Then what? Do I leave? Or wait in my car? Or let myself in and wait to surprise her when she finally gets back from the office or wherever she might be?

None of these seem like good options. The first is clearly the most advisable. I should turn around here. Or here. Or here. But I don't. I'm on the block now, pulling up to the house, and there's her car. She's home.

I let myself in, call out, "Hello!" No answer. Muffled sounds coming from upstairs. She must be on the phone.

I find her in her office, leaning back in her desk chair, cordless phone pressed to her ear, listening. She sees me, waves, and makes a gabbing motion with her free hand.

"I hear you," she says. "Just try to relax tonight, have dinner with your wife, get some sleep. We'll release a statement tomorrow. We're going to get out in front of this, don't worry."

I stand there until she hangs up. It doesn't feel like a decision. I am stuck. I can't fathom moving.

"Who was that?" I ask, though I know the answer.

"Robert," she says. Voice more energized than I've heard it in a while.

"Mom."

"What?"

"You're representing him?" I say.

She nods. "You see what lies Veronica's peddling? That Robert forced her to protect Blake? That she wanted a thorough investigation, but *he* squashed it? That's bullshit and you know it."

"Okay. But the sexual harassment. That's different."

"You believe her? She was fired fair and square. Now she's try-ing to make a scene and get money out of him. She's suing him personally. Not the network. If she sued the network, she'd have to settle it in private arbitration. It hurts women who really have been victims of sexual harassment. These false claims."

Nothing I've seen from Veronica has endeared her to me or inspired much trust, and Robert has only ever been respectful in my presence. The Blake stuff does scream of opportunism and revenge. And yet. Something feels wrong here.

"Why you? You used to tell me everyone deserves a lawyer, but not everyone deserves you."

"He's been a good friend to me, all these years, and I believe in loyalty." Her voice both fierce and shaky—a familiar precursor to tears. "For so many of these yokels in Hollywood, history and loyalty mean nothing. You're only as good as your most recent professional success—or failure. Not Robert. He has character, and he's good to his old friends. That matters. He was the first man to serve on the board of my victims' rights law center, you know."

A dark part of me thinks: *Maybe it was strategic, cultivating your friendship, serving on your board, doing you favors. Maybe this was why.* But I don't feel brave or cruel enough to say it.

"Are you officially representing him? Publicly? Or just giving him advice?"

"Officially. He's always been good to me—and to you. We owe him. He may be a lot of things, but he's not a sexual harasser. Has he ever been anything but polite to you?"

"No—"

"See? So when he called me in tears—you should have heard him, he's a mess—what was I going to say? No? After all that he's done for me. And for you. I'm doing this for you."

"That's bullshit," I say. "You are not doing this for me. If you wanted to do something for me, you would stay out of it."

"He got you a job as a favor to me."

"So you're saying I'm indebted to you, and you're indebted to him?"

"Right. That's why it pains me when I hear you talk about being unhappy at work, because I got you this job."

"No, you didn't. You got me the temp position, but they didn't have to hire me full time, and they didn't have to promote me to Coordinator, or to Manager. I did that. It's because I worked hard."

"But you wouldn't have been in a position to be promoted if it weren't for me."

"You think I owe every single thing in my life to you!"

She gives me a look that says, *Don't you?*

"You put me in a position to be noticed, to be promoted, but I did the work. We do favor hires for interns all the time, it's how this stupid nepotistic industry works. And some of these kids have really famous, really influential parents. But once they get to the office, nobody cares. If anything, we sometimes discount them at first. They have to work harder, to prove they're serious."

"I don't know about that."

"You actually think I've been included in pitches and allowed to cover projects because I'm your daughter? Nobody in my department knows that I'm your daughter. They don't even know who you are, and it wouldn't mean anything to them if they did."

The way her face crumples, then hardens. I have gone too far, but I don't know how to go back.

"Leave," she says. "Just leave."

The next day, I am in the midst of placing a phone order for lunch from Café Gratitude when I receive an instant message from Allyn: *what's a tookis?*

"I Am Dazzling, I Am Humble, I Am Thriving, and I Am Pure. Sorry, make that two I Am Pures. Can you repeat that back to me?" I say. It's impossible to order from this place without sounding like a fool. It's one of Gregory's favorites, but he doesn't like admitting to it because he thinks it makes him sound too Venice, so we've developed a cover that involves me pretending to be obsessed with their adzuki beans and him humoring me.

I type back: *That's not a word. Context?*

"Yes, I Am Whole with extra sea vegetables, but I Am Pure without cashew queso fresco."

> **Allyn:** *Um.*
> **Allyn:** *Complicated.*

"Sorry, is there a difference between adaptogenic mushrooms and regular mushrooms?"

> **Allyn:** *It might be Hebrew?*
> **Me:** *Hebrew?*

"Plus two small spirulina juices, and then that's it."

> **Allyn:** *Or what's that other one?*
> **Me:** *Yiddish?*

Allyn: *Yes!*

Me: *Tuchus means butt in Yiddish.*

Allyn starts typing. Stops. Starts typing again. The dots keep appearing, then disappearing on the chat box screen.

Finally, she presses send: *Does it have another meaning also?*

It's not the words themselves. It's how long it takes her to respond. It's the typing, stop-typing, resume-typing business. Allyn never does that. She presses send in the middle of sentences, thoughts, ideas. It's why she's sometimes so hard to understand. We all refer to it as "speaking Allyn." As in "You're so good at speaking Allyn."

The other day, she asked me, "What's the name of that place I haven't been?" And I knew the answer. It took only a moment to come up with it—a restaurant I'd briefly mentioned a few days earlier. In that moment, I felt a shock of pleasure, affection, and gratitude for my little crew, the trio of Allyn, Nick, and me.

Me: *Tell me about it offline later?*

I type and hit send before registering how presumptuous this response might seem. But Allyn responds almost immediately.

Thanks.

That afternoon, we convene in the cafeteria. It's quiet, just us and a barista preparing to close up for the day. We are in the same booth we sat in on my very first day at the network, a little more than two years ago.

"The best *tuchus* in the building?" I say, repeating Allyn's words back to her.

"Yeah, the best tuckis. How do you say it?"

"*Tuchus*. It's more guttural. The *ch*. That's not the point. How many times?"

"I don't know. A bunch."

"When did it start?"

"When I was an assistant. I used to do distro drop-off to his office."

"I'm so sorry."

Allyn shrugs, picks up her coffee. "It's not like he doesn't take me seriously, though, so that's good, right? He's been really helpful. And with this new Manager opening . . ."

Oh fuck, I think. She doesn't know that I'm getting the promotion.

"Sometimes it's worth it to put up with uncomfortable things to get what you want," she says. "Right?" The wide appeal of her kohl-rimmed eyes. She wants an answer. It's not rhetorical. Oh no.

I speak slowly. "It depends. What kinds of things?"

She shrugs, looks away, and suddenly I remember: that day going to the dry cleaners, with the goat and the duck and Julian on Tinder. She tried to tell me, but I wasn't listening. "A trust exercise?" I say now. "You mentioned once?"

I've been picking at my nails under the table. I only realize I've been doing it when I rip one off, the final tear cleaving the lavender acrylic from my weakened nail bed equal parts satisfying and shameful. I slide one hand under each thigh to keep from further damage. But the silence is too heavy, the urge too great. I slip my hands back out and resume picking. Now that I've ruined one, might as well do them all.

"He never did that with you?" she says finally.

I shake my head. "I don't think so. I can't say for sure unless you tell me what it was."

She crumples an empty Splenda packet in her hand. "Of course not. I'm so stupid."

"Allyn," I say. "Stop that." I reach a hand across the table and put it over hers, which is clenched in a fist. We don't have a touching kind of friendship; this is new. My hand looks stupid with the missing middle fingernail. There's something sticky on the bottom of my forearm from the table, but I don't move my arm. Eventually she unclenches her hand, rests her palm flat on the table. "What was it?"

She shakes her head. "I can't."

I know why she can't, why she won't. I hate myself, I hate everything. I withdraw my hand. "I have to tell you something." Why do I feel guilty? I haven't done anything wrong. I have only wanted and fought and won. It wasn't personal. So why does it feel so personal? "I'm going off-desk." As euphemistic as I could be.

"You mean?"

I nod.

She shakes her head fast, then presses both palms up against her face. Gregory would come running with Purell if he saw her like this.

"I just found out," I add. "You're the first person I've told." Technically true, since Nick guessed.

She still has her hands over her face, and it takes me too long to understand that it's because she's crying. I would venture a hand on her shoulder, but I can't reach from here.

When finally she puts a hand down, I slide a napkin across the table, and she accepts it.

"Robert told me it was mine," she says. "That's what he said."

"I'm so sorry. I had no idea."

She shakes her head, then looks around the room. The barista has disappeared, a small mercy. "He has a button, on the wall by his desk. It locks the door, he doesn't even have to get up. Did you know that?"

"What?" I thought I had broken the habit of reflexively asking "what" when I hear something I wish I hadn't. Apparently not.

"A little black button. He talked about it like it's totally normal to lock your door during a meeting, like he was showing off a cool gadget."

I think back to my meeting with him. I remember the door opening at the end. A button, he pressed a button for that.

"Was this part of the trust exercise?"

"It was before. He locked the door first. 'I'm a private person,' he said." She does an imitation of Robert's voice, his Boston accent. It comes out wrong. In any other situation, I would laugh; we both would. I feel my forearm, the stickiness. Honey? I am out of napkins.

"He had this whole speech about mutual respect and trust and stripping off protective layers. He said it would help him confirm that I'm a person to trust. 'It's all about loyalty,' he kept saying. He made it sound like something he does with everyone."

I try not to speculate. Her words come out haltingly, and it takes great effort not to fill the thick silences with words of my own. I keep going on my nails. I rip off a second, then a third. I slip them into the front pocket of my jeans as I go.

"He had me take off my clothes."

"All of them?"

"All of them. He took his off too, and he just stood there, looking at me. It was awful. I kept trying not to focus on his body, but he noticed and told me to look at him, said it didn't count unless we were both fully engaged. The lights were on. We stood there for I don't know how long, until finally his assistant knocked and he called out that he'd be done in a minute and we got dressed. He said I did a great job."

"Oh god. I am so, so sorry."

Had me take off my clothes. Told me to look at him. The wording, the attempt to soften. *Had me, told me,* as opposed to *forced me, made me.*

"I know how stupid this sounds, but he wasn't hard. So that made me think maybe it wasn't sexual, maybe it really was a trust exercise."

"There are a bunch of reasons he might not have been hard. He's over seventy. Sorry. That's not the point. This happened when . . . last winter?"

She nods. "The first time. And again last month. That's when he said the job was mine."

I wince.

"I know," she says. "I thought I could cancel out the first meeting. If the second one went differently."

"But?"

"He touched me. The second time. Not a lot, just ran his fingers down my arm, but it was creepy, and I must have looked freaked out because he said, 'Fine, fine, I won't touch, just look.'" She shakes her head quickly now; the tears are falling faster. I jump up and grab a handful of napkins from a nearby table's dispenser. Rough, brown recycled paper, but better than nothing.

"Have you told anyone?" I ask. I sit back down across from her.

"Of course not. I went to the second meeting. I fucking emailed him after, to *thank* him for everything. I followed up! I told him how much I appreciated the time he spent with me!"

I don't know what to say. I can think of responses I might offer, lines cribbed from my mother, galvanizing in the abstract or when spoken from a podium, but practically useless. Allyn doesn't need me to confirm that this was an abuse of power, that it's sexual harassment even if she said thank you.

"He kept saying it was equalizing. For us both to be naked."

"That's bullshit and he knows it."

"So what?"

"So what" is right. I shake my head.

"I can't remember if I said no. I meant to, but I don't think I did. He took my dress off. I remember standing there thinking, 'I should have worn something more complicated.'"

"I'm so sorry. I wish I'd—I feel terrible. When you asked about the trust exercises, I was wrapped up in my own shit. I should have listened."

"Knowing he created a job for you, that was part of it, I guess, but I knew how he looked at me. Before the meetings. It made it seem more attainable in a way. Like, if the way I look is the reason he learned my name and will say yes to a meeting with me, I might as well use it, right? I didn't think it would be more than weird comments, which I could handle. I literally fucking asked for it."

"Stop it. Don't say that." I tear a pinky nail off and quickly pocket it. "Do you want to report?"

"Are you kidding? I might as well move home to Indiana while I'm at it."

"You wouldn't be the first one coming forward, though. That helps."

"What, so it's me and Veronica? Great, perfect. You've heard what people are saying about her."

I have. None of it's good, though we still don't know the substance of her claims. "Horrible bitches get sexually harassed too," I say. "Equal-opportunity market out there."

"What was he like when you met with him?"

"Friendly. I don't know. We mostly talked about my mother."

"Your mother!" Allyn says. "Doesn't she specialize in this kind of thing? Do you think I could ask her for advice? Would she talk to me?"

I have to remember: it can always get worse. "Here's the thing," I say. I have to tell her. I desperately want to avoid it, to say sure, I'll ask my mother and get back to you, to defer this conflict to a later date. It wouldn't be lying. I could ask my mother if she'd speak to Allyn. That I can honestly promise to do. But I am so tired of the tense and twisted feeling of careful omission. "You know how my mom's old friends with Robert?" I say, and Allyn nods. "Well, so, he asked her to represent him."

"What?" Allyn says, her voice sharp. "She didn't say yes, did she?"

I nod.

"Are you fucking kidding me? *Your* mother is representing *Robert?*" She's shouting; her words echo in the empty cafeteria, accusatory.

"I was surprised too," I say, dropping my voice.

"How could you do this to me?"

"Me?" This is supposed to be about my mother, not me. What have I done?

"You're acting supportive, but you're probably going to go home and tell her everything I said."

"I won't," I say. "If you tell me not to, I won't." I mean it. I am pretty sure I mean it.

"Stop giving me this 'I really care' bullshit. You aren't feminists, neither of you. All you care about is being powerful and important, and you don't care who gets hurt along the way."

"I do care," I say. "I do."

"Easy for you to say. You've got no skin in the game. Sitting pretty with your promotion."

A flare of anger toward my mother, for getting involved, for taking this case. She has been feeling irrelevant and isolated, lamenting that her most important work is long behind her, that she no longer makes headlines the way she once did. You get a call from someone important, someone who needs *you*, specifically, who promises he's telling the truth . . . Not so hard to slip out of the frying pan. I've been hopping on coals for some time myself, pretending that wearing heels only some days as opposed to all and only doing my hair once in a while means I've claimed empowerment. Grinning tightly and laughing when the men in the department make sexist jokes or talk about how I'm interested in "women's subjects," as if that's a niche, as if a show focused on interpersonal relationships is somehow inferior to one with violence and explosions. Tiptoeing around my cage and pretending the door isn't locked. Policing my own body to preempt others from doing the same. Feeling like I have no right, no reason, to be angry at anyone but myself. And I'm lucky! I'm one of the lucky ones. I am so tired.

"Listen to me," I say. "I am on your side here, and I mean it.

What Robert did to you was terrible, and he should pay. I want him to pay. And—"

"And what?"

I shake my head. "I honestly don't know. Come forward and your career is probably tanked. Stay silent and he won't have to answer for any of it. Middle ground, I guess, is you file a complaint and the network offers to settle. You'd get money, enough to make a difference in your life, but only if you sign an NDA, and then they're buying your silence."

"Nobody will know."

"Nobody will know. But Robert probably won't be punished. It wouldn't even be his money paying for the settlement," I say. "If you come forward, not being the first might help with public sympathy, but there's not a lot of love for Veronica out there, and I don't think it'd stop Robert or the network or people on the inter-net from going after you."

"So I'm fucked either way. That's the answer."

"I'm not sure." My head is pounding. A throbbing headache, sudden and overwhelming.

"You think I don't know what Gregory thinks of me? That I'm some airhead bimbo who can't keep her mouth shut? Loose Lips Lucy?" A terrible nickname, one I've heard Gregory use a couple times. I didn't realize Allyn knew. "You have no idea what it's like to be treated as if you have nothing to say. Everyone takes you seriously."

"No, they don't."

"Compared to me they do."

She is right. I've often felt discounted, but rarely dismissed.

"This kind of thing would never happen to you. You're strong and empowered, and I'm just a pushover."

"That's not true."

"Yes, it is."

People have been calling me *empowered* and *outspoken* and *confident* for as long as I can remember. But why? What have I ever done to suggest or deserve it? I sat in front of the classroom and was first to raise my hand; I parroted my mother's political viewpoints with abandon, which gave me an air of precociousness. I spoke up, and I spoke with confidence—but I did that because I was good at school, because I knew I had the right answers and I was desperate to please my teachers and earn their approval. I felt comfortable making bold claims only after running them by my mother. Obedient, that's what I am and have always been, climbing from one power structure to the next. If I said as much to my mother, she would deny it, and that's part of the problem.

I try to make my mouth open, force sounds to emerge. It doesn't work.

Allyn must see the effort in my face. "What?" she says. Then, just a little gentler: "What?"

"There was a night, last fall," I say. Important to think before speaking, but if I think too much, I might not speak at all. I assumed that if I were to confide in anyone, it would be my mother, and there were several moments in the past year when I came close. I thought I was practicing self-reliance, learning how to self-soothe. I imagined a gash in the meat of my thigh, a jagged cut along my breastbone. Slowly forming scabs. *Don't pick, you'll have to start over.* I push forward. "I stayed late with Julian to help him with *Unsung* dailies. We were drinking, and it was only the two of us in the office. I got really drunk. More drunk than I realized at first."

"What happened?"

"We started talking about self-defense, and Julian said he didn't believe a woman could actually learn to take down a man, physically, and that it provides a false sense of empowerment to teach girls self-defense." Allyn looks like she's about to say something, but I have to keep charging through if I want to make it to the end. "So I called him out on that and somehow ended up agreeing to demonstrate the techniques I learned." Did I suggest it? Whose idea was it? Suddenly I can't remember. "Which obviously was stupid, but I'd been drinking. And then—he was on top of me, which is what we'd agreed to, but he was supposed to stay still so I could do the demonstration." I shake my head.

"But he didn't stay still?"

"No."

"How far . . . ? Did he . . . ?"

"I kept saying no, I know I did, but I was so drunk, so gone, and he just kept going."

"Did he . . ." She can't finish the sentence.

"Rape me?"

I am about to say no, not quite, when the phrase *digital penetration* forces its way into my mind, cold and clinical. I don't know what counts for what on the scorecard of sexual assault.

"Just his fingers," I say. "I don't know if he would have kept going, but I got sick. I threw up all over him."

She claps a hand over her mouth, muffling a laugh. "I'm sorry. It's not funny. I didn't mean to laugh. It happens when I'm nervous."

"It's okay. It was disgusting."

"Did you tell anyone?"

"No."

"Why not?"

"I was assaulted while trying to prove that I could defend myself from assault. And sure, there's no such thing as asking for it, but it felt like the world's stupidest way to get assaulted. I knew if I told, Julian would claim it was a joke or that I threw myself on him, and that story could travel all over town. I figured he'd keep quiet if I did. It's strange, thinking about it now. Because it's not that I forgot how to defend myself or was too wasted. I knew what to do, how to get him off me. But I didn't want to hurt him. They don't teach you how much damage the moves do. You're not supposed to care about that. But it's harder if it's someone you know. Not that he was concerned about hurting me. I rarely get sick from drinking, too. Thank god I did."

"So what are you going to do? You're really not going to report it?" Allyn says.

"I don't know. It's different than this Robert situation."

"How?"

"Julian's not powerful like Robert, and nobody else has accused him of anything."

"But he'll be important someday. I hear Lia Morales is about to sign a mega-deal with Netflix. He's on his way up."

"I don't want this to become who I am," I say. "I don't want that one stupid night to be my story."

"Singing to the choir," she says. She picks up her untouched coffee cup and stands. I follow suit.

I spend the following day deliberating. My mother needs to know there's more to the story. Proof of a pattern, beyond Veronica. If she is going to put her reputation on the line for this man. If he hasn't told her the whole truth. But I promised Allyn, and I meant it. My mother is responsible for her own decisions.

I want to do the right thing. I want someone to tell me what the right thing is. But that someone is usually my mother.

In the midst of this back-and-forth, the phone rings. "I hear congratulations are in order," the voice on the other end of the line says. He doesn't announce himself; he doesn't have to.

"Julian," I say, taking pains to sound calm, which I am not. "Long time no talk."

"I heard the good news, and I wanted to say I can't think of anyone more deserving. You're going to make a great executive."

"Oh! That's . . . I . . . how . . ."

Pull it together. Finish a fucking sentence.

"Thank you. And the same to you. I hear you're getting a bump as well."

There. Good. Was that so hard? (Yes.)

"Oh yeah. Thanks. To Director, actually. But we're a nimble little company, not so rigid with our hierarchies."

He's negotiated a jump straight past Manager to Director. Of course he has. It doesn't mean anything, not really, I know it doesn't, but I am frustrated nonetheless.

"That's great. Well, listen, would love to hear more, but I have a meeting and I—"

"Of course, of course. Talk soon, Miss Manager."

I throw my headset off with more force than I was intending, and Nick notices. "What's going on? You okay?"

I shake my head, then nod. I don't know where to begin.

SIXTEEN

ANOTHER DAY, ANOTHER HEADLINE. A SECOND woman with an accusation against Robert. An actress who says they had a sexual relationship, consensual, but underscored and fueled by a power imbalance. It became coercive, she says. He threatened to blackball her from XBC pilots if she stopped sleeping with him. She never got any good parts out of it anyway. All this was fifteen years ago.

On the heels of this, at 4:27 p.m., an article goes live on the *New York Times* website, asking why my mother—feminist firebrand and victims' rights advocate that she has been—is representing Robert Baum. She gives comment in the article. She says as a lawyer, it is her job to advocate for due process, to ensure justice is served. She says Robert is a longtime friend, that she feels a great deal of loyalty toward him, and that he has only ever been good to her and her daughter. Her daughter, the *New York Times* adds, works at XBC, the network run by Mr. Baum. They identify me by name.

A sudden chill as I sit at my desk, reading. That fuzzy-headed feeling of receiving news you immediately want to unhear, time sliced cleanly into a before and an after. I force myself to keep going, though I'm struggling to absorb it, lines of text swimming on the screen, and there, yes, there: Sources say this is not the first time my mother has come to Robert Baum's defense. That she helped with the Blake Peterson settlement. Sources say Blake's bad behavior was an open secret on the set of *Justice Served*. That a firm was hired to conduct an outside investigation, but it was a sham.

I scroll back up to check the byline. The name, Natalie Curtis, rings a bell. I click over to Gregory's phone sheet, and there she is, name and number in the column of calls to be returned. A voicemail from yesterday. I'm not sure whose line it came in on, mine or Gregory's. I just assumed it was for Gregory, because why would a *New York Times* reporter be calling for me?

This. This is why.

Nick is away from his desk. I consider going to find him, but instead, I go to the single-stall bathroom, close the door, and sit on the tile floor, mind spinning. I stand up and splash cool water in my face, which only has the effect of making my mascara run. I wipe the black smears away as best I can with a square of rough toilet paper.

All this work to carve out an independent identity, only to be reduced to my mother's daughter once more. But a new texture to it now. Airless in a different way.

At 5:12 p.m., Deadline strikes, with a post aggregating the news about the second woman, about my mother, and about Blake Peterson. Everybody in the office gets Deadline alerts—top headlines sent straight to our inboxes, intended to keep people abreast of who's making deals where, not actually meant for breaking news. Not usually.

Nick is back at his desk now, and I sit watching him as he reads the article. "Shit," he says when he gets to the end.

"What do I do?" I say.

"I don't know," he says.

For the rest of the workday, I alternate between checking my email and pressing refresh on the Deadline article. Hollywood people love to comment on Deadline, almost always under aliases. Most of the early comments are about Robert or Blake— alternating defenses and indictments. Then: *I hear his lawyer's daughter is getting promoted. Smells fishy to me.*

The comments pile on.

Calls come in from unfamiliar numbers. I don't pick up. By seven p.m., I've amassed voicemails from the *LA Times*, *The Hollywood Reporter*, *Variety*, the *New York Post*, and another from Natalie Curtis at the *New York Times*.

I call my mother. She doesn't pick up. I don't want to go over to her house, but I feel an urgent need to talk to her, though I don't quite know why or how that could help. Gemma would tell me to meditate, to sit with my feelings, notice them, and let them go. She would remind me that I can't control other people's behavior, only how I respond. Which, sure, fair enough, but how to respond?

That evening, I find my mother at her desk, pounding aggressively on her keyboard.

"There's an article about me in the *New York Times*. The phone's been ringing nonstop."

"I know," I say, my voice as hard as I can make it.

"I don't want to read it. Will you read it and tell me what it says?" Frustration in her voice, but also excitement.

"I've already read it," I say.

"And?" She looks up at me, her face now gentle and full of need. I feel a crack in my resolve, a powerful urge to say and do whatever I can to make her feel better, which is what I've wanted for as long as I've known how to want.

"It's not good," I say finally. "Why did you mention me?"

"I didn't."

"You did. You said Robert's only ever been good to me."

"Well, it's true, isn't it?"

"That's not the point! How could you do this to me?"

"To *you*? This isn't about you; don't you understand?"

"I wish it weren't about me. Do you realize how this could affect me?"

"What are you talking about?" The purity of her confusion.

"People are talking. My promotion. They're saying it's nepotism, or a quid pro quo."

"Well, that's not true."

"So what? People don't know that, and you're crazy if you think they aren't making assumptions. People won't take me seriously. That was half the point of getting promoted in the first place—I'd get to have my own identity, not just be Gregory's assistant, and now it's fucked."

She shakes her head with great force. "No," she says. "No. We'll fix it. Robert will fix it."

"Robert can't fix it. Don't you get it? Robert's the problem."

"Are you talking about that woman who attacked him today? That was a consensual relationship. She even admitted it. It's all going to get cleared up."

She genuinely thinks Robert is in the right, I realize. Her vision clouded, perhaps, by the allure of his need for her. A sense of control, of protection, the closer you are to power. A bulwark against victimhood: maybe that's what it comes down to in the end.

A dizzy, distancing feeling, understanding that I see something my mother does not. But I also have more, or at least different, information.

Her cell phone beeps, a muffled sound coming from her bedroom. She goes in to look for it, and I follow. Phone in hand, she takes a seat on the bed, reading, brows furrowed.

I put my hand on her arm and gently stroke the skin on the inside of her elbow. She looks up at me and smiles. "You used to love doing that," she says.

I nod. "It made me feel so safe."

"Not anymore. You don't want to be with me now."

"That's not true. I'm just trying to figure out how to have my own life too," I say, though I don't want to switch to that conversation. "Listen. About Robert."

"What about him?"

"I don't know about the woman today, or Veronica, but."

"But what?"

"I have really solid information that he did something bad."

"How bad?"

"Bad bad. Weird and specific and more than once. The kind of thing that seems like a pattern."

"Can you tell me what it is?"

"I promised I wouldn't tell anyone."

"I'm not anyone."

"I know. But she's worried about it getting out and hurting her."

"You think I would do that? Do you really think I would deliberately hurt a victim? When all my life I've fought for victims? How could you say that? I'm the one who put the kibosh on XBC's investigator. Do you know what kind of dirt we have on this actress? The texts she sent, trying to blackmail him into casting her. It's bad. I was the one who said no, absolutely not, we will not stoop to using that." Voice teetering, volume rising.

"I'm just trying to be a good friend. A loyal friend. You understand that," I say, hoping the appeal to loyalty will work, and it does, a little. She nods and goes silent for a minute, thinking.

I've been foolish. On some level, I expected her to hear this and immediately wipe her hands of Robert. To say that her loyalty was dependent on his honesty and moral decency. But no, of course not. It is too late for that. She has invested too much. He is One of the Few Good Men. The part can't be recast; the center would not hold. And she is a good lawyer—a great one, even. One who doesn't let her clients down.

"What will you do?" I ask.

"I'll talk to the general counsel. We've already discussed the need for an external investigation, a real one, not that cover-up crap from last time. This person—your friend, I'm assuming—it will be up to her whether to come forward. But she'll have the opportunity."

"And then what?"

"And then we'll see."

The next day, while Gregory is out to lunch, I ask Allyn to come down the hallway to his office. I close the door behind me and join her on the couch.

"I didn't tell my mother about you," I say.

"You promise?" she says, obviously doubtful, and I can't say I blame her.

"Yes. But I did say that I had it on good authority that Robert did something bad."

"And?"

"There'll be an investigation. You can come forward then, if you want. Or you can get a lawyer and sue. Or both."

"I don't want to sue. I want to be an exec."

"I know. And you should be. We should both be off-desk," I say, and I am surprised by how much I mean it. I was frustrated on her behalf by the way Gregory led her on. But I also thought that, were I in her position, I would have taken the hint that it was time to leave, as Julian did. When Nick and I discussed it, he agreed that he would have left too. The best explanation either of us could come up with for why she didn't was inertia. Inertia and fear. We didn't, of course, have any idea about the Robert situation.

It is only as I sit here with Allyn on the couch, sun from a daytime neither of us has seen streaming in through the windows, striping the carpet and illuminating a column of dust particles in the air, that I realize I have been unfairly derisive. I have privileged my skills over hers. I am more well read than Allyn, I write better coverage and am more articulate and better at delegating tasks. But she has talents I don't. She is a great networker, and not in just the schmoozy sense, but in the sense of connecting people, making introductions that help both parties. She finds assistants new jobs all the time. She is great at staying on top of what's happening in the industry and ferreting out secret information from other networks. Yes, she might sometimes divulge too much inside information, but she also gets intel of the sort nobody else has. I always considered these the soft skills, the silly skills, the girly high school social machinations that felt most foreign to me, and which I, long ago, decided I wouldn't beat myself up about lacking. Different people bring different skills to the game. And some are more important than others—or so I thought.

But Allyn would be a good executive too, if for different reasons than I would. And what's more, there's room for both of us. Or there *should* be room for both of us.

"But what about you?" she says. "Julian."

"I don't know yet," I say. "It's different. It's not a part of this." I gesture at the room around us, and as I do, I feel a sudden doubt. Is it actually separate? Or is that what I needed to tell myself in order to keep scraping myself against the grater of this system, watching my skin get shredded and reframing it as building calluses?

I look at the phone across the room, on Gregory's desk. Ring. Please ring.

"You knew," Allyn says, "about the Blake stuff?"

I contemplate lying, then decide against it. "I did. Not all of it. But enough."

"And you didn't say anything."

"I didn't know what to say. I wasn't involved; I wasn't even supposed to know about it. If I had said something, my mother could have gotten in trouble, because she shared privileged information with me. Would you have acted differently?" My words come out sharper than I was intending.

"Not what I meant," Allyn says. "I was just thinking, imagine how many women must know secrets about different men, and they keep quiet or only talk about it with each other, and the men carry on, feeling untouchable—"

"And we become part of a vast system of enablers," I finish.

"Right."

"Firing a few bad men won't fix that," I say, and immediately regret it when I see how visibly her face falls.

"Nope. You're right. Of course you're right," she says.

"But the alternative—doing nothing. That's just business as usual. And we've seen how that works," I add.

"I'm not going to do it unless you do too," she says.

———

THERE ARE FOLLOW-UP PIECES about Blake Peterson. A former staff writer speaks out about the culture of harassment at *Justice Served* and the open secret of Blake's predatory behavior.

Further speculation abounds online, some of it reasonable, some of it not. Someone has discovered that I was promoted to Coordinator not long before Blake received his overall deal with XBC, and a chattering group thinks it must be connected.

"I still want this for you," Gregory tells me. "But we're going to have to wait, see how the chips fall." The words land with the force of a door thundering shut, knocking me back.

This is how I know it's a no. That the promotion, once imminent, has dissolved in my hands.

I call my mother from the car, fury blinkering my vision as I drive home through Beverly Hills, where the palm tree trunks have been wrapped with twinkle lights for the holiday season. I don't want to talk to her. I don't trust myself to stay calm. But I need to tell her this. I need her to know.

"How could they do this to you?" she says.

"They?" I say. "They? This is because of you!"

I know this will set her off, but I say it anyway. I am tired of not saying things, of suppressing myself to placate others, of making sure other people feel good even if I don't. *Requires thick skin*: a phrase found in so many assistant job descriptions. Code for a difficult boss. Onus is on you to develop the skin, not on them to control their knives.

"I've only ever tried to help you," my mother says.

"You don't know the difference between helping and controlling," I say.

I hang up on her. I have never hung up on her before.

A few hours later, my righteous fury gives way to something murkier. I call her back, but she doesn't pick up. She doesn't pick up the next day, either. Or the next. I am being punished. I am expected to supplicate, to beg forgiveness.

I don't want to play this game anymore. I can't.

I'll tell her that in person, I decide. But when I visit her after work a few days later, she's apologetic, distraught. And in bed. "I ruined it," she says, hiccupping through tears. She is under the covers, in pajamas, a banana with a single bite taken out of it on the nightstand. I remain standing next to the bed. "All I ever wanted to do was help you. That's all I wanted."

I say nothing. This is it, I realize. The bed, the nightstand, the curtains drawn on the world. She will cycle, days will be better and then worse, but it will always lead back to this, her perspective expanding and contracting along with her moods. I can stand by, but I cannot spring her from this trap. And if I stand by, I'll be swallowed. I may owe her my love, but not my life.

"I was so proud of you," she wails. "You were doing such a good job, even when the assholes weren't taking you seriously. Found that great project—you should have heard me, bragging about it to Robert when he called to catch up, before I knew about any of this."

"You told Robert I found *The Color Line*?"

"Of course. He was so impressed."

A flash: Robert, rapping his fingers on my desk. *I hear you found a good one for us.* I assumed he heard from Gregory. That Gregory was being generous, giving me credit for the find.

"Is that why it happened? Did Robert tell Gregory to promote me?"

"I have no idea what Robert said. What does it matter?"

"It's the difference between me earning it on my own and not! But I guess it doesn't matter now, does it?"

"Of course you earned it." She flips the pillow over, punches it. "I was just trying to do the right thing. And now you hate me." She falls back on the pillow. Her tears grow louder, bigger, shaking her whole body.

"Stop it. Don't say that." My frustration building alongside her tears. It's my turn to be mad. It was supposed to be my turn.

"Why not? It's true. I tried my best. I was so young when I made it big. So ambitious. I really believed in the potential for change. But all these years of fighting, and what's different now? Nothing. This country still hates women. Anyone who claims otherwise needs to take a harder look."

"So what, that's it? You roll over and flip to the defense?"

"What are you talking about? I haven't flipped. I'm helping a friend is what I'm doing. Veronica Ross is no victim. She says he used to make comments about her tits. How much do you want to bet she undid an extra button on her shirt on purpose before going into his office? She knew what she was doing."

"Okay, sure, but so what? She thought it would help, and she was right. That's the problem!"

My mother sits up in bed, energized by her outrage, tears stanched for the moment. "It's tough to be an ambitious woman in a man's world. Not hard to understand why some women use their looks, their sex appeal, to their advantage. You work with what you've got. Not how I ever did it. But then again, I also never felt confident in my looks. Never had much cleavage to reveal. I'm not saying Veronica opened her legs or slept with him. You know what I've always said about women who try to sleep their way to the top."

"They end up in the middle."

"Exactly. But did Veronica know that flirting a little with Robert could get her a long way? You bet your ass she did."

"But that's the issue! That's exactly what I'm saying!"

"There are so many men who have done truly bad things, so much sexism in the world. Is it worth getting caught up in this? That's missing the forest for one old, overweight tree."

Abraham is snorting at the foot of the bed; I lean down and heave him up onto the mattress. He rewards me by sticking his wet snout into my lap and rubbing it around. "But wasn't your whole point with *Simple Rape* that it's weirdly easier to talk about the really bad black-and-white cases, since there's less stigma attached to saying you were raped by a stranger with a weapon than by someone you know? And that's part of the problem? Doesn't that mean we have to talk about the fat trees too if we want to get anywhere?"

"Do you think it was easy for me to speak up about my rape?"

"No, I didn't say that—"

"Nana told me to keep quiet, said that no man would want me if they knew. I only knew that people who are mugged or otherwise assaulted never feel ashamed talking about it, because they were victims of a crime, they weren't at fault. And why should rape be treated any differently? That was my thinking at the time. Refusing to be made small. But it was terrifying. Death threats, rape threats. Awful stuff. I don't know if you remember, but there was a trip we took to Florida, just the two of us, to visit Nana, when you were little. I was going to give a speech while we were down there, and when we checked into the hotel, there was a box of chocolates someone had delivered for me, and when I opened it, there were razor blades sticking out of the chocolates."

"That's terrible."

"It was. We switched hotels. I can't remember what I told you about why. Do you remember that trip?"

I remember some things. I remember the safe and grown-up feeling of sitting next to my mother on the plane, Bloody Mary for her, Bloody Mary mix for me. Chopped-liver sandwiches and crinkly gold-wrapped butterscotch candies and Nana taking me to have my hair permed at her beauty salon. I don't remember chocolates or changing hotels. I don't remember my mother being scared.

"There's something else," I say. "Someone else. Not Robert."

I tell her about Julian, the whole story. She listens carefully. "Oh, sweetheart," she says, pulling me tight to her chest. I'm hunched over; it's an uncomfortable position for my back, but I allow myself to lean into it all the same. Feel the beating of her heart against my cheek. Her hand on my head, smoothing my hair. "Why didn't you tell me?"

"Things were tough between us," I say. It's all I can manage. "I should report it, right?"

"This isn't a question of should," she says. I feel the vibrations of her voice, the heat of her breath. I pull back. "It's about what's best for you. People love to tell women to come forward, as if it's a moral imperative, but they aren't considering what it means to live as that woman. People will forget about this, the Robert thing, you'll see. You'll get promoted—whether at XBC or somewhere else. You're good at your job. People will push for you. You have to be patient."

Upsetting but unsurprising. Hard to believe there was a time when I expected the opposite. When the value of speaking out seemed so obvious, I didn't bother to think it through. The naivete stings.

For the next few weeks, nothing happens. It's excruciating, the waiting. A purgatory. I wish there were more headlines, more information to collect. But there isn't.

I know there's talk, but I'm marooned outside the whisper network now. To my face, in my inbox, everyone is suspiciously polite, overly accommodating to my scheduling requests. The workdays are painfully long. Time takes on the consistency of honey, sticky and slow. On the weekends, I try to distract myself. I clean out boxes in my father's garage and find one filled with old home movies. I have never seen video footage of myself from childhood. There I am, on screen, on the pink-carpeted floor of my childhood bedroom with my mother, next to a blue plastic rocking horse. Eighteen months old, according to the date stamp. The video is for Nana, my mother announces to the camera, to show her how much I've grown. My mother wants me to get on the horse, but I will not. "Let's show Nana what an expert rider you are," she says.

I walk in a circle around the horse. I sit down next to it. I stand up and look at it. Finally, my mother crawls over to the horse and stands on her knees next to me. She holds the horse's handlebar to keep it stable. "See, I'm going to put my leg over," she says, keeping her own legs still, prodding me to lift my leg. "Just like that! I'm putting my leg on the horse. That's how we get on our horse."

In a video dated six months later, Nana is visiting. She holds me in her arms, standing next to my mother. "I show you something," I say, sliding out of Nana's arms. I drag the blue rocking horse over, climb on, and begin to rock back and forth, throwing my whole body into it.

"Careful," Nana says as I increase momentum.

"See!" I say, coming to a stop. "I'm not breaking anything!" I pat the horse's blue plastic mane. "I'm not breaking anything," I repeat.

"Nobody said you were," Nana says.

"You're a good girl," my mother says.

"I'm not breaking anything," I say. I keep saying it, over and over and over again.

Amid the jumble of cassette tapes, I also find two DVDs labeled SELF-DEFENSE GRADUATION. There is a sticky note on the back of one with my name and *owes $5* in what must be the teacher's handwriting. We paid for this footage of ourselves being mock-attacked on a padded gym floor while our parents sat hushed and watching in folding chairs.

Only the graduation fights were distributed on DVD, but every fight throughout the semester was filmed. Four days a week, we did drills and learned sequences of moves and strategies for verbal de-escalation. Then, at the end of the week, the muggers came in—a series of rotating male co-teachers who we referred to as muggers because that was the goal, to send them off with only your belongings, not your body. My favorite was Mugger Dave. Each week, a different scenario: grabbed from behind, approached from the front, trapped in an elevator. Multiple assailants. Asleep in bed. The muggers wore bulbous black helmets to protect their heads.

I insert one of the DVDs into my laptop and press play. There we are, twelve girls lined up along the edge of a blue mat in the school gym. Our parents off-screen, opposite us. I'm third in line, wearing bright pink sweatpants, my hair in a high ponytail. Tenth grade, fifteen years old. I look so young. All the girls do. The teacher, a middle-aged woman with a whistle around her neck, stands at one end and urges the first girl onto the mat. She leans in to confer, then pulls back.

"Kristin is on the beach," the teacher announces to the room. The sound quality isn't great, the words swallowed by the gym's acoustics, but it's clear enough. She blows her whistle and steps back, and Mugger Dave lumbers onto the mat. I turn the volume all the way up to catch his words, garbled by the bug-eyed helmet.

"Looking good in that bikini. You wanna take it off?" he says.

Kristin puts her hands up in the ready position. I didn't know her well, she was a year behind me. "Please leave me alone," she says, voice high but steady.

He doesn't, of course. When he lunges, she strikes, first with a heel palm to the chin, then a knee to the groin. The rest of us behind her cry out in solidarity, a big group of antirape cheerleaders. "No!" we shout. "Heel palm! Groin!"

Kristin is scrappy, limbs flailing as Mugger Dave drags her down to the ground. Finally, after an axe kick to the head, she knocks him unconscious. She stands, verifies that there are no other assailants lurking, then runs to the edge of the mat. The teacher blows the whistle, and we cry out in unison, "911!"

The next girl demonstrates a reversal. She lies down on the mat in fetal position and closes her eyes. The other mugger, I can't remember his name, takes his turn on the mat. He straddles her. They remain like that, frozen, until the whistle blows, and then he leans in. "Quiet, sweetheart," he says. "This won't hurt."

I'm up next.

"Outside a restaurant," the teacher announces. The whistle blows.

Mugger Dave staggers toward me, scratching at his crotch. "Hey, baby, I got a rash. Will you check out my rash? You gotta get up close."

"I can't look at your rash," I say. Laughter from the parents in the audience. I smile, pleased. I point off the mat. "Ask that man to look at your rash," I say, riffing.

"I don't want him, I only want you," Dave says, coming closer. "Come on, bitch, get on your knees." I'm awkward, my actions jerky. It's hard to watch. Once Dave is down, as I pull myself to a stand, Mugger #2 stumbles in. There are exclamations of surprise from the parents—it's the first multiple-assailant scenario of the evening. This fight is faster; Mugger #2 is playing drunk, so he goes down easier. I stand, assess, see Mugger Dave struggling to get up. I walk over, knee him in the head, and he falls.

The parents clap. My classmates cheer. I beam, exultant.

I slam the laptop shut. So much worse than I remembered.

I took the class as my PE elective three semesters in a row, freshman and sophomore year. Three graduations my mother attended. *"No!"* I screamed, shoving my knee into the padded crotches of middle-aged men.

Junior year, I switched to yoga.

Only once did I find myself in a situation that resembled the scenarios we practiced. I was seventeen, a senior in high school, and I was outside a Starbucks, on my way to a college interview. It was a gray November afternoon, and I was feeding quarters into the meter when I felt a hand on my shoulder. I turned, and there was a man twice my size, bald and bearded, wearing a frayed denim vest, muscular arms covered in tattoos. "Hey, cutie," he said.

"Can I help you?" I asked.

"I don't know. Can you?" he said.

"I'm sorry, I'm busy," I said.

"You'd be such a good lingerie model," he said. "I can picture you in lace, lying on my bed." He nodded his head as if solidifying the image in his mind.

My simmering anxiety about the interview surged to a rolling boil. A sudden rush of adrenaline, blinkered focus. I noticed that I had shifted into the ready position, or a tentative approximation of it. Elbows bent, palms up, my feet hips-width distance apart, right leg in front of the left. So this is what they mean by muscle memory, I thought. This is how it works.

"Sir, you need to leave," I said. Never before had I called anyone sir.

"You don't mean that, baby girl," he said. Then: "Oh, the things I want to do to you."

I briefly considered my options. I could say I was waiting for my father. Brother. Boyfriend. "If you don't leave right now, I'll call the police," I said, reaching a hand down into my purse and groping for my phone without breaking eye contact. The man clocked my movements, then turned to look behind him, and with this, I felt my field of vision suddenly expand. I remembered that I was in public. That there were other people here, sitting a few yards away at the outdoor tables, under the green Starbucks umbrellas.

"You were right," the man called out. "She is good."

And then I saw him: Mugger Dave, standing alone by an empty table, smiling. "Told you so!" he called back. He sauntered over to say hello, coffee in hand.

"Dave spotted you and told me how good you are at verbals and said I should see for myself," the man said.

"I knew you could handle him," Dave said, giving his friend a soft punch on the shoulder. "He looks tough, but he's a big softy. Opposite of you." Dave winked. "I hope you're not upset."

"Of course not," I said automatically. I was creeped out, but mostly, I was proud of myself. I didn't freeze. I handled the situation well. I was flattered that Mugger Dave remembered me a year and a half later and thought so highly of my skills.

I assumed Dave knew he had pushed the boundaries of acceptable behavior, but he thought I could handle it, and I didn't want to prove him wrong. I never reported him. For all I know, he might still have the job. Might still be grabbing teenage girls and hissing threats in their ears in the name of empowerment, week after week.

———

GREGORY GETS THE BUMP to President. There's a big press release and publicity push, an attempt to shift the narrative. He says he still wants to promote me, but his hands are tied at the moment. "Optics," he says. "You understand. We have to be patient."

Entry-level exec openings around town are few and far between right now, and there are plenty of candidates unencumbered by scandal.

Allyn and I are rarely alone together. We participate in group chats and instant message about scheduling, but that's it. It's deliberate on my end, and maybe on hers as well. I can't bear to confront my inaction and uncertainty.

Lia Morales signs the Netflix deal Allyn said was coming. For $200 million, a staggering amount. Julian's promotion to Director of Development is announced in the industry trades. I try and fail to suppress my anger and envy.

Then he calls me. "Listen. I assume you saw the news about our deal," he says.

"You're not supposed to ask for congratulations," I say.

"That's not what I'm doing. Believe me, we're drowning in flowers. What I'm saying is, we have a lot of money now. Good money, and it comes with freedom and creative autonomy. Lia really wants to shake things up."

"That's very exciting," I say. Resentment probably audible in my voice. Even if I do get promoted at XBC, I'll be curtailed by bureaucracy and the tired dictates of broadcast. Lia's smart to jump ship to a digital streamer.

"It is. And you should come. Join the team. We're expanding."

I only barely stop myself from saying, "What?" Instead, I say: "Why would you want to work with me? You don't like me."

"That's not true. You were my competition. It's different."

"How would this be different?"

"Lia's splitting her development teams—features and television. I'm taking features. We'd be working together, but independently."

"What about Allyn? You two are actually friends."

"I love Allyn, but you and I both know why not Allyn. I've told Lia all about you. I know she'll love you."

"Why do you say that?"

"Because you seem sweet, but you're actually ruthless."

"Thank you?" I say. I can tell he means it as a compliment, but it doesn't sit well. *Sweet* is simpering and inoffensive, and I don't want that. But *ruthless* is a dagger; *ruthless* cuts and enjoys the slice. "Lia knows what's going on, with my mother and everything?"

"Oh yeah. That makes you sexier," he says. "Professionally sexier," he adds. How quick he is to clarify. He's being careful. "Lia loves this shit. Spitting in the face of the fools who would let political correctness keep a talented candidate from getting a job she deserves."

"I see," I say. I'm wondering how few words I can utter to get myself out of this conversation. I don't trust myself to say the right thing, and I don't want to say the wrong thing, then hate myself for it. This requires knowing what right and wrong are.

"Listen. You can think on it for a beat, but we're hiring fast."

"Okay," I say. A dream job. A devil's bargain.

"And last thing? I know I was an ass to you sometimes. But you had this whole confident thing going on, and it was like you just walked in and five seconds later got the title bump I worked

years for. It wasn't fair, and I didn't like that. But I never disliked
you."

"Well," I say, but this isn't enough. "Thanks for saying that," I
manage.

"Sure, you're welcome. Talk soon. You know where to find
me."

It's only after I hang up that I realize this wasn't an apology,
just an acknowledgment, and a vague one, at that. I shouldn't be
surprised.

In my inbox, the following day: an email from Julian, saying Lia
Morales wants to meet. *Call me*, he writes. And an email from
Natalie Curtis at the *New York Times*, asking to speak about XBC.
Call me, she writes. Throughout the afternoon, I toggle back and
forth between the emails. Reading, then promptly marking as un-
read.

I leave work early and drive to my mother's house, but by the
time I park, I'm not sure what I'm doing there or whether I want
to hear whatever she might say. A residual impulse, a shiver of preemptive guilt. Walking up the front steps, I see through the windows that all the downstairs lights are on, which is unusual. There
must be company—also unusual. I take a breath before unlock-
ing the door and try to arrange my face into something warm
and polite as opposed to thoroughly wrecked. Hoist my purse up
higher on my shoulder and turn the key. In I go, through the front
hall, into the living room, and there, sitting on the couch across
from my mother, is Robert Baum, jacket flung beside him, drink
in hand.

He rises to greet me, planting his free hand on the couch to help leverage himself to a stand. "What a wonderful surprise!" he says, opening his arms for a hug.

Like a trained monkey, I hug him back. I am midhug when I realize what I've done. I can smell the alcohol on his breath. Scotch. He's sweaty, the back of his shirt damp against my palm. I pull back.

"I'm sorry you've been dragged into this shitstorm," he says. "But don't you worry, we'll get you that promotion in no time."

"We'll be finished with business in a few minutes if you want to join us," my mother says.

"I just came to grab something I left upstairs," I say, and I hurry up the stairs as quickly as I can. Shut the door behind me, fling my bag onto the bed, and sit down. Pull out my phone, check my email.

I have seen what working within the system gets you. It gets you trapped in a building that should be burned down.

Do I want to be in that building?

But what if there are no other buildings?

On the bookshelf across from me: well-loved books, a Math Olympiads trophy, a framed photo of me on the first day of fifth grade, smiling desperately in a brand-new outfit. Eighty-nine pounds and still I wanted to lose a few more. A public service award plaque from college, a kiddush cup from my bat mitzvah, at which I tried to give a perfect speech about the importance of accepting imperfection. The program from my high school graduation, where I processed down the aisle in a floor-length white dress, bouquet of flowers in my hands, school ring on my finger. Trappings of a girl who tried, so hard, to break through without breaking anything.

And I did. Here I am. This is what it looks like.

Snaking up from downstairs, the muffled sound of my mother's voice. Robert's laugh, a loud bark.

I turn back to my phone. Open one email, then the other. I take a deep breath, and I dial.

Author's Note

This is a work of fiction. Names, characters, businesses, organizations, places, events, and incidents either are the products of the author's imagination or are used fictitiously.

Acknowledgments

To my agent, Duvall Osteen. There's above and beyond, and then there's you. I couldn't dream of a better advocate or friend. Your unwavering belief in my writing—and in me—made this possible. Thank you for talking me through countless panic spirals and texting with me eighteen hours a day during lockdown and also for shepherding my career.

To Ruby Rose Lee at Holt, and to Jess Leeke and Ruth Atkins at Penguin Michael Joseph. I feel fortunate to have had the opportunity to work with not one, not two, but three incredibly talented editors. Thank you for treating my words with such care. Your thoughtful notes led to a much stronger novel. Thank you to Hannah Campbell, Marinda Valenti, and everyone at Holt and Penguin Michael Joseph who played a part in transforming this from Word document to book.

To the NYU Creative Writing Program. Never have I felt so understood, accepted, and encouraged. Thank you to Deborah Landau for cultivating such a nurturing community.

To the professors, classmates, and friends who read early pages and gave invaluable feedback, in particular Nathan Englander, Katie Kitamura, Jonathan Safran Foer, John Freeman, Emily Barton,

Darin Strauss, Jeffrey Eugenides, Elizabeth Nicholas, Lindsey Skillen, James McAuley, Dario Diofebi, Scott Gannis, John Maher, Sam Chalsen, Jeremy Stern, and Allegra Greenland.

To my first writing teachers, Claire Messud and Jamaica Kincaid, who urged me to take risks as well as time to learn the craft and read widely. Thank you for assuring me I wouldn't be a failure if I didn't finish a second book by twenty-one.

To Kristina Moore at UTA.

To my former coworkers at Fox, especially Checka Propper, Alec Strum, Jenn Yang, and Sanjana Seelam. Assisting is a team sport, and I'm so glad to have been on yours.

To my Project 100 cofounders, Danielle Gram, Victor Garcia, and Eduardo Ortiz.

To my friends, especially Alex and Sam Drimal Barr, Jessica Ranucci, Natalie Peyser, and Kristin Rose.

To my family.

Thank you all. Your support has meant more than I can say. Please send next avails.